Flight 2O7

Scott P. Hicks

Contents

CHAPTER 1

Dr. Maya Jenkins stood amid the controlled chaos of Terminal 4 at John F. Kennedy International Airport, her gaze scanning the growing line of passengers waiting to board Flight 207. The manila folder tucked under her arm held her carefully prepared conference notes, the crisp edges a tactile anchor in the bustling crowd. Despite years of frequent travel, there was always this tension in the final hour—the kind that made her hyperaware of every sound: the hollow thud of a rolling suitcase catching a seam in the tile, a child's shrill protest echoing from the nearby Starbucks.

Beyond the glass, the evening sky hung thick with dark clouds. The departure boards still flashed ON TIME for London, but the TVs overhead carried a more unsettling forecast. Onscreen, a meteorologist, tie askew, pointed at swirling storm systems converging like fragments of a foreboding puzzle. "Once-in-a-decade conditions," he warned. Although the airline assured everyone the route would be safe, the animated swirl of crimson and violet on the radar made Maya's stomach turn.

Her phone buzzed, and she glanced at a text from her sister:

You on the plane yet? Stay safe, sis.

Maya paused before typing back:

Boarding soon. Love you.

She resisted the urge to share her unease, knowing it would only worsen Deena's natural anxiety. Slipping the phone into her purse, she reminded herself that flights went through turbulent weather all the time.

Nearby, a flight attendant navigated the crowd with practiced grace. Her name tag read **Olivia Ramos**, and beneath the professional smile lay a hint of genuine warmth. She deposited a stack of menus on the gate agent's desk, then spotted Maya, her gaze drifting to the stethoscope peeking from Maya's carry-on.

"First time flying with us?" Olivia asked, voice balanced between courtesy and reassurance.

Maya followed her glance to the stethoscope. "Not my first flight, but first time on 207."

Olivia nodded. "Good route. We'll get you there safely."

Maya tried returning the confidence in her own smile, though she couldn't help glancing at the screens displaying the storm's fierce approach. The knot in her chest tightened. *Calm down,* she told herself. *You've flown through storms before.*

Flight 207's passengers were a varied collection: exhausted parents corralling toddlers, college-age couples wearing matching *EUROTRIP 2025* sweatshirts, and professionals glued to their phones. One stood out—a woman whose tailored navy pantsuit and relentless phone alerts suggested she thrived on high-stakes deals. When the gate agent called her name—*Victoria Prescott*—Maya imagined her as a corporate lawyer who won every argument by sheer force of will.

At the terminal window, a wide-eyed boy named Ethan gaped at the planes outside. He wore a bright Captain America T-shirt, and his parents hovered close, responding to his excited questions about engines and runway lights. Their familial warmth sparked a small ache in Maya, reminding her of how wonderstruck she'd once been about traveling.

The boarding announcement startled her. She followed the line toward the jet bridge, clutching her small rolling suitcase. Behind her stood a tall man with sandy hair and broad shoulders, the name C. O'Connor stitched onto his jacket.

"Headed to London on business?" he asked, gesturing at the manila folder labeled *Medical Conference.*

Maya nodded. "I'm presenting emergency triage research. And you?"

He patted his canvas bag. "I'm Carter O'Connor, airplane mechanic, catching a ride back to Ireland by way of London. Wrapped up a contract here in the States. Tools are in the hold—though they let me bring a few on as carry-on."

Maya smiled lightly. "Well, if we run into engine trouble, at least we have an expert."

He chuckled. "Let's hope it doesn't come to that."

A steady calm radiated from him, gently easing her nerves. *Planes are safe, storms or not,* she reminded herself, though the tension in her shoulders refused to fully dissolve.

A cool draft snaked down the jet bridge, raising goosebumps on her arms. The Boeing cabin welcomed them with a soft glow. Passengers settled in, stowing bags and flipping through in-flight magazines. Maya took her window seat, 12A. Through the small window, she saw the sky deepening into bruised purple, clouds thick with unspent fury. Carter claimed 12B, folding his long frame into place.

"This your usual specialty?" he asked, nodding at the stethoscope.

"Emergency medicine," she said, snapping her seatbelt. "Never a dull day."

He offered a respectful nod. "Tough field. I admire that."

The sincerity in his voice soothed her. She glimpsed flickers of lightning beyond the wing, disquieting as the storm gathered. Carter looked too, brow tightening as thunderheads glowed in the distance.

Before she could dwell on it, the flight attendants began their safety checks. Olivia passed by, directing final stowage of belongings. At her signal, the overhead lights dimmed, the cabin taking on a hush broken by small rustles and hushed conversations.

A voice over the intercom greeted them, calm yet charged with authority. "Good evening, folks," said Captain Wheeler. "We're expecting a flight time of about six hours, fifty minutes. We'll adjust our path to avoid the brunt of this weather system. Please relax and enjoy your flight."

The plane taxied onto the runway, engines growing to a thunderous roar. Maya's pulse surged as they accelerated, inertia pressing her back against the seat until the ground dropped away beneath them. New York's skyline melted into shadowy shapes below.

She released a slow breath, forcing her mind to shift to her upcoming presentation at St. Mary's. Dinner with old classmates, a promising new research collaboration—she tried to cling to these thoughts, ignoring the swirl of storm clouds outside.

Carter flipped through a glossy aviation magazine. "You'd be amazed at the prototypes," he said. "Still, no matter how advanced, we remain at nature's mercy."

Maya managed a wry smile. "Mother Nature usually wins."

For a while, the flight found its rhythm. Drinks and trays of mediocre food appeared. Ethan giggled with his parents over a puzzle book, while Victoria Prescott alternated between phone calls and reading dense legal documents, exuding unwavering focus. Maya felt herself easing into a semblance of comfort.

Then the seatbelt sign chimed.

Her attention snapped back as the plane quivered, as if hitting a patch of rough air. Olivia's voice, steady but firmer now, came over the speakers. "Ladies and gentlemen, please return to your seats and fasten your seatbelts. We're expecting a bit of turbulence."

The sky beyond the window had turned charcoal-black, shot through with sporadic flashes of lightning. Clouds seemed to boil, their roiling shapes illuminated by pale electric flickers. A second tremor rolled through the cabin, sharper this time, drawing quick gasps from a few passengers.

Carter glanced overhead. "Doesn't feel routine," he murmured.

Maya tried not to dwell on the dread trickling into her veins. Another jolt rocked them, more forceful, and the cabin erupted in uneasy murmurs. Silverware rattled on tray tables; somewhere, a bottle clanked loudly against a seat frame.

Lightning slashed across the sky, but it was followed by something even stranger—a sudden rippling of green and violet lights, twisting through the storm like an otherworldly display. Maya's breath caught. "What on Earth...?"

Carter leaned closer to the window, eyes narrowed. "Never seen anything like that before."

Another lurch rattled the overhead compartments, snapping them open and spilling a few bags to the floor. Ethan yelped, and his mother clutched him protectively. Fear simmered in the pressurized air.

The intercom crackled. Captain Wheeler's voice, laced with tension, cut through. "Ladies and gentlemen, we're deviating course due to severe weather anomalies. Please remain calm."

The plane suddenly dropped as though yanked downward by an invisible hand, sending trays and cups flying. Shrieks and gasps broke out. Maya's water cup ricocheted off the seat in front of her, splashing her legs. She clutched the armrests, heart racing.

Lightning flared again, reflecting off those impossible auroras dancing in the clouds. A wave of electricity seemed to tremble through the cabin, making the overhead lights flicker. Maya's pulse hammered as she fought to make sense of the swirling chaos beyond the glass.

Then came another sickening drop, and the oxygen masks deployed with a mechanical *whump*, bobbing in front of shocked faces. Maya fumbled hers on, inhaling the rubbery sting of processed air. Carter strapped his on as well, eyes sharp, scanning the overhead panels as though searching for a logical explanation.

"Flight attendants, brace," Captain Wheeler announced, voice tight with urgency.

Maya's stomach flipped. Beside her, Carter gripped the seat in front. "Brace for what?" he muttered, voice muffled by the mask.

A sideways jolt slammed the cabin, throwing passengers against their seatbelts. Luggage crashed into aisles, and Ethan let out a terrified cry that pierced Maya's chest. She tried focusing on her breathing—*in, out, don't panic*—but the violent rocking shredded any sense of composure.

Then, as abruptly as it started, the turbulence cut off. The plane's engines droned steadily, as though nothing had happened. Shaken cries and whimpers filled the cabin, punctuated by the fizz of short-circuiting wires from overhead panels.

Captain Wheeler's voice returned, quieter now. "We've lost contact with Air Traffic Control. Our instruments aren't... we can't get a proper reading. We may have to attempt an emergency landing."

Maya's heart nearly stopped. *Over the Atlantic?* That made no sense. She looked at Carter, who shook his head slowly, suspicion clouding his eyes.

Minutes ticked by with excruciating slowness. Outside, the storm vanished, replaced by a blank expanse of darkness. No lights from cities or ships—just a midnight void. With labored calm, Olivia announced that they were searching for a place to put the plane down. Another voice behind Maya whispered something about open water.

But instead of water, a faint outline emerged below: a stretch of land that seemed to appear from nowhere. Captain Wheeler's instructions were urgent, nearly breathless. "We see a field. We're going down. Brace, brace, brace."

Panic rippled through the cabin. Seatbelts were yanked tighter, heads bowed. Olivia's voice rang out, instructing everyone to keep their heads down. Maya pressed her forehead to her knees, arms shielding her head. Carter's hand found her shoulder for a moment—a wordless gesture of solidarity.

The engines howled in protest. The aircraft bucked, metal shrieking as wheels and undercarriage collided with something uneven. The impact slammed Maya forward, seatbelt digging hard into her chest. Overhead bins tore open with a deafening crunch. A wash of smoke, burning fuel, and the sharp bite of ozone from sparks assaulted her senses. She clenched her teeth against the cascade of screeches and screams.

After what felt like an eternity of ripping metal and battering force, the plane lurched to a final halt, its fuselage tipped at a precarious angle. In the throbbing silence that followed, only faint moans and the crackle of unseen flames broke the stillness.

Maya sucked in a ragged breath, ears ringing. Her right shoulder throbbed fiercely. She forced herself upright, scanning for Carter. He was pinned beneath a chunk of ceiling panel but conscious. She shoved the debris aside with trembling arms.

"Alive," he wheezed, rubbing his shoulder. "Hurt, but alive."

Maya nodded, adrenaline numbing her pain. All around them, passengers stirred or lay still in disturbing positions. She heard a child's voice, quivering, calling out, "Mom? Dad?"

She scrambled over torn seats and collapsed panels toward the sound. It was Ethan, half-buried beside his unconscious mother. Blood trickled from the woman's temple, but she was breathing. Ethan's father lay just beyond, deathly still. Maya checked for a pulse—nothing.

Ethan's eyes were huge. "My dad—he won't move."

Maya fought tears. "I'm so sorry. Your mom's hurt, but we can help her if we act fast." She turned, shouting at Carter, "I need bandages—seat covers, anything!"

Olivia appeared, hair matted with blood, clutching a first-aid kit as if it were treasure. Maya pressed gauze to the mother's wound while Olivia stabilized her neck, and Carter helped distribute medical supplies. Flames flickered at the plane's ruptured side, and smoke thickened, stinging every breath.

"We have to get out," Olivia said, coughing. "Fuel's leaking. It could ignite."

Carter led the way through a jagged tear in the fuselage, clearing debris so passengers could escape. Outside, the cold night air felt almost shocking as Maya helped carry Ethan's mother to safety. Survivors stumbled onto a vast, featureless field under a sky dotted with unfamiliar constellations. No city lights, no approaching sirens—just silent darkness.

Despite a laceration on her forehead, Victoria made it out, stunned and spattered with soot. "The pilots..." she began, shaking her head. "I couldn't—there was too much debris."

Maya's chest tightened, but there was no time to grieve. She organized a makeshift triage using seat cushions and first-aid supplies. Olivia handed out water and blankets salvaged from the wreckage. Carter found flashlights and directed the uninjured to gather wood to keep a fire going—anything to stave off the bone-deep chill.

Victoria dialed her phone repeatedly, each call either dropped or answered by panicked voices insisting Flight 207 had vanished from radar. Carter got a single bar of signal long enough to leave a rushed message for his mother in Ireland. Maya tried calling her sister, but she only managed a few words on voicemail before her battery died.

Hours stretched. No rescue lights appeared. No helicopters, no sirens. Some survivors wandered the edges of the field, finding nothing but distant tree lines and more emptiness. The sky above shimmered with stars that looked oddly placed, as though they belonged to another part of the universe entirely.

Exhausted and shaking, Maya tended to the injured. She checked pulses, stabilized fractures, pressed makeshift bandages onto bleeding wounds.

Through it all, she felt Ethan's worried gaze. The boy clung to her side, trembling as he watched his mother's shallow breathing.

Sometime before dawn, they huddled around a small fire Carter and a few others managed to light. It cast flickering shadows over weary faces. Victoria, no longer the poised negotiator, stared into the flames with haunted eyes. Olivia offered hushed reassurances to an elderly man clutching a broken arm. A handful of passengers wept quietly, the shock of survival mixed with the agony of loss.

Maya cradled Ethan against the cold, her lab coat draped around his shoulders. She scanned the horizon, numb from fatigue. Logic told her a plane crash this close to any major city—let alone London—would bring help quickly. Yet the unbroken silence pressed in, reminding her how wrong everything was.

Eventually, she sank into a half-sleep, head resting on her folded arms. Nightmares of swirling green-and-violet storms haunted her: in those dreams, she heard disembodied whispers calling her name, felt an odd pull that defied explanation.

She woke to Ethan trembling beside her, his wide eyes glistening with fear. She pulled him close, her voice soft yet firm. "I've got you," she whispered. "We'll get through this." Yet as she gazed into the unfamiliar sky, she couldn't shake the feeling that the worst was yet to come.

CHAPTER 2

Maya woke to a dull ache in her shoulders and the chill of morning air pressing against her skin. The twisted remains of Flight 207 loomed behind her, a surreal monument to survival. Beneath her, a seat cushion doubled as a mattress, and the faint warmth of dying embers licked at her ankles. The sky overhead had shifted from black to a tentative gray, the horizon marked by unfamiliar outlines of trees and rolling fields.

The night had offered no mercy. Only the wounded's ragged moans and hushed cries had broken the stillness, punctuating a series of brief, restless dozes. When Maya finally pushed herself upright, her body grumbled in protest. She rolled her shoulders once, wincing as her mind lurched to more pressing matters: Ethan's mother needed her attention.

She spotted Ethan huddled at his mother's side, his knees pulled to his chest while he stared at the horizon with vacant eyes. Maya knelt beside the unconscious woman and lifted the makeshift blanket, revealing gauze stained a deep, rusty red. The sluggishly clotted edges of the gash across the woman's abdomen told Maya it had seeped all night. She pressed two fingers to the pulse point at her wrist. It was thready, weak enough to stoke Maya's own fear.

A glance at the head wound showed it wasn't actively bleeding, but her abdomen posed the greatest threat. Blood loss. Infection. A near-total lack of supplies. The odds already looked grim.

"Ethan," Maya said gently. "I'm going to search for anything we can use to help your mom. Stay with her, all right?"

He raised his face, eyes hollow with exhaustion. "Is she going to be okay?"

Maya's throat tightened. She wanted to promise success but couldn't force a lie. "I'm doing everything possible, Ethan. I don't know if it's enough."

She rose and found Carter hunched near the embers of a dying fire, poking at its glow with a twisted metal rod. Dust streaked his hair, and a fresh bruise colored his cheek in purplish blues—an unwanted souvenir from last night's desperate struggle to stabilize the survivors.

"Morning," Carter said, managing a half-smile that vanished immediately. "Though it doesn't feel like one. Still no rescue, no drone flights, no news. You'd think the UK would've sent a fleet of choppers by now."

Maya raked her fingers through her tangled hair. "It makes no sense. If we're anywhere in Britain, someone should be here. We'd at least hear sirens, or see medevac teams. It's all just... empty."

Carter shrugged, eyes scanning the distance. "We might've been blown way off course. The storm was vicious. Radar could've failed, sure. But no trace at all? I don't like it."

Victoria emerged from behind a mangled section of the fuselage, her once-elegant suit now torn and dust-streaked. She held her phone limply at her side. "I tried calling again," she said in a wavering voice. "I reached my secretary for a second. She said the news reports claim Flight 207 is lost at sea." Victoria swallowed hard. "They think we're at the bottom of the ocean."

"That's definitely a mismatch," Maya replied, gesturing at the plain of tall grass and the shadowy trees beyond. "We're very much on solid ground."

"They're looking in the wrong place," Victoria muttered, frustration strangling her composure.

Carter nodded grimly. "Storm or no storm, an entire plane doesn't just vanish. But it's been a day, and still no sign of help."

Maya crossed her arms, surveying the other survivors. Most sat slumped or lay sprawled around the broken remains of the plane, their faces ashen. "Something's off," she whispered. "But we can't wait for the perfect explanation. We have to keep people alive."

Victoria's voice hardened. "If no rescue is coming, we need to move. Organize. Scout."

Maya nodded. "I agree. But first, we stabilize anyone who's critical, then figure out how far civilization might be. Maybe we can find a road, a town, anything."

Carter huffed a faint laugh. "A traveling doctor and a knight in shining scrubs. Why not?" His expression sobered. "Still, let's not split up too recklessly."

A breeze rippled through the grass, carrying a subtle chill. Survivors stirred, stiff from cold and fear, while Flight 207's shattered hull cast long shadows in the sparse morning light. Maya eyed the unfamiliar constellations overhead, her stomach twisting with unspoken questions that loomed far larger than their immediate crisis.

At first light, a small scouting party had ventured off: Tomás, a retired history professor, along with Marcus Bryant and Olivia Ramos. Maya stayed behind to tend to the injured. An hour after sunrise, the group returned, trudging across dew-wet grass. Tomás raised an arm in greeting, but his face was grim.

They slumped onto makeshift seats fashioned from luggage. Marcus, broad-shouldered and dirt-streaked, rubbed his neck. "Just more fields," he said flatly. "That dirt path? It led to a trickle of a stream and nothing else."

Olivia massaged the dried blood on her temple. "No power lines. No roads. No phone poles. It's as if we've been dropped into the middle of nowhere. I didn't think England had anywhere this empty."

Maya swallowed her dread. "We'll make do. Right now, we sort out supplies, water, and first aid. One step at a time."

She checked on the others: Nina Patel's leg required elevation, every subtle movement sending tremors of pain through her. Paul Richards clutched his broken wrist, sweating through every breath. Nearby, Sarah Wu hovered beside her husband, Jason, who drifted in and out of a blurry consciousness.

When Maya changed the dressing on Ethan's mother, the woman stirred, eyes flickering. "Where...?" she rasped.

"Shh," Maya whispered, her voice gentle. "Stay still. We're doing everything we can to get help."

Ethan leaned forward. "Mom?"

His mother managed the faintest smile before exhaustion pulled her under once more. Maya gripped the boy's shoulder, fiercely protective. "We keep going," she whispered.

Carter suddenly rose from a wrecked section of the fuselage. He beckoned Maya and Olivia over, pointing at a scorched patch of metal. "Not your typical lightning strike. Edges are too neat, almost like some kind of energy discharge."

Maya ran her fingertips over the charred surface. "So the storm could've done this?"

Carter exhaled, frustrated. "That's my guess. But it doesn't explain why we're stranded in these endless fields."

Victoria approached with her arms crossed, her tone clipped. "Whatever caused it, we need a plan. If there's no rescue, we have to find shelter, water, and food."

Maya wiped sweat from her brow. "Right. Carter, see if you can salvage anything else from the plane. Olivia, lead a group to gather fresh water from that stream. Victoria, help me sort the wounded and ration supplies."

The survivors dispersed, tension rippling among them. Maya steeled herself, focusing on the tasks that stood between life and death. She felt the weight of every heart still beating here, and it made her hands steady despite her own inner quaking.

A brisk wind cut across the field, carrying a faint but unmistakable scent of woodsmoke. Maya stiffened, nostrils flaring as she searched the horizon. There, a thin wisp of gray curled into the sky, distant but undeniably real.

"You guys see that?" she asked, pointing. Heads turned, murmurs filled the air.

"It's not from our fire," Tomás noted. "Maybe a farmhouse or a camp."

"Could be help," Olivia said, eyes bright with sudden hope. "Or it's just another dead end."

"We need to check," Carter agreed.

Maya hesitated. She wanted to stay with the injured, but the possibility of rescue tugged at her more strongly. She turned to Tomás. "You feel up for another trek?"

Tomás offered a resolute nod. "Yes."

Within minutes, Maya, Carter, Tomás, Olivia, and Marcus started toward the drifting smoke. Victoria stayed behind to oversee the injured. Grass crunched beneath their feet as they followed a faint path, each step marked by anticipation and undercut by dread. An hour passed before they crested a low hill—and froze.

Below lay a cluster of huts with thatched roofs, each structure as foreign to their eyes as the endless fields. Wattle-and-daub walls curved beneath sagging beams, small fenced plots grew meager vegetables, and a rudimentary well sat in the center. Figures moved about the dwellings in coarse tunics and simple leather jerkins.

"This can't be real," Carter whispered.

Tomás, the historian, looked pale. "It resembles a medieval settlement. Early architecture. Exactly like the 12th or 13th century. Down to every detail."

An uneasy chill crawled up Maya's spine. The storm, the fields, and now a village from another time? She forced composure. Even if it was the strangest reenactment in history, they needed help. "Let's approach slowly," she said. "Hands visible. Don't scare anyone."

They descended toward the huts, the rustle of grass and the swirl of quiet morning routines greeting them. A woman appeared from behind one dwelling, a basket of vegetables balanced on her hip. The moment she spotted the strangers' modern clothes, her eyes went wide with alarm. The basket dropped, sending cabbages rolling.

She let out a panicked cry and fled, shouting words Maya couldn't decipher. Instantly, men emerged with pitchforks, spears, and crude clubs. They wore loose tunics on skinny frames and eyed Maya's group with grim suspicion.

Tomás stepped forward, hands up in a calming gesture. "We mean no harm," he said slowly, each syllable carefully enunciated.

The men exchanged wary glances, weapons lowering just enough to show they wouldn't kill first and ask questions later. Maya tried next, "Do you speak English?" but was met with blank stares.

One older man scowled and spat a phrase in a rough dialect. Tomás listened intently. "It sounds like a blend of Old and Middle English. I studied it, but hearing it spoken is... surreal."

The villager pointed skyward, barking more words. "Fell from the heavens," Tomás translated, swallowing hard.

Carter, still determined, raised his hands. "We crashed," he said, though they likely understood nothing. He mimed drinking and bandaging wounds, hoping universal gestures might help. "We need help."

Murmurs of confusion rippled through the villagers. Then the crowd parted for a tall figure clad in ragged chainmail, a battered sword hanging at his side. His eyes scanned the strangers with open hostility. He barked something that needed no translation—he wanted them to submit or face the consequences.

Tomás ventured another step, still trying to speak in the archaic language. The man's expression only hardened. He gestured at the wreckage on the horizon, spitting out more words that echoed with accusations of devilry. With a swift motion, he drew his sword a few inches from its scabbard, the blade glinting ominously.

Maya's heart thumped. She raised her hands, voice steady despite her panic. "We don't want trouble. Our plane crashed. People are hurt."

The soldier barked again, leveling his sword in warning. Finally, he waved over the villagers, who formed a ring around Maya's group and nudged them forward.

"Could be worse," Marcus muttered. "At least they're not running us through."

"Not yet," Tomás said, grim resignation in his eyes. "Keep calm."

They were herded past the simple huts, where smoke curled from rudimentary chimneys. A short distance away, a stone fortress rose starkly against the sky, its walls encircling a formidable keep. A wooden bridge spanned a shallow moat, tattered banners catching a faint breeze atop the battlements.

"A castle," Olivia breathed, clutching her useless phone.

All of them struggled to make sense of it. Reenactment? Hallucination? Something else entirely? None of it seemed plausible, yet no other explanation came.

The group crossed the drawbridge, the water below reeking of algae and waste. Their footfalls rang on the wood, the timbers straining under unfamiliar weight. Guards in mismatched chainmail watched from the ramparts, some with open curiosity, others with outright fear.

They entered a bustling courtyard. The clang of a blacksmith's hammer on metal, the squawk of chickens, the low hum of villagers at work—every facet of daily medieval life unfolded before their eyes. It was shockingly real, from the mud-splattered stones underfoot to the pungent stink of unwashed bodies and livestock.

Behind them, the massive wooden gates closed, sealing them inside. The guard from the village—clearly in command—led them into a grand hall lit by guttering torches. Rushes scattered across the floor crackled underfoot, and a raised dais at the far end held an imposing chair swathed in furs. A man in a dark tunic lounged on it, flanked by two grim-faced knights in battered armor.

He asked something in the ancient dialect, voice echoing off the stone walls. Tomás attempted to translate, explaining that they had crashed from the sky, that their "metal bird" was not sorcery. Each sentence earned uneasy murmurs from the watching crowd.

The man, presumably the local lord, pointed at Maya. His expression glimmered with fear and suspicion. More words flew—Tomás caught phrases like "witchcraft," "devils"—and the tension in the hall spiked. Carter tried stepping forward to deny it, but knights seized him. In moments, they were all forced to their knees under the threat of steel.

Tomás pleaded in stilted Middle English, sweat glistening on his brow. After a terse exchange, the lord snarled an order. Guards dragged Maya's group down corridors into a cramped, windowless chamber. A single torch flickered in an iron bracket, casting elongated shadows across the dank stone walls.

When the door slammed shut and the bolt slid into place, silence swallowed them. Carter paced the small room, fists clenched, while Olivia trembled, trying to make sense of the impossible. Tomás leaned against the wall, rubbing his temples.

"This is madness," Carter hissed. "We need to get back to the crash site. Our people—"

Maya nodded. "We can't help them if we're stuck here. But if these people think we're devils, we have to show them we're not."

Olivia's voice turned frantic. "What if we really are in the past? Or some twisted corner of the world that never modernized? None of it fits."

Tomás spoke up, calm but shaken. "The architecture, clothes, and language belong to another century. It's too exact for an isolated community. This is a full medieval world."

They fell silent, fear and disbelief whirling in the stale air. Maya finally drew a stabilizing breath. "Speculation won't save us. We'll try to be useful—offer medicine, healing. That's our best chance to help the others and get out of here."

Carter exhaled harshly. "All right. But I'm not going to grovel if someone waves another sword in my face."

A stretch of time passed in uneasy quiet, lit only by the smoky torch. When the door finally opened, knights marched in and ordered Maya, Carter, and Tomás to follow, leaving Olivia and Marcus behind. The corridors twisted underfoot until they emerged into dazzling sunlight. They blinked against it, hearts pounding.

Villagers murmured and stared as they were ushered beyond the fortress walls. Cresting a small rise, they saw the scattered remains of Flight 207 below. The knights stopped in their tracks, shock rippling through them as they beheld twisted metal glinting in the sun. Several crossed themselves as though confronting a portal to the underworld.

Victoria hurried forward from the wreckage. "You're back," she whispered, voice taut with relief. "People's conditions are worsening."

Carter pointed to the jagged plane fragments, addressing the knights in futility. "It's not a beast. It's technology." He tapped the fuselage for emphasis. The metallic clang echoed, causing a few knights to recoil and grip their swords. Tomás spoke in halting Middle English, trying to calm them.

Maya raced to Ethan's mother, kneeling beside her. The bandage was soaked through, her breathing shallow. A sour odor suggested the start of infection. Maya's pulse hammered. "She's in trouble," she said to Victoria. "We need actual medical supplies—antibiotics, sterile bandages. Something."

Victoria cast a worried glance at the knights. "And how do we ask them for that?"

Just then, a woman of refined bearing stepped forward. Her garments were well-made by local standards, her posture regal. She surveyed Maya's group with cool intelligence, noticing the metal wreckage, the wounded. The local physician, a wiry man in a stained apron, hovered behind her, scowling.

Lady Althea—Tomás managed her name from scattered phrases—focused on Ethan's mother, frowning at the blood-soaked gauze. Maya pressed her hands together in an appeal for aid. She pointed to the wounded woman, then to the castle, hoping the gesture would convey the need for help.

After a tense exchange of words between Lady Althea and the ranking knight, Tomás translated: "They'll let us bring some survivors to the castle for treatment—on a trial basis."

Relief and apprehension battled in Maya's chest. "Tell her thank you," she whispered.

They cobbled together stretchers from plane debris. Knights searched every bag for suspicious items. Victoria and Carter helped get the gravely injured onto improvised cots. Maya felt every second ticking away like a countdown to disaster.

By midday, a somber procession formed toward the fortress. Knights flanked the group, and weary survivors limped alongside makeshift stretchers. Ethan clung to Maya's hand, his eyes dancing with both fear and fragile hope.

Back through the village they went, drawing an even larger crowd. Children pointed, elders whispered about devils from the sky. Some villagers spit on the ground, others gazed at the wounded with compassion. Lady Althea strode ahead, chin lifted in unwavering authority, as if challenging anyone to defy her decision.

Inside the fortress, they entered a cramped infirmary reeking of dried herbs and stale air. Wooden cots lined the walls, each one lumpy and unwelcoming. The physician glared at Maya like she was an unwelcome ghost, his suspicion flaring. But Lady Althea's commanding presence left him no choice. The moment Maya began tending to Ethan's mother, the physician flinched at her modern instruments, especially when she pulled out a stethoscope.

Time blurred as Maya cleaned wounds with boiled water, used scraps of clean cloth to dress them, and did everything possible to stave off infection. When Ethan's mother's fever surged, Maya cooled her with damp rags. The woman's eyelids fluttered, a quiet moan escaping her lips. Ethan hovered, tearful but resolute.

Eventually, Lady Althea returned, motioning Maya to step aside. Tomás followed. Through a halting exchange, Lady Althea asked about airplanes, about the strange metal craft that fell from the sky. She regarded Maya's dark skin with careful fascination, questioning if her people wielded unnatural power. Maya gently explained she had no magic—only knowledge.

Their discussion cut off abruptly when a guard rushed into the infirmary, words tumbling in a frantic stream. Ethan's mother was seizing, her fever blazing through her already weak body. Maya and Carter worked together, easing her rigid limbs and trying to keep her airway clear, while Ethan cried out in horror.

At last, the seizure waned. The woman lay pale and trembling, shallow breaths rattling her lungs. Maya pressed a cloth to the woman's forehead, ignoring the sweat soaking her own temples. Lady Althea and the local physician watched in stunned silence, unsettled by the crisis that Maya fought so desperately to contain.

"She's alive," Maya whispered when the convulsions subsided. She met Ethan's gaze. Terror and hope both burned in his eyes. Outside, the fortress bristled with tension and uncertainty. But inside these walls, for the briefest moment, they had a single fragile thread of hope to cling to.

In the dim torchlight of the infirmary, the barriers between their worlds seemed to blur—ancient and modern colliding in a fragile moment of hope.

CHAPTER 3

Carter leaned against the castle's outer wall, the mingling odors of damp hay, smoke, and unwashed bodies thick in the air. The rough stone pressed into his back, reminding him how brutally real this world had become. Two knights stood watch nearby, their gazes cool, assessing. They said nothing, yet the tension radiating between them and Carter made each breath feel like a risk.

Beyond the wall, farmland rolled toward a distant horizon dotted with thatched huts and grazing animals. At least the crash site remained hidden from view, though its memory lurked in Carter's mind—a warped monument to the life they'd left behind. Now the afternoon sun sat low in the sky, stretching shadows across the fields and coloring the air with a hint of evening chill.

He rolled his stiff shoulders. "You'd think," he muttered, glancing at the nearest knight, "if you're going to keep me here, you'd at least let me help." He gestured toward the blacksmith's forge in the courtyard, where the rhythmic clang of metal on metal served as the castle's uneasy heartbeat. "I'm decent with tools," he added, pointing at himself before miming a hammering motion. "I can fix a plow, patch a fence."

The knight's scowl was the only reply. Carter sighed. "Not big on charades, are you?"

A short distance away, Tomás was deep in conversation with a younger guard near the keep. Unlike most, this guard's eyes gleamed with curiosity rather than fear. Noticing Carter's plight, Tomás beckoned him over.

"Good timing," Tomás said quietly. "This is Thomas—yes, the name's the same in their dialect, though it sounds a bit different. He's trying to learn about us, thinks we might be more interesting than dangerous."

Carter lifted an eyebrow. "That's progress. Ask if I can help at the forge. Might as well make myself useful."

Tomás translated. The guard nodded, beckoning them across the busy courtyard, where men-at-arms honed battered weapons and scrawny chickens pecked at straw. Carter's boots crackled over loose hay as they neared the blacksmith. A man with a soot-streaked face paused mid-swing, his eyes narrowing at Carter's unfamiliar clothing.

The guard spoke quickly, gesturing toward Carter. The blacksmith's stare turned appraising, drifting from Carter's jacket to his boots, then to his face. Carter held up a multi-tool from his pocket, flipping it open to show the pliers and screwdriver. He mimed tightening a bolt, then pointed at a heap of broken farm implements stacked nearby.

The blacksmith's mistrust remained, but curiosity flickered in his eyes. Without a word, he shoved a snapped pitchfork into Carter's hands, a silent dare: fix it.

Carter studied the fractured tip, aware that the blacksmith and a cluster of knights were now watching. He made his way to the forge, each step accompanied by a wave of punishing heat. He stoked the coals and laid the metal in the flames, striking carefully with the blacksmith's hammer. Every swing demanded focus and strength. Sweat trickled down his neck, his biceps burning from the strain. Finally, he quenched the red-hot metal in water, wincing at the burst of steam. Pulling the pitchfork free, he examined its reattached tine—imperfect, but serviceable.

The blacksmith eyed Carter's work, tested the pitchfork against the ground, and grunted once. Not exactly friendly, but Carter sensed a crack in the wall of distrust.

Tomás clapped him on the shoulder. "Not bad. Maybe this earns us a bit of goodwill."

Carter breathed out, letting a small grin surface. "Let's hope one pitchfork is enough to start."

In the castle infirmary, Maya knelt over her patients. The shallow rise and fall of Ethan's mother's chest worried her. Even though the fever had dropped, her lungs rattled with each breath. Ethan hovered by her side, clutching her limp hand in his.

"Can I do something?" he asked softly, voice quivering.

Maya brushed a lock of hair from his eyes. "You already are," she said. She checked the bandage on his arm—thankfully, no sign of infection. "Drink some water. You need your strength too."

Ethan obeyed, sipping from a wooden cup. Shadows flickered across the walls, cast by torches that burned low and smoky. Master Gerald, the local physician, watched from the corner, arms folded. Whenever Maya used her stethoscope or dug into her modern kit, he spat quiet curses. But Lady Althea's sharp gaze kept his muttering in check.

Maya approached him calmly, pointing to his mortar and pestle. "Show me," she coaxed, miming his grinding motion. She gestured from the herbs to Ethan's mom, hoping he'd teach her about his medieval remedies.

Gerald hesitated before lifting a sprig of something he called feverbane. Crushing it released a bitter, pungent scent, not unlike an ancient form of aspirin. Maya breathed in the sharp aroma. She offered a small smile of thanks, and for a moment, the old man's hostility lessened—two healers forging a fragile peace.

The biting scent of herbal brews dominated the cramped space as Maya and Gerald worked in tandem. She helped Ethan's mother swallow diluted remedies, alternating medieval concoctions with careful monitoring. Still, fatigue weighed on her, heightened by the steady trickle of survivors arriving from the crash site.

Paul Richards appeared, clutching his broken wrist, face ashen. Nina Patel limped in with a poorly wrapped leg wound. Sarah Wu propped up her husband, his leg crudely splinted and pain contorting his features. Each injured newcomer brought new challenges for the overcrowded infirmary, fueling Gerald's complaints about space and witchcraft. Lady Althea's presence was all that maintained order.

Sarah touched Maya's arm, voice trembling. "The knights forced us out of the wreckage. Kept repeating a word that sounded like 'bandits'... guess they're worried about raiders?"

Maya wiped sweat from her brow. "Makes sense. The castle might offer some safety, even if they don't trust us. Better than being ambushed."

Sarah gave a shaky nod. "We're their captives, but at least we're safe from whatever's out there."

Nightfall dulled the fortress corridors into an unsettling gloom. Maya lingered in the infirmary, too anxious to leave her patients. In one corner, Ethan and his mother finally slept, her breathing more even than before. Drained, Maya found a nook on a low wooden bench and dozed fitfully.

Haunting images of the plane crash unsettled her sleep—torn metal, howling wind, bizarre flashes of energy. Every time she jerked awake, the groans of wounded or the shuffle of feet grounded her in this grim reality.

She sat up when the door opened, heart thudding. Carter slipped in, accompanied by Thomas—the friendly guard. Carter set down a small satchel: fresh bandages, dried fruit, a chunk of coarse bread. He crouched beside Maya, exhaustion carving lines into his face.

"Been busy making friends at the forge," he whispered. "Bartered for these supplies. You okay?"

Maya rubbed her eyes. "Exhausted, but Ethan's mother is stable. That's... everything right now."

His expression softened. "You're keeping a lot of people alive. Don't sell yourself short."

She wanted to smile, but the weight of uncertainty smothered her. Instead, she thanked him and forced herself to eat a little of the bread. Each swallow tasted of desperation.

When daylight returned, Maya's first action was to check on Ethan's mother. To her relief, the woman's fever had dropped, her breathing steadier. Maya brushed the back of her hand over the woman's forehead, murmuring praise for her resilience. "Keep fighting," she whispered.

Lady Althea arrived soon after, accompanied by Tomás, who looked both tired and intrigued. Through Tomás's translation, Althea wanted to know if it was Maya's potions or Gerald's herbs that saved the woman. Maya insisted it was both. Althea gave a thoughtful nod, then turned to Master Gerald with something like approval in her eyes. Gerald merely frowned, though not as fiercely as before.

Althea beckoned Maya and Tomás along a winding corridor that opened onto a high balcony over the courtyard. Below, peasants gathered near the main gate, their faces weary and hollow. Carter's hammering rang out from the forge, echoing like a slow heartbeat through the stony enclosure. Althea gestured to the throng below, then to Maya.

"She wants you to treat them," Tomás explained, brow creasing. "A test, maybe. To see if you'll help her people."

Maya's gaze traveled across the sick and malnourished forming a ragged line. Children with sunken cheeks clung to mothers who carried festering wounds. "I'll do what I can," Maya murmured.

She spent the rest of the day tending the ill in the courtyard—cleaning cuts, wrapping sprains, and dispensing simple hygiene tips. Most peasants stared at her in awe and apprehension, as if she were a sorceress in disguise. Gerald lurked on the sidelines, making comments under his breath, but not interfering.

Carter appeared near sundown with a small stool and a flask of water. His face was etched with something close to despair, but he tried to hide it as he offered them to Maya. She sipped the water, her back stiff from hours of crouching over patients.

"How are the others?" she asked quietly.

He lowered himself onto a stone ledge, shoulders slumping. "No new word. Everyone's inside these walls, as far as I know. And we've buried those who didn't make it."

Maya bowed her head, the courtyard's chill settling into her bones. The meager fortress walls might protect them from external threats, but they also penned them in. "Doesn't feel like we have a choice," she murmured. "We're stuck."

Carter nodded in agreement. "We are. But at least we're alive."

She exhaled and gazed around at the knot of survivors scattered among the locals. "No plan. No rescue. Just... this." She waved at the fortress's craggy stones.

He offered the flask again. "Drink. You need energy."

Maya's hands trembled around the container. "To do what?" she murmured bitterly.

"You know what," Carter said, his voice quiet but firm. "Keep fighting. For them. For us."

Maya let his words settle, then took a long drink.

Later, Maya trudged back to the infirmary. She found Ethan curled beside his mother, the pair clinging to each other in uneasy sleep. The sight twisted her heart, stirring a fierce protectiveness. Outside the narrow window, knights patrolled the ramparts, steel helmets glinting under moonlight. The castle loomed like a prison on one hand, a fortress on the other—keeping them in while keeping countless threats out.

By the next morning, the survivors had quietly settled into a new rhythm. Carter, grim-faced but determined, worked alongside the blacksmith. Victoria, with stubborn persistence, tried bargaining for better bedding. Her efforts earned little more than sneers from the steward. Nina helped Maya in the infirmary despite a limp that made every step a trial. Paul, still hampered by a splinted wrist, gathered firewood in stiff silence. Each routine felt like an anchor in the swirling chaos, even as dread simmered beneath the surface.

Ethan rarely strayed from Maya's side, fetching water, gathering scraps of cloth, or simply watching her with worried eyes. His resilience warmed her heart, providing a spark of hope when her own faith wavered.

Any sense of relative peace shattered one morning when a guard summoned all survivors to the great hall. They trudged across the courtyard, the weight of unspoken fears slowing their steps. Inside, the vaulted ceilings seemed to swallow the faint daylight. Lord WilCarter perched at the far end on a fur-draped throne, his stance exuding ownership of every stone in sight. Lady Althea sat to his right, posture regal and calm, her eyes darting between the visitors and her husband.

Knights stood along the walls, armor mismatched and ancient, but their unwavering gazes signaled readiness. A long, scarred table bisected the hall, remnants of bread and cheese scattered across its surface. A musty tapestry depicting a hunting scene hung lopsidedly, its colors dulled by the centuries.

WilCarter spoke, his tone clipped, each syllable echoing in the cavernous hall. Tomás translated haltingly. "He says we've proven... moderately useful. He's allowing us more freedom—within the castle and the village."

Lady Althea spoke next, her voice almost gentle, gesturing to the survivors. Tomás relayed, "She says we're still under their rule and protection. If we want to leave, we must wait for his permission."

Victoria stepped forward, her voice steady but threaded with desperation. "Thank you for your hospitality," she said, pausing for Tomás to translate. "But we need safe passage. Our families—"

WilCarter cut in, stiffening at the mention of distant lands. He responded tersely; Tomás explained: "He can't spare knights. His borders are threatened by a rival baron. He won't risk his men on a journey across unknown seas."

The mention of conflict sent a ripple of unease through the survivors. Maya remembered Sarah's talk of bandits and warring lords. Even if they were granted permission, stepping outside these walls might be more perilous than staying.

Eventually, the survivors were led to a cramped space near the stables, where they fashioned tents from tarps salvaged from the wreckage. Knights stood watch, ever vigilant, but the arrangement was still an improvement over a cell. Over the following days, Ethan's mother slowly regained her strength. One morning, Maya helped her shuffle across the infirmary floor, while Ethan darted around them like a nervous sparrow.

The woman's voice, faint but steady, broke the silence. "Thank you," she whispered. "For saving my life."

Maya squeezed her hand, uncertain how to respond. Saving a life should have felt monumental, but here, it seemed like a single droplet in an ocean of needs. "I don't think we've been formally introduced. I'm Maya."

"I'm Anna."

"Anna, it was a group effort," Maya replied with a small smile, ruffling Ethan's hair. "This one hasn't left your side."

Ethan giggled shyly, hiding his face against his mother's arm.

Word of Maya's skills spread quickly among the peasants, and more began trickling in for help: infected wounds, high fevers, children weakened by malnutrition. She worked tirelessly, though her supplies dwindled by the day. Master Gerald watched her efforts with a mix of grudging acceptance and quiet approval. Occasionally, he stepped in to demonstrate an age-old remedy or correct her application of local herbs. Together, they forged a weary synergy, blending medieval traditions with modern ingenuity.

Carter hammered and shaped metal in the forge, forging a shaky rapport with the blacksmith. Tomás pushed himself to learn the local tongue, scribbling down every phrase. Victoria tried to charge her phone with a jury-rigged solar panel, leaving frantic voicemails that went unanswered. Paul, once a tech executive, offered grim ideas about documenting their knowledge in case no rescue ever arrived. The suggestion unsettled them all.

Maya, though, found comfort in glimpses of progress—each time Anna took an extra step, or a child's infection subsided. Small triumphs, overshadowed by rumors of war. Lord Braxton, a rival, had begun raiding border villages. The knights sharpened weapons while the local villagers handed over grain and livestock to meet higher levies. Whispers of ill fortune clung to the survivors like a shadow.

Late one afternoon, Maya was startled by commotion in the courtyard. Shouting guards, the thunder of hooves. She hurried outside to see knights dragging in two wounded soldiers, both bearing arrow wounds that seeped red. Her heart spiked with dread. Dropping beside them, she slashed through blood-soaked cloth and pressed clean bandages against gaping flesh. Gerald loomed, calling for a red-hot iron to cauterize. Maya insisted on cleaning the wounds first with boiled water, sparking an urgent argument.

In the end, they split the difference: Maya scrubbed as best she could, then stepped back as the iron seared the wounds. The men's screams ricocheted through the courtyard, chilling her. Once the branding was done, she wrapped their injuries in fresh linens. Lord WilCarter arrived, a storm in his eyes, demanding to know if they could be saved. Maya answered with measured calm, "I'll do everything possible. But it's in fate's hands now."

The lord's gaze flickered from desperation to respect. Their survival might dictate whether the survivors were seen as allies or devils. That night, Maya and Gerald stood vigil, listening to the men's ragged breathing. If they lived, the castle's gratitude might buy the survivors more time. If they died, the whisper of "witchcraft" would return.

Carter checked on Maya, exhaustion etched into his every step. "If fighting ramps up, the wounded will keep pouring in."

She stared at her bloody hands, longing for the clean efficiency of a modern ER. "We're too valuable to lose. They'll never let us go."

He said nothing, but the truth weighed on them both.

Over the following days, Maya's efforts pulled the knights back from death's door. Word spread of her skill. Suspicion shifted toward a precarious gratitude. The peasants offered small tokens—a few eggs, a clay jug of goat's milk. This fragile acceptance eased some of the survivors' hardships.

One late afternoon, Lady Althea requested Maya's company on the ramparts. Tomás served as translator. Althea pointed toward a cluster of distant huts, explaining that disease ran rampant there. Their crops had failed; the people were desperate. Would Maya help?

Fear rippled through her at the idea of leaving the castle's meager safety. Yet people were suffering. And maybe beyond that village lay a clue—some explanation for the storm that had propelled them through time. "I'll go," she said, heart thudding.

Althea rested a hand on Maya's shoulder, murmuring words that Tomás turned into thanks. The next evening, Maya and Carter made careful preparations. She gathered her battered medical supplies, a canteen, and the stethoscope she refused to abandon. Carter assembled what he could with the blacksmith's assistance: a crude but serviceable knife, a reinforced pouch for food, a coil of rope. Tension crackled in the air—no one knew what awaited them outside these walls.

Anna insisted on letting Maya go. "I'm strong enough now," she managed, though her voice wavered. "Ethan will stay here. Help them. Save whoever you can."

Ethan clutched Maya's waist, voice trembling. "You don't have to leave, do you?"

Her heart twisted. "I do," she whispered. "Like I helped your mom, I'll try to help other people too." She forced a steadiness she didn't feel. "Stay with her, okay? She needs you."

He sniffed, nodding while Carter knelt beside him. "I'll look after her," Carter said to the boy, ruffling his hair lightly. "Don't worry."

Victoria placed a hand on Maya's shoulder. "Watch your back out there. Come back in one piece."

Before dawn, the party assembled in the courtyard, breaths puffing in the frosty air. Pale sunlight stretched over the ramparts, making the forest in the distance look both sinister and inviting. Each survivor had a borrowed horse, the animals stamping restless hooves against the cobbles. Maya, unaccustomed to riding, clung to the saddle on a tall gray gelding that tossed its head in irritation.

Carter eased his horse closer, noticing her white-knuckled grip. "Relax," he murmured. "If you panic, the horse will know."

Maya exhaled shakily. "Easier said than done." She held the reins with trembling hands, trying not to pull too hard.

A scarred knight trotted up, barking an order. Tomás spoke softly. "He says don't yank on the reins, you're confusing it."

"Got it," Maya muttered, loosening her grip bit by bit.

The knights took the lead, armor clinking as they rode under the raised portcullis. Maya's horse lurched forward, testing her balance. She glanced back at the receding castle walls, fear gnawing at her. One part of her wanted to stay behind those thick stones, but a stronger part recognized the urgency of the mission.

Carter leaned over. "You'll get the hang of it, Doc."

She gave a tight nod, guiding the horse onto the winding dirt path. The forest's edge loomed ahead, tall trees bathed in the rising sun. Her heart pounded, yet she pressed on.

Above them, Lady Althea stood on the battlements, watching in silence as they rode away. Maya couldn't tell if it was a blessing or a test. Probably both.

They entered the open countryside, where the ground lay frozen and rutted. Each hoofbeat drummed a somber rhythm. The knights remained alert, scanning the treeline for potential threats. Carter offered Maya a reassuring look. "Ready?" he asked.

She swallowed hard. "As I'll ever be. If there's a chance to help that village—or find any clues to our situation—I have to try."

His grin was brief but genuine. "That's what you do, Doc. You try. You save people."

The sun inched higher, lending weak warmth to the frosty air. Yet as they neared the shadowy woods, Maya felt a chill of unease. This land held more secrets than she could fathom. But she urged her horse onward, determined to face whatever waited.

CHAPTER 4

The sun climbed higher as Maya urged her borrowed mare down the uneven road, her heart pounding every time the horse stumbled on loose stones. She clutched the reins, still uneasy atop the powerful creature. Riding wasn't just unfamiliar—it rattled her nerves. Beside her, Carter seemed to glide in a practiced rhythm, seated with a confidence that made her clench her jaw. Four knights flanked them, chainmail clinking in soft, rhythmic warnings. Their gazes swept across the horizon for threats.

Fields stretched on both sides, punctuated by distant cottages and sparse clusters of forest. Villagers paused their morning chores to stare at the odd procession. Maya heard their hushed chatter—sharp, uneasy murmurs about the strange pair under the lord's protection. She kept her focus ahead, hoping to avoid their eyes.

"I never thought I'd be a mechanic on horseback," Carter muttered, shattering the uneasy stillness. "And I sure didn't think my first Middle Ages gig would be fixing wheels."

Maya offered a wry smile. "At least you're useful. Half the time, I feel like I'm throwing Band-Aids at bullet wounds."

He glanced her way, expression softening. "You're keeping people alive. That's more than anyone here expected." His voice dropped, solemn. "You sure this trip is worth the risk?"

Her shoulders stiffened in the saddle, legs aching from the unfamiliar strain. "If there's any chance we can stop that illness from spreading, we have to try."

He nodded, though his jaw set with concern. The knights remained silent, a reminder of the hazards ahead.

They reached the village by mid-afternoon. It was a husk of life. The air hung thick with decay, a sour scent clinging to the back of Maya's throat. Crooked huts leaned on each other like exhausted drunks, while gaunt villagers peered from behind warped shutters. Flies buzzed over a mound of refuse near the road, a constant drone in the heavy hush.

When Maya dismounted, her legs screamed in protest. She was grateful to stand on solid ground again, though the feeling of relief vanished almost instantly. A frail elder shuffled out from a hovel, urgency plain in every step. He barked words in a dialect that differed from the castle's, pointing from the knights to Maya. One knight responded curtly, gesturing at her in turn.

The elder's gaze landed on her with a mixture of bafflement and hope. He motioned for them to follow, and they trailed him deeper into the village.

A row of dim huts waited, filled with the low, unending moans of the sick. Stale air carried the stench of unwashed bodies and festering wounds. Maya swallowed, forcing her stomach to steady. Harsh coughs echoed from corners lost in gloom, and a child's frail whimper prickled her skin. She didn't need lab work to know this was an outbreak.

She flung open her medical kit, her mind tallying every supply. "We need boiled water—lots of it," she told Carter, her tone clipped but calm. "If they have a pot or kettle, anything we can use to make the water safe, find it."

He hurried off. The knights shifted uncertainly, but one or two barked orders at the villagers to help. Maya moved with deliberate focus—checking pulses, feeling for fever, listening with her stethoscope. At first, the villagers drew away in alarm. One even crossed himself, muttering under his breath.

"Easy," she murmured, though it was unlikely they understood. She used gestures and a gentle tone to convey her intention.

She soon identified the source of the sickness: a stagnant pond the villagers relied on for water. Filthy, no question. Her frustration spiked. Treating the sick would help, but without a safe water supply, they were fighting a losing battle.

By nightfall, she'd ministered to dozens of patients, using the knights' halting translations to outline basic sanitation. Carter finally returned, sweat and soot marking his face. "We boiled a decent batch of water," he said, voice thick with fatigue. "It's not much, but it's something."

"It's a start," she agreed, though a heavy weight pressed on her. A few patients showed faint improvements—a child with a calmer fever, an old woman sipping water without coughing—but it felt like bailing water out of a sinking ship.

They camped at the village that night, the knights setting a wary guard. By the fire's glow, Maya sifted through her dwindling medical supplies. Fever-reducers, antiseptic wipes—she rationed them like precious coins. Across from her, Carter stirred a pot of thin broth, looking troubled.

"You saved lives today," he said softly.

She grimaced, the words comforting yet hollow. "It's never enough. I can't fix everything with a few pills and bandages."

He met her gaze. "You're doing more than anyone else here ever could."

The following days blurred into a haze of backbreaking labor and exhaustion. Maya taught a handful of villagers how to boil water and keep their dwellings cleaner. Carter fixed broken tools, patched leaks in a battered well bucket. At first, the knights watched them with cool detachment, but gradually they began to show grudging respect for the foreigners determined to help.

Then the merchant arrived.

His wagons rattled into the village on the fourth day. They were loaded with sacks of grain, though the man himself looked modest—ordinary clothes, sharp glint in his eye. He studied the sick with a curious mix of pity and calculation.

Carter was repairing a wagon wheel when the merchant spotted him, pointing at his modern jacket, then at Maya who was bent over a patient. He spoke rapidly with the guards, who flinched at his tone.

Soon, the merchant beckoned Maya and Carter behind a wagon. Under a stained tarp lay a small wooden chest. When the merchant pried it open, Maya's heart lurched. Nestled inside were objects that shouldn't exist here—coins with odd symbols, a cracked plastic compass. Artifacts from another time.

"Where did you find these?" she asked, knowing he wouldn't understand. The merchant gestured west, hands mimicking swirling winds.

"Storms," Carter translated cautiously, his voice hushed. "He says storms bring... strange things."

The merchant's warning was evident: items like these invited suspicion and danger, especially from powerful men. He gave them to Maya without fanfare, snapped the chest shut, then melted into the gathering dusk, leaving Maya and Carter speechless.

That evening, they huddled in the small hut that served as their base. The broken compass rested on a rickety table, its cracked face catching the flicker of the oil lamp. Maya ran a fingertip over it. "This is definitely from modern times," she murmured. "He said it blew in with storms from the west."

Carter folded his arms, hesitation and hope mingling in his expression. "If these storms have happened before, maybe there's a chance they'll happen again—and maybe we can go back."

Her pulse leapt at the thought. "How do we look for them? Lord WilCarter barely lets us out of sight these days. We're under constant surveillance."

He set his jaw. "We could try negotiating. Offer him technology, better tools. Or..." He paused, voice lowering. "We slip away."

The dangerous idea hung between them. Maya closed her eyes, wondering about the objects' previous owners. Did they escape, or did they die here in the past? The question chilled her.

Slowly, the village's health improved under Maya's relentless care. People still died, but not nearly so many. Hygiene efforts and safe drinking water practices took hold. Some villagers whispered about the "strange healer," reverent or fearful depending on who told the story. Maya barely registered their murmurs, focused on saving whoever she could. When Lord WilCarter's messenger arrived with a summons to return to the castle, she left the villagers with instructions—boil water, keep distance between the sick and healthy, dispose of waste away from living areas. She could only pray they followed her advice.

The journey back was tense. Carter scanned every bend in the road, as though bracing for an ambush. Maya couldn't stop replaying the merchant's warning, picturing the cracked plastic compass. If the storms offered a path home, how could they reach it under the lord's scrutiny?

When they entered the castle courtyard, the atmosphere crackled with urgency. Knights sharpened swords while peasants hauled crates. Word had spread about clashes on the border between WilCarter and a neighboring lord named Braxton. A siege loomed like a specter over the fortress.

Victoria greeted them, visibly relieved. "Thank God you're back," she whispered. "WilCarter's been impossible. Tempers are high."

Maya asked after Ethan and his mother. Victoria assured her they were safe, but then pulled her aside. "There's a complication. WilCarter discovered Carter's talent for forging. He wants him to make better weapons."

Carter's lips thinned. "So I'm an arms dealer now?"

Victoria nodded. "If you refuse, he might lock us up. Or let Braxton storm the place and take us all."

That night, they gathered in the makeshift camp in the castle stables—Maya, Carter, Victoria, Tomás, and the rest—faces grim in the glow of torchlight.

"If we help him make weapons, we fuel a medieval war," Paul said, voice rough. "That has to break every rule of time travel ever written."

Tomás exhaled. "We might be meddling with history either way. And if WilCarter loses, Braxton might wipe us out."

Maya rubbed her temples. "We can't win if we're dead. We need the lord's protection until we figure out how to find these storms. But we shouldn't lose sight of our bigger goal."

She showed them the compass, describing the merchant's account of strange storms in the west. They clung to that sliver of hope. Meanwhile, they cooperated with Lord WilCarter, though uneasily. Carter toiled in the smithy, shaping spearheads and arrow tips. Maya patched up wounded knights, hoping each act of mercy earned them a little more security. Still, guilt churned in her whenever she pictured those new weapons in battle.

One afternoon, Anna approached Maya, moving with renewed strength. The grief in her eyes smoldered beneath her gratitude. "Thank you," she said softly. "But we can't stay like this forever. Ethan deserves more."

Maya squeezed her hand. "We're trying. I promise."

Each day brought more tension. One evening, as they shared a meager meal in the stable, a guard appeared, frantic. He babbled to Tomás, pointing at the gate.

Tomás paled. "Braxton's banners are outside."

They hurried to the ramparts, finding the castle in chaos. Knights formed defensive lines, crossbows loaded, swords unsheathed. Beyond the moat, six riders in dark surcoats sat astride restive horses under a crimson banner with a snarling beast. Their leader shouted a challenge in guttural tones.

Tomás translated: "They demand WilCarter turn us over or face an attack."

Maya's heart jumped. "They want us?"

Carter muttered a curse. "We're chess pieces in a medieval arms race."

From the battlements, WilCarter roared his response. Tomás caught words like "my domain," "sworn charges," and "no right to claim them." Braxton's riders traded insults before galloping away into the night.

Tomás turned to them, face drawn. "They gave WilCarter three days. If he doesn't hand us over, they'll attack. They think we have advanced knowledge—things they can exploit."

Victoria's hands curled into fists. "That's just perfect. We're the ultimate trophy."

Maya's stomach churned. "If we stay, we risk open war. But if we leave, who knows what Braxton will do to us?"

Lord WilCarter descended the steps, his expression grim. He addressed the group, speaking with a clipped edge. Through Tomás, he warned them: this was their doing, but he wouldn't give them up. In exchange, they owed him total loyalty, especially in the face of impending battle.

Carter's face darkened. "So I keep churning out weapons."

Maya sighed. "Either that or end up in Braxton's clutches."

They exchanged glances laced with dread. War was coming, and they were at the heart of it.

Preparations swallowed the castle in a frenzy. Carter hammered out more arrowheads. Maya stocked the infirmary, bracing for incoming casualties. The atmosphere weighed on everyone, tension vibrating like a plucked string.

Anna approached Maya in a shadowy alcove near the infirmary. "A battle is coming, isn't it?" Her voice trembled.

Maya nodded. "It looks that way. All we can do is survive."

Knights patrolled incessantly. Scouts brought word of Braxton's troops massing nearby. Civilians huddled together, praying or slipping into corners of the courtyard to weep. In their cramped stable quarters, Victoria labored over a torn scrap of parchment dotted with messy phonetic Middle English that Tomás had taught her. She dipped a quill in ink, forcing her hand steady:

To Lord Braxton, We are the sky-people, strangers not of this land. We do not seek conflict. We have knowledge to share. Spare this castle and its people. We wish to speak for peace.

She folded the note and sealed it with a drop of wax from a dripping candle. It wasn't flawless—Tomás had warned her—but perhaps it could avert needless bloodshed. She slipped it to a jittery stable boy along with a few silver coins that Carter had gotten from a merchant.

"Take this to Braxton's camp," she whispered. "Make sure his men see it. Hurry, and don't be caught."

He nodded, though fear flickered in his eyes. He tucked the note under his tunic and disappeared into the night.

Morning brought disaster. WilCarter's men caught the stable boy slipping out and confiscated the letter, delivering it straight to the lord. His rage boiled over. He marched into the survivors' camp with two heavily armed knights, eyes flashing.

Tomás stepped forward, hands raised. "My lord, what is this about?"

WilCarter thrust the crumpled parchment at him. After reading it, Tomás swallowed. "He's accusing us of conspiracy with Braxton. He demands to know who wrote this."

The group fell silent, glancing at one another. At last, Victoria stepped forward, trembling but defiant. "I did. I was trying to prevent war."

Tomás relayed her words, but WilCarter's anger didn't relent. He snarled that her action jeopardized the castle, might have encouraged the enemy to think them weak. It was treason.

Victoria's voice shook with emotion. "I only wanted to stop the fighting. To save lives."

Tomás conveyed her plea. WilCarter spat a final warning, then stormed out with his knights.

"What did he say?" Carter asked tightly.

Tomás exhaled. "No more second chances. Any sign of further contact with Braxton will bring severe punishment."

Everyone stared at Victoria. She sank onto a wooden crate, hands pressed to her temples. "I just wanted peace. We can't stay trapped here forever."

Maya rested a hand on her shoulder. "We know. But right now, WilCarter's protection is all that keeps us from Braxton's reach."

Victoria nodded numbly. Her attempt had failed; tension in the castle soared. Time ticked toward the deadline Braxton had set, and the survivors could almost taste the dread in the air.

The final day arrived under a bruise-colored sky. Torches dotted the walls while crossbowmen and knights took positions. Maya waited near the infirmary, a sick ache rolling in her gut. Her table held bandages, simple herbs, and the last of her antiseptic wipes. She organized them by priority, recalling her emergency room training.

Ethan hovered by her side, gripping her sleeve. His mother knelt next to him, eyes clouded with fear. Maya crouched and took his hands. "Stay inside. Find somewhere safe. Keep quiet, and don't move until I come for you. Got it?"

He nodded, tears threatening to spill. "Be careful."

At first light, Braxton's army gathered in a ragged line along the horizon. Crimson banners flapped in a biting wind. WilCarter's knights fidgeted, outnumbered yet determined to hold. Maya stood beside Carter on the ramparts, scanning the enemy. The tension was suffocating.

A trumpet blasted, ripping apart the stillness. A volley of arrows arced overhead, rattling off the stone walls. The siege was on.

Maya sprinted back to the courtyard where the wounded soon poured in. Screams, shouts, and the clash of swords merged into a nightmarish symphony. She triaged men with arrow wounds, knives to the gut, shattered bones. Carter dashed around, carrying water, pressing bandages against gushing injuries. The forge master, helped by heating irons to cauterize the worst of it.

Blood soaked the cobblestones. Maya's hands didn't stop moving—stitching, cleaning, pressing clean rags against seeping wounds. Even her busiest shifts in the ER had never matched this sheer scale of carnage.

Carter slumped against a wall, chest heaving. "We helped WilCarter's men get stronger," he said, voice hollow. "They used that strength to kill. But if we hadn't, they'd all be dead. It's madness."

Maya stared at her bloodstained palms. "No perfect choices here." She turned toward another injured knight, her voice hoarse. "Let's keep going."

By midday, Braxton's trumpet calls sounded a retreat. Shattered bodies littered the battlefield beyond the moat. Inside the castle, the courtyard became a makeshift morgue. Some knights cheered, but their triumph sounded feeble. Too many had fallen. Maya toiled on until her hands cramped, saving who she could.

WilCarter trudged through the carnage, grime and soot clinging to his face, eyes rimmed with fatigue. He inclined his head toward Maya—a wordless thanks. Yet the unspoken message rang loud and clear: this was only the first battle. More waited on the horizon.

That evening, the survivors gathered in their corner of the stables, silent and pale as ghosts. Ethan cradled in his mother's arms, Victoria stared at the floor, Tomás sat with his head bowed, and Carter stared at the distant stars. At length, Tomás breathed, "We're altering everything here—lives, wars, the course of history. And we're still stranded."

Maya tipped her gaze to the sky. "Then we keep trying," she whispered.

She imagined the rumored storms in the west—portals, maybe, or cosmic disturbances that had dragged them here. Were they still swirling, waiting for the right moment to fling them home? She found it hard to believe in miracles with the stench of blood everywhere. Yet a fragile sliver of hope flickered. She squeezed Ethan's little hand in hers, summoning the only comfort she could muster: the will to endure another day.

CHAPTER 5

Smoke still wreathed the castle courtyard in pale coils, drifting from the smoldering remnants of pitched arrows. Maya stood near the makeshift infirmary, rubbing the ache between her eyes. Dawn had turned the sky a hazy gold, revealing the scarred landscape that stretched beyond Kentwood's walls. The acrid smell of scorched wood clung to everything, a harsh reminder of yesterday's battle against Lord Braxton's forces.

Lord WilCarter's victory had been just enough to repel the attack—for now—but the price lay in a row of fresh graves near the outer ramparts. Inside the infirmary, more wounded knights moaned with fever or bled through bandages. Maya had worked through the night, pressing gauze against injuries, doing her best to ease delirium with limited supplies.

Carter appeared from the courtyard. His sleeves were shoved up past his elbows, revealing bruises from hauling injured men to safety. Soot streaked his stubbled jaw. "Mornin', Doc," he said, voice low and strained. "How is it in there?"

Maya released a mirthless breath. "Holding by a thread. Another knight died an hour ago. Sepsis or shock—couldn't save him."

He exhaled slowly, gaze drifting to the bandaged men in the infirmary's open doorway. "If Braxton rallies his troops, the next assault could be worse. Word is he's gathering an even bigger army."

A sick lurch twisted Maya's stomach. Another battle would mean another surge of casualties. She was an ER physician armed with future knowledge, yet her resources in this age were paltry. Already, she felt like she was running a 12th-century clinic while confronting 21st-century injuries. "I can't keep this pace forever. We need real solutions."

Carter clenched his jaw. "We might have to leave."

Their exchange was interrupted by the sharp sound of boots on stone. Victoria rounded the corner, hair pinned in a makeshift style that still somehow looked businesslike. She'd discarded her ruined suit jacket for a practical tunic, though her eyes still shone with fierce intelligence.

"Lord WilCarter is calling everyone to the great hall," she said breathlessly. "He wants a meeting with all survivors to discuss new defensive plans—something about us, too." She smoothed a stray lock of hair, regaining her composure. "We should go."

Carter and Maya shared grim looks, then fell in step behind Victoria across the courtyard. They passed the stables, where other survivors—Paul, Nina, Sarah, and the newly mobile Jason Wu—lingered. Ethan and his mother stood by the entrance, the boy's eyes dark with worry.

"You're coming?" Maya asked softly, addressing Anna. The woman looked pale but steadier than before.

She swallowed. "Yes. If WilCarter wants a headcount of these 'sky-people,' I'd rather stand with the rest of you."

They walked as a group, weaving among the castle's tense knights. Most wore bloodstained surcoats from the previous day's battle. Anxious glances confirmed Kentwood had survived once, but few believed the danger had passed.

The great hall, normally alive with idle chatter or feasts, felt oppressive. Torches spat orange light across the high stone walls. At the dais stood Lord WilCarter, draped in a fur-trimmed cloak, his face carved with exhaustion and a sense of purpose. Lady Althea hovered at his right, expression impenetrable. Knights and stewards hovered around them like statues.

When the survivors had gathered, a steward struck the floor with the butt of a polearm, calling for silence. WilCarter's gaze swept over the group—Maya, Carter, Victoria, Tomás, and the rest. His eyes held the weight of a man who had lost soldiers and might lose more if he couldn't control the situation.

Tomás cleared his throat, ready to interpret. WilCarter spoke in archaic English, gesturing forcefully at points. After a pause, Tomás offered the translation:

"He says we've proven helpful with healing and forging, and that was crucial in defending Kentwood. But Lord Braxton remains a grave threat, demanding we be handed over. WilCarter refuses, believing our knowledge is too valuable to sacrifice. He also fears we might draw future attacks."

A ripple of tension moved among the survivors. Carter's shoulders tightened. Guilt twisted Maya's insides. Their presence here had triggered at least part of this conflict.

Tomás continued, voice trembling. "So WilCarter intends to keep us under his protection but also under tighter supervision. He wants a formal oath of loyalty."

Victoria frowned. "An oath of loyalty? Feudal style, where we swear fealty to him as our liege lord?"

Tomás gave a curt nod. "Exactly. If we swear, we're bound to his laws and expected to support him in battles. He sees it as the only way to ensure we won't defect to Braxton or vanish into the countryside."

Sarah gripped Jason's hand. "Then we're endorsing his war. We'll have to fight or heal his soldiers."

Victoria's gaze flicked to Maya and Carter. "We can't survive alone out there, but we'll lose autonomy if we do this."

Lady Althea spoke softly, her words directed at Maya in reference to the healing she'd provided. Tomás interpreted: "She says she understands we come from a distant land with strange customs. But WilCarter can't protect us unless we stand with him wholeheartedly. She asks that we consider forging this alliance."

The hall fell silent. Maya's mind spun, recalling the siege's brutality. Refusing WilCarter's protection would place them at Braxton's mercy—or in the path of roving bandits. Swearing fealty in the 21st-century sense felt impossible, but they were trapped in a medieval reality that demanded it.

Carter cleared his throat. "Tomás, tell him we need a little time to discuss this among ourselves—just a day to decide."

Tomás translated. WilCarter's brow lifted, then he nodded briskly. The steward announced something, and a collective breath was released in the hall. The survivors were ushered back into the courtyard, knights shifting to let them pass.

They regrouped near the stables, hearts pounding at the thought of this pivotal decision.

Beneath the rafters, they formed a tense circle around a single flickering torch on the wall. Maya crossed her arms, leaning against a wooden post.

"We have one day to choose. If we reject the oath, WilCarter might see us as a threat or let Braxton come after us."

Tomás rubbed his forehead. "In a feudal setting, refusing a liege-lord's demand is practically suicide. He might imprison us or withdraw protection entirely."

Nina smoothed a crease in her tunic. "What about the reports of a strange storm phenomenon in the west? If we're stuck under house arrest, we can't investigate."

Victoria let out a soft, wry laugh. "Hard to investigate if we're dead."

Anna pulled the boy closer. "He's only ten. I can't let him live like this, always looking over his shoulder. If taking the oath keeps us out of Braxton's hands, it might be our best shot."

Maya closed her eyes, recalling the chaos of the past days. "It buys us time to survive, though it means forging weapons and tending soldiers for a war we never wanted. But maybe this is the only way forward until we can find a real way home."

Paul cleared his throat. "Yes, we may be forging war tools and healing knights, but it gives us cover. Once we're more free to move, we can keep an eye out for any rift or anomaly."

Jason, braced on a rough-hewn cane, nodded. "I agree. We'll never make it out there alone."

Maya exhaled shakily. "Let's vote."

The survivors, uneasy with turning such a momentous choice into a show of hands, still knew they had little choice. One by one, they voiced reluctant approval. Only Sarah faltered, whispering that it felt like betraying their world. Ultimately, she conceded, determined to safeguard her husband.

Next morning, they informed WilCarter of their conclusion. He summoned them to a smaller council room near the great hall. Torches lit the chamber, revealing a massive oak table. WilCarter, Lady Althea, and several knights stood waiting.

Tomás bowed slightly. "We accept the oath, my lord," he said in stilted medieval phrasing. "We only ask for some freedom to keep our own crafts and beliefs."

WilCarter's stern features remained steady as he spoke in hushed tones. Tomás relayed: "As long as your crafts don't undermine the realm or aid Braxton, you may continue. But you serve me and my cause."

Ceremony followed—each survivor knelt, albeit awkwardly, before WilCarter. Carter bristled at the humiliation of bowing, but forced himself to endure. Maya's chest tightened. She was a modern physician, sworn to save lives under the Hippocratic Oath, and now had to swear fealty to a medieval lord. The contradiction made her pulse pound.

When it came her turn, she lowered her gaze. WilCarter placed his callused palm on her shoulder and recited the formal words. Tomás silently translated: "I receive your vow. May your skill serve Kentwood." Maya felt the intangible bonds of fealty coil around her. Rising, she caught Lady Althea's faint smile, as if the woman recognized how alien this moment was for them.

The days that followed showed WilCarter's promise of protection in a concrete way: instead of tents in the stable yard, the survivors were assigned a cluster of small rooms near the south tower. Though spartan—wooden beds and shuttered windows—they were at least more private. Knights guarded them, but the atmosphere felt less like imprisonment and more like lodging for crucial aides.

Carter's forging responsibilities multiplied. Working with the castle blacksmith, he churned out arrowheads and spear tips in preparation for another conflict. He returned to the tower exhausted each evening, a bleak scowl marking his face. "I'm making tools for war," he murmured to Maya one night. "It goes against everything in me, but I see no other way."

Maya squeezed his soot-blackened hand. "I know. Just keep reminding yourself this is only temporary. Eventually, we'll find a path out. Right?"

He tried to nod, though his eyes remained clouded with doubt.

Maya, meanwhile, became the go-to physician for both survivors and local peasants. WilCarter's men increasingly brought her villagers with fevers or infected wounds. Word of her previous medical triumphs had spread. Her makeshift clinic drew a steady flow of the injured. Master Gerald, the resident healer, had grown more cooperative—perhaps begrudgingly impressed by her successes. He began offering local herbs known to ease pain or slow infection.

One afternoon, she treated a teenage girl with a severe leg abscess. Maya carefully drained and irrigated it with boiled water, using the remnants of her antibiotic ointment. As she wrapped the wound, Gerald watched with intense focus, scribbling notes on parchment, trying to capture her methods.

Lady Althea observed quietly from the corner. Afterward, she asked Tomás whether Maya had more "magic salves." Maya admitted her modern stock was nearly gone. A flicker of concern crossed Althea's face. That day, Maya resolved to experiment with medieval plants, trying to formulate substitutes for her dwindling antiseptics.

Despite the oath and new rooms, tension lingered among the survivors. Paul, in particular, despised his new role as WilCarter's adviser on supply management—using modern knowledge to ration grain and store water. Over a meager supper, he grumbled:

"He's squeezing every modern idea out of me. Once he's learned all he can, who's to say he'll keep us around?"

Victoria sighed in agreement. She'd been roped into drafting official letters and negotiations for WilCarter's distant allies. Though she tried to nudge him toward peaceful options, he seemed fixed on readying for more clashes with Braxton.

Anna listened without speaking until she finally murmured, "So we're basically fueling a medieval arms race with our knowledge?"

Sarah's expression hardened. "We might be. But if we stop cooperating, we lose what little protection we have."

Their situation shifted one morning when a scout arrived, breathless, reporting that Braxton hadn't yet regrouped—but a new danger had arisen. A group of ruthless raiders, possibly mercenaries, was ravaging farmland near Kentwood's western borders, burning fields, attacking peasants, and stealing livestock. Terrified villagers begged for help from Lord WilCarter.

He summoned Maya, Carter, and Tomás to the great hall. Pacing, fists clenched, he described the raiders' brutality. Lady Althea stood by, uneasy, while Master Gerald fiddled with his wooden staff, lost in thought.

WilCarter spoke quickly, eyes flaring as he pointed at Tomás. Tomás relayed: "The raiders are led by a rogue knight rumored to own strange objects from 'beyond.' Possibly from the same storm that brought us here."

Maya's pulse skipped. "Strange objects... like that odd compass the merchant showed us?"

Carter frowned. "If these raiders collected artifacts from another wreck, it could be a clue about how we got here—or how we get back."

Tomás nodded, turning to WilCarter. "We'll help, but how do we proceed?"

Through Tomás, WilCarter explained: a small contingent of knights would ride out to confront the raiders. He wanted Carter along for on-the-spot forging or repairs, and Maya for medical care if there were casualties. The survivors exchanged tense glances. Another military excursion—yet now they had a real motive to investigate possible modern artifacts.

Within hours, the expedition was ready. Five knights, two squires, and three mules laden with supplies gathered in the courtyard. Carter lugged a sack of blacksmithing tools and a kit for quick repairs. Maya carried what remained of her bandages, a few antibiotic pills, and the herbs Master Gerald had given her. Tomás would accompany them as translator. Paul, Nina, Victoria, and the others stayed behind to manage fortress life.

Before Maya mounted her horse, Ethan clutched her sleeve. "Please... be careful."

She brushed a hand gently over his hair, offering what she hoped was a reassuring smile. "I promise. Watch after the infirmary with your mom."

He nodded, eyes bright with fear. Maya hated leaving him behind, but the mission could bring them closer to answers. Urging her horse forward, she joined Carter and Tomás, following the knights through Kentwood's gates.

They rode across rolling farmland into a rugged stretch of woodland. The knights kept their eyes peeled for smoke or signs of pillaging. Maya and Carter exchanged hushed words about what might lie ahead. Carter's voice carried a tight edge:

"If these raiders have a modern weapon, it'll be devastating against people who've never seen anything like it."

Maya nodded, remembering the merchant's dire warnings. "We should be cautious. If they realize we're from the same place, we could become targets."

Tomás, overhearing, guided his horse closer. "Let's try to gather any clues, but not advertise who we really are."

By dusk, they reached a scorched farmstead—a cottage reduced to charred rubble. Several livestock lay slaughtered, the scene brutal. The knights dismounted in disgust. Maya stepped carefully among the debris. A lone peasant woman stood trembling behind a wrecked cart. She approached them, voice ragged with terror, describing men who carried a black sword and a device that shot flames.

Maya's heart hammered. "A gun?" she whispered. Carter's stunned look confirmed he was thinking the same.

They continued, the forest looming around them, torches lighting their path. Tension coiled in the air. Near midnight, they made camp by a shallow stream, posting sentries. Maya examined the knights' old wounds but found nothing critical aside from the lingering injuries from Braxton's siege.

In hushed tones, Carter repeated the possibility of a firearm. "A single gun in this era is unimaginable. They could dominate entire villages."

Maya winced. "They might be short on ammo, though. Still dangerous enough to terrorize people."

They tried to sleep but found little rest. At daybreak, they pressed on, following footprints and ransacked cottages. Around midday, they caught sight of smoke beyond a ridge. The lead knight lifted a clenched fist, halting them. They crept through undergrowth until they saw a clearing.

Below, around a low fire, waited ten raiders. Their horses grazed near the treeline. A hulking figure paced among them, a black sword strapped across his back. Off to one side lay a twisted metal object, possibly part of an airplane's remains: an engine panel or a chunk of fuselage.

Maya's breath caught. "They must've salvaged that from another crash."

Carter's face hardened. "There might be more planes out there. More travelers like us."

Then one raider came into view, wielding something shaped like a gun, cobbled from medieval iron and modern parts, duct tape glinting in a patch of sunlight. Maya's stomach tightened.

The knights conferred in tense whispers. They had fewer men, but they hoped to use surprise. Maya's heart pounded. She was no warrior. She needed a closer look at that wreckage, but not at the cost of a violent clash.

Carter hunched beside her. "If that thing fires bullets, we're in real danger."

Tomás grimaced. "We might try negotiation... but it's a long shot."

The lead knight signaled for half the group to move into position around the clearing. Carter and Maya stayed with the main force, waiting for a signal. The silence felt electric. Finally, the knight whistled sharply. They emerged, swords drawn, calling on the raiders to surrender in Lord WilCarter's name.

Chaos erupted. The raider with the gun fired, the blast echoing through the trees. A knight screamed, clutching his thigh. Another knight hurled a spear, striking a raider's shoulder. In seconds, everyone was shouting, blades swinging.

Maya ducked behind a tree, yanking Carter with her. Tomás huddled by a fallen log, pale with shock. Maya peeked out to see the raider leader swinging that black sword at a knight.

Her instincts demanded she help the wounded. She fumbled in her bag for gauze and antiseptic. "Carter, cover me," she hissed. "I'm going to help that knight who got shot."

He nodded tautly. "Be careful."

Maya sprinted, crouched low, reaching the knight writhing in agony. She pressed cloth to his bleeding thigh, trying not to recoil at his anguished cries. She prayed the bullet hadn't shattered a major artery.

Gunfire roared again, splitting the air. A shot missed its target by inches. Carter yelled at Tomás, "We have to disarm that lunatic with the gun!"

Tomás signaled to two knights who lunged at the raider, knocking him down with their shields. The gun fired once more, and a young squire collapsed. Yet the raider, pinned under chainmail, lost his grip on the weapon.

Roaring, the leader tried to hack at the pinned knight. Carter, desperation fueling him, swung a broken spear shaft at the raider's helmet. The man reeled, giving the knight time to scramble free. Steel rang on steel.

Maya focused on the wounded knight, dragging him behind a stump. Blood soaked her hands. She fought to stanch the flow, glancing up only when the clamor began to subside. Several raiders lay unmoving, while a few darted for the woods. The leader, calling for retreat, took an arrow to the back and collapsed with a ragged cry.

When the fighting ended, three knights were wounded. The raider leader lay dying, trapped under a broken wagon. Two raiders had escaped, leaving their injured and dead behind. Carter, breathing hard, came over to Maya. Tomás stumbled forward, his face ashen.

"God, that was horrible," Tomás breathed.

Maya pressed a final bandage on the knight's thigh. "We need to triage. Now."

Carter nodded, scanning the aftermath. The knights who could still stand began rounding up the remaining raiders, many of whom moaned in pain or lay unmoving. Maya hurried from one fallen knight to another, assessing bleeding and broken bones.

Eventually, she found the bullet-wounded knight again. He was feverish and losing blood. She cleaned the area with precious antiseptic, cursing medieval limitations. The bullet seemed lodged near his femur, but she lacked proper tools for a clean extraction. She packed it and prayed he'd hold on.

A rattling cough drew her attention. The raider leader, pinned, coughed up blood. The black sword rested just beyond his reach. Maya hesitated, then inched closer, Carter at her shoulder. The man glared, rage flickering in his eyes. Then he rasped in half-garbled English, "You... came from the storm too?"

Maya's blood ran cold. "Yes. Where did you find the gun?"

He coughed, spitting red. "Wreck... not just you... more storms... north hills..." His eyes rolled. "No... escape... only war." A final shudder racked him, and his head lolled back.

Maya stared at the corpse, heart hammering.

Carter crouched beside her, breathing raggedly. "He knew about us."

Maya swallowed hard. "He said others have come through the storms. The gun came from a different wreck. And he mentioned more storms to the north."

Tomás approached, having heard enough. "We have to investigate those hills. This could be our way home."

Maya felt a chill. "Or a dead end, just like this one. He warned there's no escape, only constant fighting."

Her gaze shifted to the jagged chunk of metal near the fire. Knights rummaged for anything of value, ignoring that plane debris. Carter and Maya edged closer, spotting what looked like a partial airline logo scoured by time. Different from Flight 207's. Maya's heart pounded—evidence they weren't the only travelers ripped out of their timeline.

In the aftermath, they treated the knights and tied up the surviving raiders. Tomás tried to interrogate a whimpering prisoner, who only babbled about "devils falling from the skies." He had no real knowledge of the gun's origin. The knights decided he was worthless but took him anyway for questioning at Kentwood.

Before leaving, Maya lingered over the twisted fuselage. She yearned to examine it more thoroughly, to find any piece of instrumentation or black box. Carter kneeled beside the wreckage, discovering a partial seatbelt buckle under a layer of rust. It bore an Airbus manufacturer's code. Maya felt sick. So many planes had disappeared, lost in storms that scattered wreckage across centuries.

By dusk, the knights insisted on heading back to Kentwood. They fashioned makeshift stretchers for the wounded, including the knight with the bullet wound. Maya hovered, trying to keep him stable. Carter and Tomás helped as she attempted to remove the bullet with medieval tongs and her own scalpel. His screams filled the forest until she finally succeeded, trembling as she stitched the hole. She dropped the slug into her hand with a grimace.

The forest seemed to close in on them as they marched. More blood. More horror. And the final words of a dying raider echoing in Maya's mind: "No escape... only war."

Two days later, they returned to Kentwood, slowed by the injured. The bullet-wounded knight burned with fever, and Maya used every scrap of penicillin left to fight infection. She managed to stop the bleeding and keep him alive. The castle inhabitants hailed her as a miracle worker again. Master Gerald lingered nearby, watching each step, no doubt memorizing her methods.

When WilCarter himself visited the infirmary to check on the wounded, he thanked Maya stiffly. Then he asked about the "black metal tube" used by the raiders. Carter claimed it was a "dangerous contraption" that required strange magic. WilCarter wanted to know if Carter could replicate it. Carter lied outright, insisting it was impossible without powers beyond human skill. WilCarter seemed to accept the explanation, although a flicker of suspicion lurked in his eyes.

He also asked about the twisted scrap of metal found in the clearing. Maya and Carter shrugged it off as useless junk. The lord, consumed by more pressing concerns, let it drop.

That evening, the survivors gathered in their cramped tower quarters. Paul, Nina, and Sarah bombarded Maya, Carter, and Tomás with questions about the gun. Carter described the chaotic fight, while Maya spoke of the raider leader's final words and the unsettling revelation that other crashes existed. Tension simmered as they realized this phenomenon stretched beyond Flight 207.

Victoria drummed her fingers on the rough table. "If multiple storms are pulling planes here, maybe we can find one to get us back. Or maybe it's too random. People scattered through time and space."

Tomás paced, eyes flicking over his notes. "History might be peppered with travelers nobody recognized. But in this savage century, they'd be labeled devils or witches."

Paul rubbed his temples. "So do we wait for the next storm? Seek one in the north? We're trapped between warring lords, forging weapons to survive."

Maya swallowed. "We take small steps. Maybe we can request an 'official mission' to the north, pretending we're scouting for more sky-people threats. WilCarter might allow it if he sees strategic value."

They fell silent. A single lantern lit the chamber, shadows dancing on the walls. Outside, the wind curled around the tower as though whispering of distant storms. Each day, they seemed to sink deeper into medieval life, stitched more tightly into the tapestry of this world.

***

Weeks crawled by. The knight with the bullet wound lived, though he'd never fight as he once did. WilCarter's men dubbed Maya a miracle worker again, while Master Gerald watched every procedure keenly. Carter continued forging weapons, weighed down by the moral burden. Victoria negotiated trade alliances to bolster Kentwood's power against Braxton.

Tomás meticulously documented the raider's confessions, the black sword, and rumors of storms in the north.

Every night, the survivors whispered about a clandestine trip to the hills. Should they slip away? Or try to secure WilCarter's approval for a scouting mission? Either path felt fraught.

Anna offered her help in the infirmary, learning basic care and comforting wounded peasants. Maya, grateful for the assistance, felt a tiny thread of normalcy as they established a routine. Yet the question lingered: would they remain in this brutal time forever?

Then, news arrived that rocked the castle's uneasy balance. A messenger from a neighboring domain appeared at Kentwood's gates, announcing that a lesser baron had heard tales of the "sky-people" and wanted to discuss alliances. WilCarter, displeased by outside meddling, still agreed to a meeting in a week.

The survivors realized that their existence was no longer a secret. Rumors about their strange origins were seeping into the wider realm. Rival lords and even rogue knights might try to claim them—or destroy them. Tension crackled through Kentwood.

But a flicker of hope glimmered in Maya's thoughts. If new alliances formed, perhaps they could negotiate safe passage north to investigate the rumored storms. Unless this was another trap.

Late that night, Maya sat alone in her cramped tower room, head in her hands. She couldn't shake the memory of the raider's dying statement: "No escape... only war." That phrase haunted her. She thought of Ethan, of everyone who still believed they might one day return to modern civilization—of planes that soared without disappearing. She forced the dread back, refusing to accept the raider's grim certainty.

A soft knock broke her reverie. Carter stood at the threshold, exhaustion etched into his face. "Mind if I come in?"

She managed a nod, blinking back tears. He settled on a low stool, turning a battered scrap of fuselage in his hands. Its faint markings read "Flight 65—," the rest peeled away by time. They stared at it, both pondering the incomplete story. Another ill-fated flight, lost to an impossible phenomenon.

"We'll figure this out, Doc," Carter whispered. "We didn't survive a plane crash into the Middle Ages just to give up."

She offered a wavering smile. "I know. But it feels like we're sinking deeper each day. Our oath to WilCarter, forging these weapons, all this bloodshed—are we changing this world or letting it change us?"

He slid a comforting hand over her shoulder. "We have to trust there's a way out. If we can find a rift, we'll take it."

She closed her eyes, letting the warmth of his presence steady her. She remembered the swirling violet sky, the jolt when Flight 207 had suddenly vanished from its own time. Did that storm function like some cosmic funnel, sucking in unsuspecting souls? Or was there a grander design behind it all? She didn't know. But she refused to abandon hope.

Together, they held the worn metal piece in the torchlight. It was a relic of another plane, a silent testament to the countless others who had fallen prey to these storms. One day, they might decode this puzzle. Or they might, as the raider had warned, find no escape—only war.

CHAPTER 6

The midday sun angled sharply through the narrow windows of the south tower's second-floor chamber. Maya stood there with Anna, rearranging crude wooden chairs so they could greet the newest arrivals—two peasants with minor injuries. Sunbeams revealed floating motes of dust, a reminder of the fortress's ancient stones. Outside, the clang of smithing rose from the courtyard, courtesy of Carter's unrelenting forge work.

Maya pressed a hand to her temple, inhaling slowly. Sleep had been scarce since her return from that brutal encounter with the raiders. A battered airplane scrap and a dying leader's words about more modern wreckage haunted her thoughts, proving they weren't alone in this medieval world—and that terror lurked everywhere.

One of the peasants, a middle-aged woman clutching a cloth-wrapped hand, shuffled forward with lowered eyes. "M'lady," she whispered. "Come closer," Maya said softly, offering a bowl of boiled water. She unwound the soiled bandage to find a deep splinter festering in the woman's palm.

Anna knelt beside them, ready with a clean cloth. "We'll be gentle," she murmured. While she dabbed around the wound, Maya used tweezers from her dwindling med kit to extract the splinter. The peasant winced, tears welling, but stayed still. When the fragment finally came free, Maya spread a simple herbal paste, taught to her by Master Gerald, over the injured skin. Relief shone on the woman's face.

"You'll heal," Maya said, summoning a reassuring tone. "Just keep the area as clean as possible."

The woman bobbed her head. "Bless you, Sky-Doctor," she whispered, her voice trembling with gratitude. Maya's shoulders tensed at the title, but she let it pass. They'd all grown used to these strange labels.

Ethan hovered nearby, handing over fresh strips of linen. Once the woman's hand was secure, the second peasant—a wiry man with a twisted ankle—hobbled forward. He glanced around the makeshift clinic in awe, eyeing the salvaged airplane blankets on the walls and the jumbled mix of modern textbooks beside archaic scrolls. Maya and Anna tended him with a methodical routine, guiding his foot into a shallow water soak. It all felt like a small-town doctor's office—except for the torch brackets along the walls and the rattle of chainmail echoing in the corridor.

By the time both peasants departed, dusk had settled. Anna gave a faint smile while tidying leftover linens. "Feels good to be useful," she said, her voice quiet but steady. "My own wound's healed, and Ethan needs me steady on my feet."

Maya nodded, rubbing stiff muscles in her neck. "You're invaluable. I couldn't manage half of this without you." She meant it, and a flicker of warmth passed between them.

Outside, the hallway buzzed with rumor. Maya picked up snippets of archaic English referencing Lord Braxton's potential regrouping and a new messenger from a lesser baron sniffing around for alliances. A steward arrived moments later, breathless and insistent, beckoning Maya by name.

She glanced at Anna. "Sounds like they want me again. You can stay here or come along—your call."

The woman hesitated, then exhaled. "Let's see what fresh crisis looms."

They climbed the winding stairs behind the steward. Knights lined the upper landing, muttering about foreigners and glancing warily at the newcomers. Maya tried not to let annoyance flare. After months, acceptance was still fragile.

At the top, they entered the lord's council chamber—a high-ceilinged space dominated by a polished wooden table. Sunlight filtering through narrow windows fell in slanted stripes across the floor. Around that table sat Lord WilCarter, Lady Althea, Master Gerald, Tomás, Carter, and, to Maya's surprise, Paul. He gave her a tense nod from his seat beside the lord.

WilCarter frowned, gesturing for her to join them. Tomás leaned close, lowering his voice. "A messenger from Baron Harlow arrived, asking for an audience... maybe an alliance. He knows about us, apparently wants to harness our knowledge."

Maya's stomach gave a small flip. More feudal powers wanting to exploit them. "So what does WilCarter expect from us?"

Tomás sighed. "He wants us to meet Harlow's messenger and prove we're loyal to Kentwood. Maybe impress them enough to secure a diplomatic edge. If we refuse, Harlow might side with Braxton."

Carter muttered under his breath. "We're the new pawns in medieval politics."

Paul tapped the table. "I've been helping WilCarter with resource distribution, and now this. Every day, it gets more tangled. But we can't ignore potential allies, even if it does lock us deeper into the feudal framework."

Maya tried to ignore the knot in her gut. "So how do we handle this?"

WilCarter spoke with firm composure, scanning the survivors. Tomás translated: "He wants you, Carter, Paul, and possibly Victoria to join tonight's feast and meet the baron's messenger. Show them you're civilized, not devils or demons. Impress them with your skills so they'll think twice about allying with Braxton."

A grim chuckle slipped from Carter. "So we're dinner entertainment now."

Paul shrugged. "If it keeps us alive and maybe opens a few doors, I'm in."

WilCarter's gaze then shifted to Anna, delivering a pointed request through Tomás: "He hopes for a demonstration—healing or some display of knowledge to underscore Kentwood's advantage."

Maya stiffened. Being put on stage again. But refusing would spark conflict. "Fine. A small medical demonstration. Nothing too dramatic." She recalled showing her stethoscope to WilCarter's knights, how they shrank back at the amplified heartbeat. She'd do the same if needed.

Lady Althea watched, face thoughtful. Tomás relayed that she appreciated their cooperation. Maya offered a tight smile in return. None of them believed it was a real partnership; they were weapons of knowledge to be brandished at the baron.

That evening, the castle's great hall blazed with torchlight and the bustle of servants spreading out trenchers and earthenware cups on long wooden tables. Knights milled around the dais where WilCarter presided, and Lady Althea supervised with cool elegance. Maya, Carter, Paul, and Anna waited off to one side with Victoria, who had just arrived, hair braided and expression harried.

"Rewriting their trade agreements in archaic script all day," Victoria said, frustrated. "Now playing hostess to a baron's envoy. This never ends."

Carter ran a hand over his stubble. "Better than them deciding we're witches and throwing us in irons. Small mercies."

A trumpet call echoed through the vaulted space, and a steward announced Sir Lionel, Baron Harlow's messenger. The man swept in with three guards wearing green-and-white surcoats. He had a narrow face and a carefully trimmed beard that hinted at vanity. He sized up the hall, lip curling slightly.

WilCarter greeted him, speaking with stiff courtesy. Sir Lionel responded in fluid archaic English, voice carrying a subtle condescension. After a round of pleasantries, WilCarter beckoned the survivors forward. Sir Lionel's eyes brightened with curiosity.

Tomás introduced them: Carter O'Connor, master of forging; Dr. Maya Jenkins, a skilled healer; Victoria Prescott and Paul Richards, experts in law and trade from a far-off land. Sir Lionel asked Carter if he could craft armor stronger than steel—he'd heard rumors of metal beasts from the sky. Carter offered a careful explanation that Tomás rephrased into diplomatic terms. Sir Lionel's polite smile suggested he'd press for more later.

Next came questions about Maya's ability to mend "mortal" wounds and whether she practiced witchcraft. Heat rose in her cheeks. "No witchcraft," she said, letting Tomás translate. "Just knowledge from my homeland."

She pulled out her stethoscope, placing it against a guard's chest so Sir Lionel could hear the amplified heartbeat. Shock rippled across the onlookers. Some knights stared in wide-eyed alarm, a few whispering prayers. Sir Lionel exchanged a sharp glance with his men, clearly intrigued.

When the demonstration ended, Sir Lionel turned back to WilCarter, speaking in a measured tone. Tomás murmured, "He's impressed. He invites you to visit Baron Harlow's court, possibly to perform this healing magic there. The baron would offer gifts and an alliance."

WilCarter stiffened. Refusing might offend Harlow, but agreeing meant risking his precious resource—these sky-people. Sir Lionel's faint smirk suggested he knew the tension he'd created.

Victoria leaned closer to Maya. "If we travel there, maybe we can find out if Harlow is friend or foe. And if his domain nudges closer to those rumored storms... we could investigate."

Paul nodded, voice subdued. "We'll strengthen trade ties, gather intel. We can't progress while stuck in Kentwood forever."

WilCarter finally spoke, and Tomás translated: "He'll consider sending a small envoy in a week. But the survivors remain loyal to Kentwood, under my protection. No double-dealing. No secrets."

Maya glanced at Carter, who gave a minute shrug. That oath to WilCarter weighed on them all. Still, traveling might unlock new clues about returning to their own time.

A feast followed. The visitors devoured roast venison and spiced wine under the blaze of torches, while knights swapped boasts about battles. WilCarter made occasional remarks, posture guarded. Lady Althea gleaned scraps of detail about Baron Harlow's territory, though Sir Lionel revealed little. Meanwhile, the survivors fielded questions about "flying ships," forging wonders, and potions that saved the dying. Maya answered carefully, hiding how limited her supplies truly were. Carter offered vague explanations about forging steel. Victoria parried trade-related queries, refusing to divulge too much modern knowledge.

Eventually, Sir Lionel and his entourage retired to guest chambers, intending to depart at first light. WilCarter beckoned the survivors and spoke in a low voice. Tomás relayed the message: If they travel to Harlow's domain, they do so as Kentwood's representatives. They owe complete loyalty. Carter is also expected to finish forging new arrowheads before they leave. Carter's grim nod betrayed exhaustion at the thought of more weapon-making.

They exited the hall beneath the moon's muted glow, a single guard escorting them through the courtyard to the tower steps. At the top, they paused in the dim corridor.

"Intense," Victoria murmured, exchanging a glance with Carter. "But maybe useful."

Paul rubbed the back of his neck. "Let's hope so. If Harlow's territory touches the north, we might sneak closer to those storms."

Maya sighed. "One week until we leave. Let's rest while we can."

She climbed the last steps to her cramped room, finding Ethan asleep near the window, his mother dozing beside him. Slipping off her boots, Maya slouched against the cold stone wall, the stethoscope still a tangible reminder of her lost world. How many times would they have to appease medieval lords before finding a path home?

Dawn arrived with the echo of horses' hooves as Sir Lionel and his men departed, carrying WilCarter's cautious acceptance. Castle life soon returned to its routine of repairs, forging, and farmland maintenance. Maya spent her days tending illnesses in her makeshift clinic, Carter wore himself out at the forge.

On the second morning, the castle stirred with excitement when a group of traveling merchants arrived at the gates. They promised exotic wares—spices, dyes, strange curiosities. Sensing an opportunity for supplies, WilCarter granted them entry, and the courtyard bustled with peasants, knights, and the colorful merchant stalls. Maya watched from a tower window, curiosity sparked.

She hurried down to join the throng, passing men in armor arguing over prices. Stalls offered bolts of cloth in vivid saffron or red, crates of dried herbs, and pungent spices in clay jars. One merchant boasted of "miracle seeds." Another had carved talismans claiming mystical powers.

Carter sidled up, wiping sweat from his brow. "Think we'll find anything like modern medicine here?"

"Not likely," Maya answered, "but it's worth a look. We need any antiseptic or analgesic we can get."

They wandered from stall to stall, Tomás sometimes stepping in to help translate. One merchant recognized them as the "sky-people" and tried hawking a piece of battered metal, insisting it fell from the heavens. Carter tested it and found it was just old local scrap. They moved on.

A slender female merchant in a patched cloak caught their eye, beckoning them over. Her sharp gaze suggested a cunning mind. She spoke in a heavy accent. Tomás translated: "She sells powerful healing salves."

Maya's pulse quickened. "Ask if she has anything that helps infections or high fevers," she said. The woman dug around, finally producing a clay jar sealed with wax. A sharp, acrid scent wafted out when she cracked it open, and flecks of dark residue floated in the oily mixture.

Carter winced. "That doesn't smell pleasant."

Maya leaned in, nose wrinkling. Beneath the rancid odor, she detected something herbal that might inhibit bacteria or at least disinfect wounds. When the woman named an exorbitant price, Maya tried haggling.

Carter offered a handful of silver from the forge allowance. Eventually, they reached a deal, though Maya felt the merchant's triumphant stare. Clutching the jar, she breathed a guarded hope: maybe this was the antiseptic they desperately needed.

They parted, passing more rows of merchants. Knights demanded bargains; peasants marveled at foreign fabrics. The courtyard pulsed with color and noise, an all-too-brief respite from the bleak realities of war.

Later, as midday waned, Maya returned to her clinic, Carter to his anvil. Both reconvened at dusk for a hasty meal in the tower hallway. She showed him a small pot of crushed herbs she'd also bought, hoping to replicate modern treatments. He reported steady progress on arrowheads, though exhaustion rimmed his eyes.

"Just a few more days of forging," he mumbled, chewing on hard bread. "Then off to Harlow's domain. God knows what awaits us there."

Maya gave a wan smile. "Another trap, maybe. But we can't ignore the chance to scout for more rifts."

Their small group continued working and waiting. Anna had started teaching local girls basic reading with salvaged airplane pamphlets. The Wu couple helped plan farmland improvements to stave off famine. Everyone contributed, yet hope for a real return home glimmered faintly at best.

Three days later, the merchants prepared to depart. Maya and Carter rushed to the courtyard for any last-minute deals or hints. That same cunning woman beckoned them behind her cart, rummaging under a blanket to produce a smooth, cylindrical piece of metal—modern steel by the look of it.

Carter's heart jolted. "That's part of a thermos."

Tomás demanded to know its origin. The merchant shrugged, muttering about a forest glen in the north, swirling storms, vanished travelers. She called the land cursed. Maya's pulse throbbed. North—where the raider's dying words had pointed. Could this confirm the storms' location?

Carter tried to purchase it, but the merchant refused coins. Instead, she pointed at her wagon's cracked wheel, indicating she wanted Carter's forging skills in exchange. He heaved a sigh and obliged, rolling up his sleeves to make repairs. While he worked, Maya pressed for more information. The woman repeated rumors of lights in the sky, strange wreckage, travelers who never returned. It matched everything they'd heard from the raider and the merchant who'd shown them a modern compass before.

When Carter finished, she handed over the thermos cylinder. He and Maya examined the faint brand name etched in the steel. Relief mingled with dread. Another artifact from the modern era. The merchant smirked, urging them to be wary of "cursed metal" before she packed up and rode off.

That night, the survivors gathered in the tower's largest room. Carter laid out the thermos piece beside the battered fuselage scrap. Nina and Paul stared at both, eyes full of wonder and fear. Tomás repeated the merchant's tale about swirling lights and travelers lost in the northern hills, where modern debris occasionally surfaced.

Victoria exhaled slowly. "So more evidence of storms to the north. We already heard about storms west. Bits of technology are scattered across this era. But how do we get there?"

Maya laced her fingers, tension clawing at her chest. "We're about to head east to Harlow's domain. Maybe from there, if we gain his favor, we can push north."

Sarah grimaced. "And if that fails, we keep forging war gear for WilCarter, waiting for some miracle?"

Jason shifted his weight on his cane. "We have to try. It's better than surrendering."

Paul, looking weary, said, "Chasing these storms might be chasing illusions, but I'd rather try than do nothing."

Maya glanced at Ethan, who seemed both hopeful and wary, as if he'd heard too many false promises. She forced a steady voice. "We'll keep looking for answers. Maybe one day we'll find a rift home."

They dispersed, each wrestling with doubt yet clinging to a thread of optimism. The constant demands of medieval life pressed in, but these artifacts suggested a bigger puzzle—one they refused to abandon.

Finally, the morning of departure arrived. WilCarter assembled a traveling party in the courtyard: four knights, two squires, and a wagon loaded with goods for trade. The survivors assigned—Maya, Carter, Victoria, Paul, and Tomás—would ride out under Kentwood's banner. Ethan and his mother stayed behind, as did the Wu couple and others, to keep the castle running. Ethan's tearful goodbye nearly broke Maya's heart. She promised to return quickly.

In the crisp dawn, they set off. WilCarter watched from the ramparts, Lady Althea at his side, both figures etched against the sky. Maya felt torn; she'd built a strange empathy for these people, yet needed to leave if she had any chance of getting home.

They traveled east, passing farmland that soon gave way to dense forests. Villagers doffed caps or stared warily as the small caravan moved along. They camped beneath brilliant stars each night, knights standing guard. Tomás practiced archaic dialects around the fire, while Carter and Paul talked forging methods. Victoria quietly mapped negotiation points in her head.

On the third day, they crossed a broad river spanned by a sturdy wooden bridge. Baron Harlow's castle came into view—less imposing than Kentwood's fortress, but well-fortified. Guards in crisp livery stood atop the walls, arrows glinting. A hawk emblem fluttered on the highest turret.

After a trumpet call at the gate, Harlow's men admitted them into a bustling courtyard. The place felt strangely prosperous, with well-maintained storehouses and carefully tended gardens. A steward in a fine tunic escorted them into a grand hall. Thick rugs covered the floor, tapestries of hunting scenes hung on the walls, and the aroma of roasted meat and perfumed oil permeated the air.

Baron Harlow sat upon a carved wooden seat, perhaps fifty years old, beard streaked with gray, sharp eyes assessing everything. At his side stood Sir Lionel, smug as ever.

"Welcome, guests from Kentwood and beyond," Harlow said in a refined tone, letting Tomás translate. "I've heard tales of your metal birds and healing arts. Let us dine and see if our domains might find common cause."

Maya bowed slightly, absorbing the rose-oil scent that drifted in the air. The baron's hall felt like a polished stage for intrigues.

A midday feast followed. Servants brought platters of poultry, fresh bread, spiced stew. Musicians played a soft tune on a lute, giving the proceedings a veneer of civility. Harlow peppered the survivors with questions about forging, healing, and WilCarter's intentions. Carter gave his standard disclaimers about refining steel; Harlow seemed disappointed they had no recipe for "unbreakable armor."

He next turned to Maya, pressing for details on her alleged miracles. She responded guardedly, citing the limitations of medieval tools. Harlow's intense gaze suggested he wanted more than she was offering.

As the meal wound down, Harlow dismissed most of his retinue and summoned the survivors, Sir Lionel, and a few guards into a smaller chamber with a single stained-glass window. Rainbow light spilled onto the stone floor, casting an eerie glow.

"WilCarter claims your loyalty," Harlow said slowly, "yet I see you carry secrets neither of us fully know. Braxton lurks in the west, but these rumors of storms and strangers trouble me. I must decide if they're a threat or an opportunity."

Victoria explained (through Tomás) that travelers like them arrived through these storms without warning, some bearing dangerous relics—possibly firearms. Harlow listened, face unreadable.

"If these storms keep bringing new artifacts," he said, "the balance of power changes. I'd prefer to harness that power myself rather than let enemies snatch it. Give me reason to trust you."

Maya resisted a shudder, thinking of the crude gun used by the raiders. "We can't control these storms, only adapt and help where we can."

Harlow gave her a knowing look. "Knowledge is power. If you truly seek peace, share more about your forging and healing. Otherwise, men like Braxton will claw it out of you."

Silence hung. Carter cleared his throat. "We're not hiding anything that could stabilize the realm, my lord. We face serious limits with local resources. Our healing might seem miraculous, but it's not omnipotent."

Harlow studied them as if deciding how best to use this new piece on his chessboard. Then Sir Lionel cut in, focusing on Maya. "Prove your sincerity. A knight here was badly injured months ago and can barely walk. Heal him, and Baron Harlow will see your worth."

Dread fluttered in Maya's stomach. Another test. But perhaps a path to some goodwill. She nodded stiffly. "I'll do everything I can."

Harlow's expression brightened at the prospect. "If he walks again, perhaps I'll see a reason to unite with Kentwood—and grant you privileges."

The unspoken threat: fail, and we'll find other uses for you. Maya felt her heartbeat spike. "I'll do my best, my lord."

They were shown to small stone rooms for the evening—cramped, but better than a dungeon. That night, Carter, Tomás, Victoria, and Paul met with Maya in a drafty antechamber. Victoria paced, eyes glittering. "This baron is sly, more refined than WilCarter but just as dangerous."

Paul exhaled. "At least we're not thrown in a dungeon. If Maya heals his knight, we might earn his favor. But it won't end there."

Carter's jaw tightened. "If we succeed, Harlow might demand we create guns next. We can't give him that kind of advantage."

Maya rubbed her temples. "Let's get through tomorrow. I've never done surgery with these tools on a badly set leg. Our patient could die of shock or infection."

Tomás offered a thin smile. "If it works, maybe we'll gain permission to travel north in Harlow's realm. That's our best shot at the storms, right?"

They dispersed, weighed by tense possibilities. Medieval ambitions loomed around them, and only a precarious balancing act held them safe.

The next morning, a guard led Maya to a courtyard behind the keep. She found a makeshift infirmary under a canopy, with two cots and a table of crude implements. A large, grim-faced knight lay on one cot, his left leg twisted from a poorly healed fracture. Sir Lionel stood nearby, arms folded.

"His leg was crushed by a war hammer," Sir Lionel explained curtly. "If you can fix it, Harlow will be... appreciative."

Maya knelt by the knight, gently pressing around the scarred, crooked bone. She realized she'd have to break and reset it. In modern times, even with anesthesia and modern hardware, this was risky. Here, it could be catastrophic. She requested hot water, cloth, and any sedation they could muster. The knight glared at her stethoscope, but she focused on the job.

Eventually, she told Sir Lionel, "I'll have to re-break the bone, realign it, then immobilize it. He'll need strict care. No one can promise perfect results."

He relayed this to the knight, who cursed until Lionel reminded him of the baron's command. Resentfully, the man agreed. Maya's pulse throbbed with dread.

Harlow appeared, arms folded. Carter and Victoria hurried in, drawn by the commotion. Maya looked to them for reassurance. Carter gave a supportive nod, though his face was ashen.

She had the knight drink strong wine and ingest a mix of sedative herbs. Guards pinned his shoulders and leg. With a trembling hand, she made a shallow incision over the old break, exposing malformed bone. The knight screamed into a leather strap Carter offered. Sir Lionel watched with clinical detachment. Maya grimaced as she chiseled away the bad callus, then forced the bone into alignment. The wet crack of bone made her stomach lurch.

At last, she pressed the ends together, bound them with splints, and wrapped the leg in cloth. She coated the incisions with her new salve, praying it would stave off infection. The knight's screams faded into ragged sobs. Carter helped mop up blood, pale as chalk.

Maya finished with shaky hands, turning to Harlow. "He'll need weeks of careful rest. The risk of fever is high. Daily bandage changes. If the bone sets well, he may regain some mobility."

Harlow gave a curt nod. "We'll see how well your skill holds up."

They retreated, leaving the knight in the canopy with guards posted. Maya slumped onto a bench, adrenaline spent. Victoria handed her water. Carter whispered, "That was heroic, doc."

She managed a wry laugh. "Welcome to medieval orthopedic surgery."

Paul frowned. "Let's hope it buys us enough goodwill for the north."

So began another vigil. Each morning, Maya changed the knight's bandages and applied salve. His fever rose and fell, sometimes spiking into delirious curses. She coaxed him to sip water and weak broth, Carter or Victoria lending a hand. Paul probed Harlow's stewards for any mention of roads leading north. Tomás offered quiet moral support, bridging language barriers.

Slowly, the swelling eased. The leg held alignment, miraculously. By the fifth day, the knight's fever broke. He could speak through clenched teeth, and though pain etched every breath, he was alive. Harlow came by to inspect, and this time a grudging respect lit his eyes. He told Maya, through Tomás, that if the man walked again, he would owe her a boon.

Her pulse leapt. A boon might mean access to the northern hills, rumored storms, and the chance to find a portal home. She bowed her head, keeping her voice steady. "He has far to go, my lord. But I'll do all I can."

Harlow nodded and walked off, calculating gaze never leaving her. Sir Lionel followed, inscrutable as ever. Maya felt tension coil through her muscles. If this knight regained his stride, it could open a door—or lock them further into feudal politics. Success might lead to freedom. Failure could seal their fate.

CHAPTER 7

A hush draped Baron Harlow's courtyard like a premonition of distant thunder. In the makeshift infirmary near the keep's rear wall, Maya rose from the knight's bedside, exhaustion etching deep lines beneath her eyes. She pressed a final clean dressing to the man's freshly set leg, an improvised splint of padded wood bound with hammered metal rods bracing bone that might—if fortune allowed—heal straighter than before. The patient's labored breaths ebbed and flowed, each inhalation a tenuous link to the possibility of recovery.

Maya closed her eyes for a moment, letting her own breathing settle. Outside, a breeze stirred the edges of the pavilion, carrying the aromas of straw and fading embers from the kitchens. She pictured home, a place centuries beyond this time, where sterile hospital corridors and advanced orthopedic wards could have eased this man's suffering. Yet here she stood, in an era of flickering torchlight and half-miraculous ointments. Despite her best efforts, dread gnawed at her mind. Even small triumphs might not hold back the rising tide of medieval ambition.

Stepping onto the stone path bordering the infirmary area, Maya listened to the crunch beneath her boots. Dawn's pale glow traced the keep's ramparts. She had spent the past week tending this knight—Roderick—monitoring every fever spike with increasing anxiety.

An unchecked infection could take him overnight, and she refused to let her knowledge be meaningless in this age. Not when it might save him.

Midway down the path, she nearly collided with Carter, who carried a clay mug of thin porridge. His tunic bore the blacksmith's marks, soot smudged across threadbare fabric. Concern flickered in his eyes. "Have you eaten?"

She shook her head and accepted the mug. The porridge tasted bland but soothed her hunger. "Roderick's stable for now," she said. "The fever broke. If we keep managing his care, he might walk again—though not perfectly."

Carter's broad shoulders eased. "That's better than anyone hoped. Word is spreading among Harlow's men, too. They're calling it enchantment—or a curse, depending on who you ask." His mouth twitched with a hint of humor, then grew serious. "We need to use this. If Roderick recovers, the baron might finally grant our request to travel north."

Maya exhaled, her gaze drifting toward the keep's spires. North meant rumored storms, lost remnants of modern wreckage, and maybe—just maybe—a way home. The raiders' last taunt still replayed in her thoughts: No escape...only war. A chill coursed through her. "We'll do what we must," she murmured.

They headed inside the keep's main hall, past tall pillars carved with hawk-headed crests. The entire space felt hushed, as though waking from a night of uneasy sleep. Victoria and Paul stood by a heavy oak table, poring over pages of archaic script. Their conversation fell quiet at Maya and Carter's approach.

Victoria's eyes gleamed with cautious triumph. "We found a clue. Tomás and I cornered one of Harlow's stewards. He let slip there's an old watchtower two days' ride north, near a mountain pass. Locals report eerie lights during violent storms. They call it cursed."

Carter's eyebrows rose. "Isn't that the same region the traveling merchant mentioned? Where she saw scraps of a modern thermos?"

He turned to Maya, unspoken questions swirling in his gaze. If this tower was indeed a gateway or held signs of one, they couldn't ignore it.

"If Harlow lets us go, we'll investigate," Maya said. "But will he agree?"

Paul's expression hardened. "He's suspicious. Still, if Roderick's leg heals, the baron might owe you. We could ask for a scouting party—though if he says no, we might sneak away." His face darkened. "But that risks being branded traitors."

Tomás appeared then, an air of optimism about him. "The baron wants an update on Sir Roderick," he announced. "Also, he's planning a grand hunt tomorrow to celebrate forging ties with WilCarter's domain. He expects us to attend."

Maya's mouth twisted. "A hunt? Boar, deer? Or just a chance to show off his 'sky-people'?"

Victoria's lips tightened. "We can't offend him by refusing. Besides, maybe we'll glean more information if we play our roles. Any knowledge about that watchtower helps."

Maya's sigh carried her frustration. She loathed more displays of violence, but their position was precarious. "All right. One more performance. Then we push for permission to head north."

That evening, their group assembled in a guest chamber along a dim corridor. Flickering sconces lit the damp stone walls. A single candle on a small wooden table threw exaggerated shadows. Paul pressed his palm on the tabletop. "We need a united approach when we talk to Harlow. If Roderick improves, we request a scouting mission. We'll claim it's to search for bandits or stolen relics. But really, we're headed for that tower."

Tomás leaned forward. "Mention the risk of Braxton's raiders finding more 'sky-metal.' That'll get Harlow's attention."

Carter looked at Maya. "If the baron insists on sending his own men, we'll be under watch. Let's hope we can dodge them if we discover something like a rift."

Maya studied the candle's quivering flame. "The route will be dangerous. Storms could catch us in the mountains. Braxton's men might prowl the passes."

Victoria rested her hand on Maya's forearm. "One step at a time. We survive the hunt. If the surgery continues to help Roderick, Harlow may grant our request."

They parted to snatch what sleep they could, all too aware that their future might hinge on the baron's goodwill—and that north lay the threat of storms and war.

Morning brought swirling gray clouds. Baron Harlow's courtyard bustled with anticipation for the hunt. Grooms led sleek horses, eager hounds yelped, and knights bragged about what they'd take down. Maya and the others stood aside, forced to participate if they wanted to keep Harlow's favor.

She found herself mounted next to Carter, uneasy in the saddle. She'd only ridden a handful of times in her own era. Now the stakes felt higher. She spotted Victoria adjusting her reins with a tense jaw. Paul looked like he'd rather walk, while Tomás seemed the most composed, having practiced since their arrival.

Harlow, astride a powerful stallion, observed them with an amused gleam. "You ride with us?" he asked, voice laced with mock cordiality.

Maya dipped her head. "Yes, my lord. We're honored." She gripped the reins, determined not to show fear. Perhaps buoyed by Roderick's improved condition, the baron seemed almost gracious.

At a horn's blast, the hunting party cantered out through the gates, crossing farmland that soon gave way to a dense forest. Towering trees stretched half-bare branches like skeletal arms. The air smelled of damp leaves and wet earth, a promise of hidden hazards. Harlow rode at the forefront, accompanied by knights in green-and-white surcoats. Sir Lionel followed, ever vigilant.

Maya fought to keep her horse steady over root-choked ground. Carter edged closer with a quick smile. "If we survived medieval skirmishes, we can handle this."

She forced a wry grin. "I'd still rather be tending the clinic." Memories of a squire ripped open by a boar in Kentwood flitted through her thoughts. She hoped not to see a similar injury today.

The deeper they ventured, the more the forest quieted. Knights peered at tracks, hounds sniffed the underbrush. A gust of wind rattled dead branches. Harlow motioned for silence. The group spread out, hunting for prey.

Suddenly, a hound barked. Another answered. The knights tensed, gripping weapons. Maya's pulse soared. She glimpsed a swift blur of gray-brown fur among the trees—maybe a boar or a deer. Sir Lionel lunged after it, three knights on his heels. Harlow waved for Carter and Victoria to search another patch of brush, while Maya and Tomás followed the baron toward a clearing. Everything felt too charged, as if they hunted each other rather than wild game.

A large stag burst from the brush, wide-eyed and desperate. Its hooves pounded the ground. Harlow fired his crossbow in one smooth action. The bolt missed, splintering bark from an old trunk. The stag veered, bounding farther into the forest.

With a frustrated oath, Harlow urged his horse ahead. Maya and Tomás thundered after him, ducking branches that whipped at their arms. Her horse stumbled over a twisted root, nearly sending her tumbling. She clenched the reins, refusing to be unseated.

In the chaos, she lost sight of Carter's green tunic. She heard him call her name, distant and muffled. The forest's labyrinth swallowed the other hunters. At last, Harlow reined in his stallion, scanning for movement. They were alone. Maya's own mount snorted, restless.

"We've lost them," Harlow growled. "I heard the hounds to the east."

Maya steadied her horse. "We should backtrack—maybe fire a signal arrow."

Harlow dismissed the idea with a flick of his crossbow. "The stag might have circled back. Stay alert, Maya." The quiet command in his tone set her teeth on edge, but she hid it well.

They trotted through a narrow lane of ancient oaks, shadows heavy beneath thick branches. Just as Maya prepared to insist on rejoining the group, a savage squeal shattered the silence—a boar, surging from tangled undergrowth, bristling and infuriated. Harlow's stallion reared, hooves pawing the air. He struggled to steady the reins and raise his crossbow simultaneously.

Maya's mind flashed with images of men gutted by boar tusks. Instinct overwhelmed caution. She forced her horse between the beast and the baron, spear rattling at her side. The boar let out a vicious roar, launching itself. She snatched the short hunting spear from its holster and thrust forward. The wood struck coarse hide, wrenching from her grip. She nearly fell from the saddle.

Harlow regained control, loosing a bolt that struck the boar behind the shoulder. With a guttural shriek, it dropped, twitching in a spreading pool of blood. Maya sucked in breath, heart drumming. The baron turned, eyes still wild, crossbow quivering.

"Reckless," he said, but relief flickered in his gaze. "You nearly got yourself killed."

Her voice wavered. "Couldn't watch it rip you open. I'd be the one treating you afterward."

His tense posture eased into a short laugh. "Bravery or madness, I'm not sure which. Either way, you saved me." A begrudging respect glinted in his eyes.

They eased their mounts to a drier patch of ground. The boar still twitched, and Harlow finished it with another bolt. Then he sounded a horn, summoning the scattered knights. Maya dismounted carefully, legs trembling. The baron swung off his stallion and surveyed the carcass, its tusks razor-sharp. "You have my thanks," he said, voice subdued.

Within minutes, riders converged, marveling at the wounded boar and eyeing Maya in surprise. Carter arrived last, relief illuminating his face. She gave him a faint smile, aware that in saving Harlow she might have gained a valuable bargaining chip.

By early afternoon, the hunting party gathered in a sunlit glade. Servants began dressing the boar for transport. Harlow regaled everyone with the story of the kill, emphasizing Maya's intervention. She felt uneasy in the glow of the knights' attention but knew it might serve them well. Carter hovered protectively, whispering, "You were inches from disaster." She offered a tense nod, still shaken by the beast's fury.

They returned to the castle at a measured pace. Harlow maintained a thoughtful silence, as though reevaluating the "sky-people." Maya prayed it would give them leverage for the mission north.

That evening, a modest feast took place in the great hall. The roasted boar took center stage. Knights praised the baron's perfect shot, casually downplaying Maya's role—something she accepted, relieved not to be the focus. She picked at her meal, attention drifting to Tomás, who quietly pumped a steward for more details about the watchtower.

Toward the meal's end, Harlow rose, goblet in hand. The chatter subsided. He singled out Maya with a raised hand. "To the lady healer who spared me from a terrible fate today." Murmured applause followed. She managed a courteous nod.

He took a long sip of wine. "May her skill extend to Sir Roderick's recovery. If he walks again, I shall have cause to trust these travelers from far away." Low murmurs stirred in the hall.

Maya caught Carter's encouraging glance, and beyond him Victoria and Paul exchanged silent looks. Whatever Harlow's true feelings, he seemed slightly more open. That might be enough.

Later, she left the feast to check on Roderick. He lay in a small chamber lit by a single torch. Though restive, the fever had not returned. She touched his forehead, relief kindling. He blinked at her, voice hoarse. "Am I...better?"

Her smile was gentle. "Too soon to be sure, but the fever's gone. That's a start." She examined the bandages. No new seepage. The boneset contraption had held. With luck, he might recover a measure of mobility.

Tears glistened in Roderick's eyes. "I want to serve again. Not be cast aside." His vulnerability made her heart twist. She squeezed his hand. "You've got hope. Rest now."

She rose and found Sir Lionel in the doorway, arms folded across his chest. He regarded her with suspicion and grudging respect. "He rests?"

She nodded. "He's stable."

Lionel's expression remained unreadable. "The baron appreciates what you've done, but he won't drop his guard. Remember that."

Her shoulders tensed. "I have no illusions."

He allowed himself a faint smirk. "Good." Then he stepped aside, letting her leave. His presence was a stark reminder that every favor she earned from Harlow carried a layer of watchfulness.

By the next day, Roderick's condition had improved further—no sign of infection. The baron, pleased and still remembering how Maya had stepped between him and the boar, summoned the group to a smaller council chamber draped in hawk-themed tapestries. Sir Lionel stood at his side. Unfurled maps depicting farmland, forests, and mountains lay across the table. Maya's pulse quickened. This had to be about the watchtower.

Harlow didn't waste time. "You saved my life, and you may have saved Roderick's. I owe you—cautiously." He swept his hand over the maps. "My scouts speak of unsettling events to the north: strange lights, rumored bandits, unnatural storms. WilCarter's domain shares these rumors. I want answers, but I have limited men."

Victoria spoke calmly. "If you allow us north, we can investigate on your behalf. These storms sometimes deposit relics...objects we've glimpsed before."

Harlow's gaze shifted to Carter, expecting confirmation. Carter dipped his head. "We believe storms carry dangerous items. If Braxton or others seize them, the balance of power changes. We want to prevent that."

Harlow studied them, clearly calculating. At last, he tapped a winding route on the map. "Near these foothills stands an abandoned watchtower. Locals fear it. If you ride there, confirm the nature of these storms, and return with proof, I'll consider deeper ties with WilCarter. But you must remain loyal."

Tomás cleared his throat. "We can do that, my lord. We only request a small escort and freedom to conduct a thorough search."

Lionel cut in, voice sharp. "My knights will accompany you. If you disappear or deceive us, we'll consider it treason."

Paul's jaw clenched. "Understood."

Maya exhaled with cautious optimism. A sanctioned trip north, albeit with watchers. "When do we leave?" she asked, eager to go before Roderick's condition could change or Harlow's disposition cooled.

Harlow motioned at the map. "Depart in two days. Gather what you need. Bring back evidence of these strange relics. If you vanish, I'll hold WilCarter accountable."

They left the council room weighed down by tension. Outside, Carter murmured, "We're doing it. We're headed north to see if these storms connect to a rift. But Lionel's knights will stay on our heels."

Victoria gave a grim nod. "We'll tread lightly. One slip, we'll be labeled traitors. If we do find a real lead, maybe we can get home. Or maybe these storms will trap us."

Maya glanced at a tapestry showing hawks in mid-flight, their threads telling stories of ancient battles. "Let's pray we're not walking into a bloodier conflict. If the storms are as destructive as rumors say, we may not return at all."

They spent the next two days stocking supplies: dried provisions, bandages, a few precious vials of antibiotic salve, and a map copied from Harlow's archives. They marked the tower's location, a blot on inked mountains. Locals told tales of storms swirling with unnatural light.

Maya entrusted Roderick to local healers, giving them strict instructions for cleaning his wound. He thanked her in a broken whisper. She could only hope no infection took hold during her absence.

At dawn, two of Harlow's knights—Sir Arnolt and Sir Beric—came to escort them. Their eyes were guarded, as though expecting treachery. Maya, Carter, Victoria, Paul, and Tomás mounted their horses, heartbeats throbbing with determination and unease. Two mules bore extra gear.

From a rampart, Sir Lionel watched, face grim. Harlow gave a final nod. "Return with truth," he commanded, "or don't return at all."

They set out on a winding road through farmland that yielded to gentle hills dotted with pine. Arnolt and Beric hung back, though they eavesdropped whenever the survivors spoke. Sensing that scrutiny, Victoria and Tomás avoided overt references to "time rifts" or modern technology.

At twilight, they made camp in a shallow valley by a trickling stream. Paul set up tents while Carter gathered firewood. Maya massaged her horse's sore muscles, feeling a dull ache in her own limbs. A short distance away, the knights murmured among themselves, as if worried about devils in the northern mountains.

That night, Maya dozed fitfully, haunted by images of swirling violet lights tearing airplanes from the sky. She jolted awake near midnight, heart pounding. The forest loomed, dark and watchful. She slipped outside and scanned the treeline under faint starlight. Carter stirred from his bedroll, offering a silent nod of reassurance. Maya forced her breathing steady and returned to her tent, bracing for the next day's hardships.

On the second day, the path climbed steeper slopes. Craggy outcrops jutted against a brooding sky. Rain threatened, and the wind grew sharper. By midday, the knights urged caution. Dark clouds pressed overhead like an ominous prophecy.

Tomás rode alongside Maya, voice hushed. "Feels like a storm. According to the map, we're close to the tower."

A jagged spire of rock loomed on the horizon. Thunder rumbled in the distance. Tension tightened her chest. Carter, just behind them, met her eyes and gave a brief nod. Up ahead, the road curved around a rock face, revealing a crumbling tower perched on a cliff. One wall had collapsed, vines strangling ruined stones. The place seemed abandoned to centuries of neglect.

Sir Arnolt raised his hand, halting them at the warped wooden gate. Beric ventured forward with his crossbow. The rest dismounted, tethering their horses to a battered post. Beric and Arnolt insisted on going first, so Carter and Tomás trailed after them. Maya's nerves twitched as she stepped over knee-high weeds and broken stones. The air smelled of rot and rain.

Victoria joined her, scanning the courtyard. "No sign of modern debris."

Thunder growled overhead. Arnolt pointed to the tower's fractured upper levels. "I'll check inside. Beric, keep watch." He disappeared through a dark archway, footsteps echoing on creaky stairs.

Paul circled the courtyard's perimeter. Maya knelt by a shallow depression filled with decaying leaves. A glint of metal caught her eye. Carefully, she pried it free—a twisted scrap of wiring, crusted with rust but unmistakably modern. She shot Carter a tense look and slipped it behind a stone.

A raven burst from the tower's crumbled ramparts, launching into the sky with a harsh cry. Beric jumped, crossbow rattling. Wind whipped stronger, flicking droplets of rain that quickly intensified. Thunder boomed, closer now. Arnolt emerged from the tower, shaking his head. "No sign of squatters or bandits. Only rot."

He noticed the wire in Maya's hand. "What's that?"

She dropped it. "Scrap metal." Suspicion flickered in his eyes, but before he could press further, lightning flashed. The sky opened with a roar.

Tomás's horse whinnied, straining at its tether. "We should shelter inside," he yelled over the rising gale.

Another burst of lightning tore across the clouds. Maya thought she glimpsed a distant flicker of purple light. Her pulse jumped. Arnolt barked an order to hurry. Rain slashed sideways, turning the courtyard into a mire. They ducked into the tower's ground level, battered walls providing partial refuge. Water dripped through gashes in the ceiling. Paul and Victoria huddled near Tomás, while the knights paced, weapons at the ready. Carter fumbled with a lantern, the wind threatening to snuff out its tiny flame. Each thunderclap vibrated in Maya's chest.

Then she heard it—a distant, resonant hum beneath the storm's roar. A violet flash flared beyond the tower walls, bright enough to light the chamber. The knights recoiled, swords and crossbows raised. Maya's heart thudded. Was this a rift in action?

Rain hammered the roof. Another violet pulse shimmered, growing more intense. Beric shouted in alarm, stepping toward a jagged opening. "Devilry!" he cried.

"We have to see," Victoria urged, glancing at Maya. "If this is a gateway—"

Arnolt blocked her path. "No one moves until the storm clears!" But a fresh flash of purple startled them, and the knights faltered, fear unraveling their composure.

Seizing that moment, Maya and Carter slipped past Arnolt, lantern clutched. The knights stuck close, too frightened to let these travelers roam unchecked. In a rear courtyard hammered by howling wind, jagged stones littered the ground. The violet glow pulsed again, revealing a swirling distortion in the storm-darkened air. Thunder rocked the tower's foundations.

Maya's eyes locked on the churning haze, its edges crackling with electric fury. A low roar echoed, reminiscent of an engine heard from a great distance. Carter knelt beside her, water streaming down his face. "It's real," he breathed.

Beric, face ashen, tried to steady his crossbow. "Is this your witchcraft?" he shouted at them. Lightning clawed the sky, setting the swirling energy ablaze with brilliant purple light.

Suddenly, a wave of pressure exploded outward, driving them to their knees. Maya gasped, ears ringing. Debris hurtled through the air—a twisted hunk of metal that skittered across the stones, half recognizable as part of an airplane seat. Beric shrank back, muttering oaths. With a final, earsplitting crack of thunder, the vortex collapsed in on itself, leaving only howling wind and driving rain.

Silence took hold. Rain pounded in curtains. The seat frame lay on the ground, seatbelt hanging like a torn ribbon. Maya trembled, overwhelmed by questions. Could that vortex be used intentionally to go home, or would it shred them to pieces as it had done with whatever wreckage lay strewn across time?

Arnolt approached, sword shaking in his hand. "Explain," he demanded through clenched teeth. "What power is this?"

Carter steadied himself. "It's the phenomenon we told you about—storms that bring dangerous fragments from another place." Lightning flickered again. "We warned you."

Beric kneeled beside the twisted seat, his crossbow abandoned. He stared at the unfamiliar metal and rivets. "No blacksmith here could craft this," he whispered, fear in every syllable.

Victoria stepped in. "Baron Harlow must see this. If more storms throw debris into his lands, it poses a threat to everyone."

Tomás translated, and both knights nodded, determined to bring proof to the baron. Arnolt shuddered and tore his gaze from the seat. "We leave at first light."

They retreated to the tower's interior, where a small fire crackled amid the dripping stone walls. Carter and Tomás hauled the seat frame inside, setting it near the meager flames to keep it in sight. Paul stood nearby, face wan. Victoria rubbed her arms, voice trembling yet steady. "Now we know it's real."

Maya slumped beside the fire. "It's more than real. The question is, can we cross such a storm intentionally, or would it kill us?"

Carter placed a hand on her shoulder. "No one should rush into that. It's too dangerous." Torn scraps of metal danced through her mind, haunting her.

The knights kept a wary distance, offering a few hushed prayers. Outside, thunder rumbled again before fading into a murmur. Maya stared at the twisted seat frame, uncertain whether she should fear it or see it as a beacon of hope. Either way, they'd found exactly what they came for—and it was terrifying.

By dawn, the storm had passed. The courtyard was a sodden wreck, littered with broken stones. They quietly saddled their horses, while Arnolt and Beric avoided looking at the seat frame as if it might curse them simply by existing. Still, they secured it to a mule's pack, a trophy of evidence for Harlow.

They rode away from the tower without lingering. Once on the path, the knights took the lead, muttering about demons and witchcraft. Maya followed at the rear, mind replaying the sight of that swirling vortex. They had come so close to discovering a way home—or to meeting the same fate as the twisted metal at her side.

Victoria fell in beside her. "Are you all right?"

Maya managed a nod. "Shaken. That thing...was beyond anything I've seen."

Victoria's gaze drifted to the distant peaks. "We found what we were looking for. Now Harlow can't dismiss our story."

Paul guided his horse near them. "But will he let us harness it or lock us up to preserve his secrets? We shouldn't be naïve."

Carter overheard and responded in a muted tone. "We keep building alliances. These storms are real. If they keep emerging, there might be a pattern. Someday, maybe we slip through—if it's stable. Or we stay here, if there's no other choice."

Maya's throat tightened at that last possibility. The image of modern streets felt more distant with each passing moment. Still, she squared her shoulders. They continued down the mountain road, resolute, each step carrying them toward the baron—and the uncertain promise he'd offered.

They rode on, resolute, each step down the mountain reinforcing the vow to survive—and to see if the baron's promise of a boon might yield a chance at freedom.

CHAPTER 8

They arrived at Baron Harlow's castle under a sky thick with clouds, as if the storm from the watchtower had followed them home. Rain loomed overhead, poised on the brink of descent. The knights, Arnolt and Beric, led the way through the gatehouse, their tense shoulders drawing the guard's curious glances. Behind them, Carter guided the mule bearing a warped seat frame. Maya rode close, her heartbeat echoing the anxious rhythm that had accompanied her down the jagged mountain paths.

Once the portcullis groaned shut, the group dismounted. Stable-hands hurried forward to collect the horses. Arnolt gestured sharply at the seat frame. "Make sure you deliver this directly to the baron's private hall," he warned in a low tone. His unease rippled through the servants, who gawked at the twisted metal.

Victoria and Paul said little as they slid from their saddles, eyes combing the courtyard for anyone paying too much attention. Tomás, still nursing an old bruise, joined them. They headed toward the keep's large doors, aware that the battered relic from another world weighed heavily on their thoughts—and their future.

Inside the keep, Baron Harlow waited in a smaller reception hall, talking in hushed tones with Sir Lionel and a pair of stewards. Flames flickered along the walls, casting dancing shadows across the floor. A charge hung in the air, as if the atmosphere anticipated a single spark that could change everything. When the survivors entered—exhausted, soaked from near-constant drizzle, and visibly uneasy—Harlow's eyes narrowed. He raised a hand, beckoning them forward.

Arnolt spoke first, describing the cursed watchtower's swirling lights, the barrage of unnatural wind, and the hunk of "sky-metal" hurled from the vortex. Lionel's face lost its color. Harlow's knuckles blanched as he gripped the arm of his heavy wooden chair. He demanded to see the strange artifact at once.

Carter gestured to the open doorway. Two servants trudged in, carrying the bent seat frame, its metal torn and twisted. The ragged seatbelt reeked of rust and dampness. The stewards watched, aghast. Harlow stepped closer, eyes filled with wary fascination.

"This isn't fashioned by any blacksmith here," he muttered, running a gloved fingertip over the peculiar buckle. "No craftsman in these lands could dream up such an object."

Maya drew a steadying breath. "My lord, it supports our belief that storms bring items from far beyond your borders. If this falls into the wrong hands, who knows what weapons might appear next?"

He studied her expression, torn between disbelief and a growing sense of awe. "You saw no one attached to this thing? No living soul cast out from the skies?"

"None," she said softly. "But the storms could bring more—maybe bigger pieces of machinery, or people." A memory flitted through her mind: the shattered fuselage of a downed aircraft, lodged in medieval soil. She forced it away.

Harlow turned aside, exhaling hard. Lionel's grim visage reflected the same disquiet. "If storms drop such devilish creations," Lionel said, "how do we protect ourselves? And how do we prevent Braxton from seizing them first?"

Paul cleared his throat. "We'll need to watch likely storm sites. The watchtower might be only the beginning. If storms appear there frequently, we have to monitor or guard it." He paused, letting that sink in. "We're prepared to help, as long as you don't keep us locked away."

Baron Harlow's gaze flicked to Maya. "Freedom of movement, is that what you ask?"

She dipped her head. "If you want to protect your domain—and WilCarter's—allow us to research these storms without being confined."

Silence gathered, a razor-thin tension slicing through the hall. Lionel's posture grew taut. At last Harlow tapped the seat frame thoughtfully. "I recall owing you a boon," he said, voice subdued, "for saving my knight—and saving me. Very well. The boon is this: You and your companions may travel my lands and WilCarter's, keeping watch for storms. But on one condition." He raised a hand. "Any relic you find must be brought here first."

A ripple of relief skimmed through the group. Yet caution lingered. Maya inclined her head. "We'll do our best to secure them before enemies exploit their power, and we'll bring them to you if it's safe."

"Then so be it," Harlow said. He looked at Lionel. "Prepare letters of passage for these travelers. Let it be known they have my leave." His thin smile tugged at the corners of his mouth. "Lady healer, this is your boon. Do not waste it."

They left Harlow's presence with hearts pounding, weighed by the baron's demand. In the corridor, Victoria let out a long breath. "We're officially storm-chasers now."

Paul shot her a wry glance. "Still better than being caged."

Maya nodded, though the image of that violet vortex and the raw, unearthly power behind it loomed large. Even if they were free to roam, controlling such storms—or finding a route back to their own century—felt as precarious as walking a cliff's edge.

They split up for a time, each person needing a moment to collect thoughts. Maya made her way to the small infirmary, where Roderick lay recovering from wounds sustained in previous battles. He was awake, bleary-eyed but stable, and she checked his injuries for infection. He grumbled thanks, pride hurt by his frailty. She reminded him that patience was crucial for healing.

Late that night, Maya stood at a high window, gazing across Harlow's courtyard. Raindrops tapped the glass like fingernails, a soft hush after days of violence. She wondered if a portal might tear open the sky again. The memory of a battered plane fuselage haunted her. She pressed her palm to the cold stone, whispering that there had to be more than unending conflict in this world.

Two days later, the survivors prepared to depart for Kentwood, the warped seat frame strapped to a wagon to serve as proof. Harlow gave them letters bearing his hawk seal, granting free passage through his land and WilCarter's. Lionel remained stiff and cold, but he managed a curt, "Travel safely."

Roderick, still weak, stayed behind in the care of local healers. Maya left him with instructions and the last of her antibiotic ointment. He thanked her with a solemn nod, grudging respect in his eyes. "Tell your baron I owe him no small debt," he managed. She grasped his hand once, then rejoined her companions.

They started at dawn. A handful of Harlow's knights escorted them just beyond the gates, then peeled away. Freed from the castle's shadow, the group let out a collective sigh. A crisp wind played through the roadside trees, hinting at the next chapter of their uncertain future.

Traveling east to west, they passed farmland where shoots of springtime growth peeked through the soil. The gentler terrain contrasted sharply with the storm-lashed mountains. Carter guided the wagon, cautious with each bump lest the seat frame topple. Victoria and Paul discussed how to approach WilCarter with the bizarre relic. Tomás rode ahead, eyes sharp for danger. Maya brought up the rear, scanning the skies for any glimmer of swirling violet.

By the second afternoon, they entered Kentwood territory. A patrol of WilCarter's knights greeted them near a small outpost, initial suspicion giving way to shock when they glimpsed the metal frame. Soon they arrived at Kentwood's fortress, relief and apprehension mingling as familiar faces came into view.

In the courtyard, Anna embraced Maya with shining eyes. "We worried," she whispered. Ethan himself flew toward Carter, clinging around his waist. The Wu couple hovered, anxious for answers. Nina's gaze caught on the relic. "This emerged from a storm?"

Maya inclined her head. "Ripped from somewhere far away. Another plane, maybe. We can't be certain."

They were summoned promptly before Lord WilCarter in the grand hall. He stood with a small retinue of knights and Lady Althea by his side, her expression solemn. When the seat frame was revealed, low gasps and murmurs spread. WilCarter descended from his dais, authority in every step.

Carter explained the journey, how they had convinced Harlow to grant them passage, and the terror of the watchtower storm. When Maya mentioned the agreement to share relics with Harlow, WilCarter's face shadowed. "You swore yourselves to him as well?"

Victoria bristled. "We pledged no disloyalty, my lord. We simply offered the same courtesy to him that we offer you: our knowledge. In exchange, we can move freely."

WilCarter regarded the seat frame with a clenched jaw. "If Harlow tries to claim you, that courtesy might prove... problematic." Lady Althea laid a calming hand on his arm before he continued. "Nonetheless, storms threaten us all. Braxton, Harlow—any might attempt to harness such power. Very well. You have permission to travel, provided you remember your duty to Kentwood. Am I clear?"

They bowed their heads, keenly aware that both domains now held a stake in their loyalty. Nothing about their predicament felt simple or safe.

Later, they gathered in the tower rooms WilCarter had granted them as living quarters. Candles illuminated the exhausted group. Carter's hands were smeared with soot from the road, Victoria and Paul sat close, and Tomás sorted through new maps. Nina hovered, her gaze fixed on the seat frame's twisted metal. Ethan and his mother listened with rapt attention as Maya described the watchtower's terrifying vortex, the driving rain, the seat belt still strapped to the relic.

Ethan shuddered. "Like another crash?"

Maya nodded, her voice subdued. "Yes. Yet no survivors, only this broken seat. We can't guess what else might drop into our world next."

Sarah's voice trembled. "If more planes fall from the sky... God, how do we stop it?"

Carter placed a reassuring hand on her shoulder. "We can't, not yet. Our mission is to observe and warn Harlow or WilCarter if anything new appears."

Victoria exhaled slowly. "And if we find a stable vortex—assuming that's even possible—do we dare cross? It might tear us apart."

Maya's heart felt heavy. "We need a plan, but nothing is certain. For now, we survive here. Maybe we figure out a safe route home... or maybe we accept that this realm has become our life."

A hush draped over them. No one spoke of the possibility that they might remain forever in this medieval tapestry. Yet the thought flickered among them like a single candle flame in a drafty corridor.

Days blurred into weeks. The group adapted to daily responsibilities in Kentwood: Maya oversaw the clinic, healing knights and villagers alike. Carter spent hours at the forge, wrestling with the moral burden of crafting ever-more-lethal weaponry. Victoria and Paul negotiated for better supplies, while Tomás taught reading lessons to local children. Though they functioned in this feudal society, the promise of unexplained storms never quite let them rest.

Occasional messages arrived from Harlow, reporting no additional signs of the swirling lights. The seat frame, locked away in WilCarter's storehouse, served as a silent reminder of the cataclysm that could return at any moment. Yet talk of Braxton's aggression overshadowed all else. War drew near, the lords hunkering down for further conflict.

One evening, the survivors gathered in a small chamber they had claimed as a communal space. Only a single window allowed starlight to slip through. A ragged trunk in the corner held diaries and strange objects they'd salvaged: the merchant's thermos cylinder, the seat-belt buckle from the watchtower. Ethan dozed in a corner, lulled by low voices. His mother sipped tea by the open shutter. Carter sorted scraps of parchment near the flickering candle. Maya sat on the cold floor, her old stethoscope coiled in her lap like a relic of another life.

Victoria cleared her throat. "We've built an uneasy alliance with two feudal lords, but storms aren't predictable. We can't see a clear path home."

Paul, leaning against the wall, nodded. "We record every rumor and observation about weather patterns. Maybe we'll find signs—certain lunar phases or atmospheric shifts—something that signals these rifts."

Tomás spread out a worn map. "If another war flares, we won't travel freely. We might be forced to choose sides. That could destroy any chance to observe storms."

Carter ran a hand over his face. "I can't stop forging weapons if WilCarter demands them. But each sword I craft weighs on me, knowing it will be used on some battlefield."

Maya lifted her gaze. "Let's do what we must to keep the peace while we watch the skies. If a stable rift appears, we'll decide then whether to risk it."

Silence followed, filled with the unspoken awareness that they were as bound to this world now as any knight or peasant. Still, they yearned to see modern city lights, hear the hum of engines, and feel the neat cleanliness of a hospital. One by one, they whispered goodnight and slipped away to their separate corners of the tower.

Dawn broke with turmoil. A messenger barreled into Kentwood, reporting a Braxton raid on a nearby village. WilCarter's knights scrambled. The survivors observed from the windows, dread pooling in their stomachs. Again, war overshadowed their search for cosmic anomalies.

Maya worked tirelessly in the infirmary, prepping bandages and boiling cloth in a frantic bid to maintain cleanliness. Carter hammered swords and mended dented armor for knights ready to fight. Victoria and Paul strategized with the advisors, controlling supply lines. Tomás helped the peasants barricade their homes. Days vanished into nights of anxious waiting. Wounded men trickled back, and Maya treated arrow punctures and savage cuts. She missed modern antiseptics with a bitter ache.

After weeks of skirmishes, WilCarter's forces limped back victorious—or at least not defeated. Braxton had been held at bay, but at the cost of burned fields and injured soldiers. WilCarter's domain needed time to recover. The weight of that war settled upon Maya, who spent the nights in the infirmary, cleaning wounds amid the odor of blood and herbs.

One evening, Lady Althea came to her. Althea's eyes were shadowed. "Your healing made all the difference," she said softly. "Lord WilCarter wishes to know if there've been any new storms or relics. If Braxton unearths something powerful, we could lose everything."

Maya's throat constricted. "No new sightings. Our watchers remain vigilant, but the sky's been calm. All we can do is keep looking."

Althea offered a weary nod, then left, carrying her own burdens of loss. This was life in medieval conflict: no illusions of quick endings, only the slow acceptance of each day's demands.

Summer arrived, warmth replacing springtime chill. The survivors integrated further into Kentwood's daily routines. Carter experimented with forging superior farming tools, hoping to improve the harvest. Victoria advocated for trade reforms to elevate local peasants. Paul helped create basic surpluses for the winter months. Nina assisted Maya in the clinic, while Anna taught the young how to read. Tomás bridged cultures, forging relationships with local elders. Their modern knowledge seeped into this archaic realm, changing it in subtle but undeniable ways.

They never stopped watching for storms. Late at night, from the highest towers, they combed the horizon for flickering lights or thunder without clouds. Harlow sent occasional reports of bandit attacks but no mention of swirling skies at the watchtower. The battered seat frame sat in WilCarter's storeroom, an artifact that seemed to belong neither to their old world nor their new.

As the months passed, they measured time by medieval seasons rather than the digital calendars they once relied on. A year crept by since their plane crash, though they spoke of it only in hushed tones. Ethan had grown taller, Carter's once-pristine coat was patched all over, and Maya had memorized half a dozen local medical texts, merging medieval theories with modern practice. She sometimes caught herself calling it "time-lost medicine."

One warm evening, while the sun melted into the horizon, Maya climbed to the top of Kentwood's highest tower. She gazed out at rolling fields of gold. Ethan arrived, a lantern in hand. He peered up at her, eyes bright with unspoken questions.

"You said we might go home," he reminded her, voice quavering. "Is that still true?"

Maya's heart clenched. She knelt, smoothing his hair. "I wish I could promise it. We watch for storms, hoping for a stable gateway... but there's no sign yet."

He pressed his lips together, blinking fast. "I like it here sometimes. Mom's happier teaching. It's not all bad, right?"

She embraced him, tears burning the back of her eyes. "It's different. You're strong, Ethan. We'll face whatever comes."

He stayed by her side as the sunset flared into embers of color, then died away, leaving a hush. Acceptance ghosted around the edges of her thoughts. She stood, letting the boy lead her down from the tower, a small flame dancing in the lantern, a reflection of hope that might never be fully snuffed.

Autumn came early with cool winds. One night, the survivors gathered around a small fireplace in their tower chamber. The Wu family served a hearty meal of bread and stew. Nina chuckled about a local festival. Tomás shared tales from village elders who believed storms were omens from the heavens. Paul flipped through old journals, rereading notes about the fuselage remains. Victoria sipped spiced cider and turned to Maya.

"Heard anything about storms next month?"

Maya shook her head. "We've posted watchers, but the sky's silent. Maybe winter will bring something, maybe not."

Carter added a log to the fire, sparks dancing upward. "Even if another vortex opened, we have no guarantee it'd be safe. The last thing we want is more wreckage." He forced a tight grin. "We're not in a story with magic slippers or guaranteed happy endings."

A gentle laughter rippled around them, though it held an undercurrent of sorrow. They shifted to lighter conversation—village gossip, new forging techniques, orchard yields. For a brief while, they felt like part of the local tapestry, neighbors sharing an evening meal. Candlelight softened their expressions, forging a temporary sense of family across time and circumstance.

When the company had dispersed for the night, Maya stood by the window with Carter, watching moonlight spill into the courtyard. He settled an arm around her shoulders. "It's been a year," he said, voice thick with memory. "If another storm came tomorrow, I don't know if I'd celebrate a chance to return home or fear what it might destroy."

She leaned into him. "Sometimes I'd rather no new storm came at all. The seat frame was horrifying enough. If another plane fell... more grief, more lives lost."

He nodded, his features etched with the same conflict in her own heart. "Still, if we had a real shot at going back—"

She closed her eyes. The dilemma cut to her core: would they trade all they'd built here for the uncertain chance to reclaim modern life? She said nothing, only held his hand more tightly, as though that gesture might tether her between two worlds.

A crow's caw echoed through the darkness, wings sweeping over the parapets. Beneath that hush, Maya eased her head onto Carter's shoulder. They had once clung to hope that the next storm might open a corridor home. Now, though, a new kind of acceptance was taking root. The war had delayed their research, and time itself seemed determined to weave them into this realm's fabric.

In that moonlit tower, she listened to the soft thud of her own pulse, felt Carter's warmth at her side, and remembered the swirling vortex that had once flung a broken seat from the skies. If another came, she would meet it without illusions. But if it never arrived, she would endure here, with Ethan and the others. Maybe, in a sense, they already belonged.

For now, they waited. War might reignite, storms might tear open the heavens, allies might shift loyalties. But in that moment, their hearts found a calm acceptance that might outlast all uncertainty. The moon drifted behind a veil of clouds. No thunder, no unnatural lights, only the hushed breathing of a land that, for better or worse, had become home.

CHAPTER 9

A hush clung to Kentwood Castle in the predawn chill, its high towers black silhouettes against a sky tinted faintly by emerging starlight. Maya stood alone atop the north rampart, pulling her cloak tight against a biting wind. The courtyard below was peaceful—carts of grain, stalls stacked with supplies—but in the looming stillness of the horizon, she sensed a fragile calm. She tilted her head, scanning for the faintest flicker of violet lightning or the swirl of unnatural clouds. Nothing. Only the steady exhale of a world edging into dawn.

She'd come here each morning for weeks now, compelled by the quiet ritual. Something about these ramparts gave her the space she needed to weigh the tension that had become her life: modern knowledge in an ancient era, two feudal lords vying for her allegiance, and a year's worth of crushed hopes that a stable rift might appear. She breathed in, then out, letting the cold air steady her. No swirling storms yet. Perhaps that was both mercy and regret.

Behind her, boots scraped against the stone. Carter approached, hair ruffled by the breeze. He offered a lopsided smile and a mug of steaming herbal tea. "I figured you'd be up here," he said in a gentle voice. "Same as always."

"Thanks." She sipped the tea, warmth easing into her chest. He leaned against the rampart, the early light picking out the angles of his face. Together, they surveyed the courtyard—where the daily routine would soon begin—and the farmland beyond, neat patches nurtured by the survivors' modern insights. Looking at those irrigated rows and improved tools, Maya felt pride mingled with resignation. Every innovation braided them deeper into this medieval corner of the world.

"Any sign?" Carter asked, though he clearly expected none.

She shook her head. "All quiet. No eerie lights on the horizon."

He exhaled. "Winter's coming. Storm season could kick up more phenomenon...assuming they ever come back."

They shared a somber silence. Both recalled how the storms had once seemed like a lifeline home; now, after seeing the toll they took, hope felt tainted by dread.

***

When they descended to the courtyard, the bustle had already started—laborers setting up for market, castle guards readying supplies. Victoria emerged from the stable tower in a practical wool tunic. She waved them over, eyes sharp.

"We have visitors," she said quietly. "Two men who claim to be from Harlow's domain. They arrived early, talking to Tomás at the main gate. Seem jittery about strange rumors to the west."

Carter frowned. "Rumors of storms? Or Braxton's raiders?"

Victoria lifted one shoulder in a shrug. "They wouldn't say with me there, insisted Tomás translate alone. But they're clearly on edge."

They made their way past villagers bartering sacks of oats and halted near the gatehouse, where Tomás spoke with two travelers in dusty cloaks. The men glanced around as if the castle walls themselves could leap up to snare them.

Tomás beckoned them close. "These fellows are from a village near the southwestern border of Harlow's territory," he murmured. "They claim there've been 'demonic lights' in the skies over an old abbey—strange glows at night, thunderous noises. They're worried it's either Braxton's witchcraft or something far worse."

Maya's pulse fluttered. Another potential storm site? She kept her voice calm. "How long have these rumors circulated?"

Tomás asked in the local dialect. One man answered in hushed tones. Tomás nodded. "They say it started a few days ago. An orchard near the abbey was found scorched as if by lightning, but the sky was clear that night."

Victoria scowled. "Could be arson, a freak event, or something else. Are we about to walk into another vortex fiasco?"

Maya recalled the watchtower storm that had spat out airplane fragments. "We need to investigate," she said softly. "If it's a rift, ignoring it won't help. Braxton might exploit it, or more wreckage might come through."

***

WilCarter convened a short council in the great hall. He listened to the travelers' urgent tales, his expression impassive. Maya, Carter, Victoria, Tomás, and Paul stood by, braced for a verdict. The travelers finished with anxious pleas—they needed someone to determine if the scorched orchard was an omen of doom.

WilCarter tapped his fingers on his armrest. "Harlow's men, always trouble," he muttered, eyeing Maya. "You'd run to investigate? Could be Braxton's ruse to draw you away."

Victoria spoke carefully. "We can't dismiss it. If it's another storm phenomenon, leaving it unchecked is dangerous. We do have Harlow's permission to move freely in his domain."

Murmuring rippled among the knights. WilCarter, torn by suspicion and the memory of past storms, finally relented. "Very well. Take a small group. Confirm what's going on. But don't get tangled in Harlow's politics. Report back quickly."

Relief flickered among the survivors. Another expedition, another shot at unraveling these storm portals. Maya bowed respectfully. "Thank you, my lord. We'll return as soon as we know more."

***

By midday, the two travelers led the way, accompanied by Maya, Carter, Victoria, Paul, Tomás, and a pair of Kentwood knights assigned as escorts. They rode out onto roads tinted by the first hints of autumn. No thunderheads darkened the sky, yet the men's unsettled whispers about "demonic" sightings put everyone on edge.

Maya quizzed the travelers about the orchard, once belonging to a crumbling monastery. Locals claimed to see shimmering lights at night, accompanied by booming echoes. One man insisted the grove smelled of sulfur, "like devils' breath," though Maya suspected it was ozone or burnt metal. She shared a significant look with Carter. The watchers of this era might label any advanced phenomenon as black magic.

Victoria drew her horse alongside Carter's. "We're neck-deep in another storm chase. I hope it's not a trick."

Carter offered a quick grin. "If there's a real vortex, we have to document it. If not, we lose a couple of days, but at least we keep Braxton from scooping up modern debris for his war."

The knights, riding ahead, cast uneasy glances behind them. As they traveled deeper into lands claimed by Harlow, the risk of bandits increased. Yet Maya steeled her nerves. Their duty was twofold: safeguarding the local population from lethal anomalies and, in some sliver of hope, finding a doorway home.

***

Two days later, they passed through a patchwork of hamlets that recognized Harlow's seal. At night, they slept in village corners or alongside quiet streams, gleaning rumors from curious locals. Tales of the orchard multiplied—some said it was a demon's lair, others believed it an omen of looming war. Whispered accounts even mentioned fragments of "strange metal" strewn among the charred trees, fueling Maya's racing thoughts.

On the third afternoon, the terrain changed. Hills rose up, crowned by old oaks. A narrow lane curved toward the relic of a monastery wall. Beyond it stretched a slope where rows of trees stood stark and blackened. One look at that orchard made Maya's stomach twist. Ash coated the ground, and the trunks appeared seared from within.

They reined their horses at the edge. Carter's voice came out hushed. "This is no ordinary burn."

Maya dismounted, picking her way over brittle grass. "Check for modern debris," she told the group. "Anything out of place."

Victoria and Paul moved toward the broken monastery gate, scanning the rubble. Tomás gently encouraged the wary travelers to stay behind, while the knights stood guard, swords at the ready. The orchard itself felt eerie, as though the air still hummed with aftershocks of immense energy.

Maya crouched near a trunk while Carter ran a hand over splintered bark. Beneath the ash, she spotted a faint glimmer. Carefully brushing it aside, she teased out a twisted thread of metal. A closer look confirmed her suspicion: a scrap of modern wiring. Her pulse quickened.

Carter's face hardened. "Looks like another piece of an airplane. Enough force to set the orchard ablaze."

She nodded grimly, gesturing for Tomás. She held up the thread. "Ask the travelers if anyone found more of this. We'll need every clue."

At Tomás's prompting, one man admitted orchard workers had unearthed "evil lumps of iron," which they discarded. Another heard of a black-lacquered panel carried away by an old woman who believed it cursed. Victoria jogged back from the monastery, breath ragged. "Stone walls are scorched, too. Some partial collapse—no obvious sign of sabotage, but it's definitely not normal fire."

Maya's mind whirred. Another vortex must have opened here, scorching everything in a surge of heat. She pictured the watchtower's terrifying storm, the twisted seat frame spat into the courtyard. These events were no random illusions.

***

They spent the afternoon searching. Among the ashen remains, they uncovered shards of melted plastic and scraps of foam that might have been seat padding. A curved steel rod that resembled part of an airline seat brace. The knights muttered in alarm, calling it sorcery. By dusk, the travelers flatly refused to camp near the orchard, fleeing to a nearby village. Maya and her companions, however, remained. Someone needed to keep watch in case another phenomenon flared.

They made a modest fire in the monastery courtyard. A swirling wind scattered ash across the lifeless grove. Carter held up fragments under the fading light, a shadow crossing his features. "If this was part of the fuselage, we're seeing only the smallest pieces. The rest...could be anywhere, or maybe obliterated by the vortex."

Paul knelt by the relics, brow creased. "We can't be sure. At the watchtower, some big chunks survived. Here, it looks like the orchard was hammered by extreme heat."

Maya stared into the orchard's blackened silhouette. "We'll keep vigil. If it returns, we need to witness it."

The knights stationed themselves a short distance away, uneasy but unwilling to disobey WilCarter's orders. Tomás passed around meager rations and water. Night settled in, the moon half-lost behind drifting clouds. An unsettling calm hung over the orchard, as though the land still smoldered with untapped power.

***

Carter volunteered for first watch, pacing at the orchard edge. Maya tried to rest, but her sleep was fragmented by tension. Around midnight, she awoke to a faint crackling on the wind. Alarmed, she lit a lantern and crept away from the still-glowing embers of their fire. The orchard, ghostly and cold, loomed like a row of skeletal fingers stretching toward the night sky.

Then she spotted Carter's silhouette near a collapsed wall. He waved her over, his voice hushed. "I heard something. Not sure if it's just wind…" He trailed off, gaze sliding behind her.

She pivoted. A subtle luminescence shimmered among the central trees. A pale violet glow pulsed like the heartbeat of some spectral creature. Maya's breath constricted. "Is it another storm?"

Carter grabbed her hand. "Get the others."

Within moments, Victoria, Paul, Tomás, and the knights rushed over. They doused the fire, letting their eyes adapt to the orchard's dark. Still, the violet light remained, a wavering haze about fifty yards in. The knights murmured prayers, their swords seeming feeble against what was essentially raw energy.

"It's smaller than the watchtower vortex," Paul breathed. "But definitely something."

They approached in tense formation. The faint glow rose from a cluster of charred stumps. Sparks danced in the air like errant fireflies. Maya's skin tingled with static, a memory of the watchtower swirling in her mind. Carter touched the ground, found it strangely warm.

Victoria moved close, stretching a hand toward the glow. Little arcs of energy zapped her fingertips, forcing her to recoil. "That stings," she muttered, eyes wide.

A continuous low hum threaded the silence. The knights looked desperate to fight, yet how does one battle shimmering air? One stammered, "What do we do?"

Maya swallowed. "Observe. See if it expands or vanishes. If it flares, stay clear."

They formed a wary circle, rotating watch throughout the night. The flickering glow never erupted into a full vortex. Instead, it faded toward dawn, dissipating with the morning's first light. By the time the sun rose, the orchard was plain scorched timber once again, its menacing aura replaced by a profound exhaustion in the watchers.

***

Late morning found them huddled around the sparse remains of their camp. Maya rubbed her eyes. "We'll have to warn Harlow's people," she told the group. "This area needs to be off-limits. That residual field could still be dangerous."

Carter nodded. "And no obvious sign of a stable portal. Another dead end."

Tomás sighed. "At least the orchard might be quarantined if we get word out. Keeps villagers safe from wandering into it."

Victoria folded her arms, expression grim. "So it's another near miss. No crossing to our time. Just more heartbreak."

Paul ran a hand through his hair. "These storms tease us, dropping scraps of our world but never offering a way back."

Maya felt the sting of that truth. "We do what we can. Let's move on and report."

***

They rode to the closest village, warning the locals of the orchard's "cursed lights." The peasants were all too eager to promise they'd avoid the place. An elderly woman invited them to see a large piece of black-lacquered metal she'd found. In her humble hut, she reverently unveiled what looked like the top portion of an overhead bin—charred, with half-melted instructions for oxygen masks.

Maya's throat constricted. Words like "Emergency Exit" and "Cabin Pressure" were still faintly visible under the scorched surface. She gently accepted it, offering silver coins in thanks. Another relic from a world that felt more distant with each day.

***

They continued east, bound for Harlow's seat to deliver their findings. The baron himself was absent, quelling unrest on distant fronts, so his steward, Sir Lionel, received them. He listened gravely, eyes widening at the twisted plane fragments they produced. At length, he rubbed his temples.

"We'll seal off the orchard and warn the villages," he promised. "Though we can't hope to control these forces."

Victoria dipped her head. "No one can. But at least fewer people will wander into danger."

They spent a restless night in Harlow's fortress, listening to hushed talk of Braxton's raids. The novelty of "sky-people" had dulled to an undercurrent of awe and fear. By dawn, they mounted their horses and began the journey back to Kentwood. For all the risk, they carried only scraps of scorched plastic and metal. No victory, no solution, just more puzzle pieces that led nowhere.

***

On their return to Kentwood, they rode in near-silence. Each person was lost in thought—about swirling vortexes that offered neither rescue nor relief. Their hope wore thinner with each disheartening expedition.

At the castle gates, WilCarter's steward escorted them inside. Lady Althea received their report, her face tight with worry. She thanked them with solemn gratitude, seeing the fragments of modern wreckage that served only to underscore how random and violent the storms could be. Once again, no stable crossing, no path home.

***

Days turned to a subdued routine. Maya returned to tending wounded knights, many injured in Braxton's small-scale clashes. Carter hammered out plow blades and scythes when he wasn't forced to forge more swords. Victoria managed trade logistics, Paul cataloged storehouse inventories, Tomás tutored peasants. The survivors' role in Kentwood's prosperity grew every week, a testament to the synergy of modern knowledge with medieval resources.

Not long after, Ethan—now older, bolder—found Maya in a modest orchard behind the castle, where she cultivated herbs for the clinic. He squatted beside her while she tested leaves for antiseptic qualities.

"You're finished with lessons early?" she asked softly.

He shrugged. "Mom's busy with younger kids. She said I could come help." He pointed at her small pile of leaves. "Those any better than last year's crop?"

She managed a tired smile. "Yes, I think they'll reduce infection. Could save lives."

He nodded, then looked up at her. "Do you still want to go back? To our time?"

Her heart gave a painful twinge. She set aside the herbs. "I used to dream about returning every single night. But the longer we're here, the more people rely on us. The storms are so unpredictable. We might never find a safe path."

Ethan bit his lip. "If we stay, is that really so awful?"

Maya's throat tightened. She pulled him into a gentle hug. "We'll make the best of wherever we are, okay?"

He nodded against her shoulder, and she felt both a fragile hope and a quiet ache.

***

As autumn gave way to cooler nights, the castle's rhythm felt almost normal. A hush of tension still lingered—Braxton's raids never truly stopped, and Harlow's alliances were tenuous—but Kentwood remained unscathed for now. Letters arrived praising the survivors' contributions: new farming techniques, improved medical care, improved record-keeping. The notion of belonging took subtle root.

Occasionally, the survivors whispered among themselves about possible storms. Each inquiry to the orchard near Harlow turned up the same news: no new lights, no fresh damage, no sign of a portal. WilCarter's knights seemed only half-convinced the orchard had ever been anything more than an unlucky lightning strike.

***

One crisp afternoon, a traveling troupe of minstrels entered Kentwood, bringing laughter and music for the harvest festival. People gathered in the courtyard to hear spirited ballads about knights, dragons, and devils. Maya watched from the edges as children clapped to the tune. The orchard fiasco was already morphing into a tale of "demonic apples," woven for entertainment rather than caution.

In that moment, she recognized how swiftly life moved on for most residents. Even storms that tore open the fabric of time could fade into legend if they remained unseen. The twisted seat brace in a storeroom, the overhead panel scorched beyond recognition—these were reminders of a different world that few here truly understood.

When evening settled over the courtyard, lanterns flickered in the swirling cool air. The survivors retreated to their usual tasks or found quiet corners to reflect on the day's festivities. Maya stayed back until the last minstrel packed up, pondering how ephemeral all these wonders and terrors could be in a place that embraced myth more readily than fact.

***

Later that night, she made her way to the tower, footsteps echoing in torchlit corridors. She remembered how the watchtower once roared with swirling energies, that single instance of raw possibility. Now, it was silent, as though the castle itself had decided no more storms would intrude upon daily life. At the top, she found Carter gazing out a narrow window into the star-flecked sky.

She joined him, resting a hand on the ledge. The hush wrapped around them, comforting in its own way. At length, he said, "I'm considering building a new workshop—something bigger. I want to craft more advanced equipment for everyday life: water pumps, improved weaving looms. We can ease people's burdens, maybe even spark more prosperity."

Maya placed a gentle hand on his shoulder. "That's a wonderful idea. We can be more than instruments of war."

He glanced at her. "We may never find a stable rift. The storms...they come and go on their own terms."

She felt that pang of sorrow again. But his resolve also steadied her. "If they never open for us, we still have each other. We still have a purpose."

He turned to her, forehead lightly pressing against hers, his words soft. "That's enough for me."

They lingered there, hearts quietly synced, the wind carrying the scent of woodsmoke and apples from the harvest festival. Maybe, somewhere, a vortex still churned. Maybe it would remain elusive forever. For this moment, she allowed acceptance to warm her heart, content to shape a better world in the only place they truly inhabited—the here and now.

CHAPTER 10

In the hush of predawn, Ethan crept through the corridors of Kentwood Castle, careful not to wake slumbering knights. The stone floors chilled his feet through thin shoes. A sense of purpose guided him—he had a plan, albeit a half-formed one. He'd overheard whispers about another orchard mishap near the southwestern fields. Perhaps he could slip out quietly and see if any odd lights flared before dawn. Adults might have grown resigned, but he hadn't. At almost twelve, he refused to believe all hope was lost.

He slipped into the courtyard, stars blinking overhead, the castle's great wooden gate sealed for the night. Two weary guards stood watch, half-drowsing on the walls. Ethan scanned for a smaller sally port, reasoning that if only the grown-ups understood, they'd see he was old enough to help. Instead, they coddled him. Enough was enough.

He ducked into the stable yard, searching for an unlatched side gate. Then he froze—his mother emerged from behind a stack of hay bales, her face stern but not unkind. "What do you think you're doing?" she whispered.

Caught. His cheeks burned. "Mom, I—I just wanted to check the orchard. There might be new storms. I'm not a baby." He folded his arms, frustration turning his voice sharp.

She softened at the sight of his earnest expression. "I know you're not. But sneaking out alone is dangerous." She exhaled, pulling him into a shadowed corner. "If there are signs to find, we'll look together. We don't hide things from each other."

He blinked, caught between relief and embarrassment. "Promise? You won't just say no?"

She nodded, offering a gentle hug. "We'll talk to Maya and Carter in the morning. If something odd is brewing, we'll handle it as a team."

Ethan's shoulders loosened. Only months ago, she'd been so fragile, still grieving his father's death. Now, she was a calm presence in a medieval storm. He returned her embrace. "Okay. But we can't ignore the storms anymore."

Later that morning, Maya met Ethan and his mother by the orchard behind the castle. Their expressions were resolute. After hearing Ethan's fervent desire to watch for any new vortex sites, Maya's gaze softened.

"He's grown," she admitted, resting a hand on his shoulder. "We haven't told you everything, but maybe we should start. If new rumors crop up, we'll involve you. Agreed?"

Ethan's eyes lit with gratitude. "Agreed."

Carter soon arrived, wiping sweat from his brow after an early session at the forge. He ruffled Ethan's hair. "He's not wrong. We've barely kept tabs on those southwestern fields for months."

Maya caught the flicker of concern in Carter's eyes. The looming war had overshadowed their storm investigations. But Ethan's fierce determination reminded them that complacency could be costly. "Let's gather everyone and see," she said. "If there's truth behind these rumors, we'll know soon enough."

They convened in the tower's communal chamber as morning light slanted through narrow windows. Victoria, Paul, Tomás, Nina, Sarah Wu, and Jason Wu listened intently while Tomás described a snippet he'd overheard: a far orchard with scorched ground, echoes of earlier incidents. No actual sightings, but enough to raise eyebrows.

Nina rubbed her chin. "Whether it's sabotage or the real deal, we should confirm. We can't ignore any oddities."

Jason, leaning carefully on his cane, chimed in. "I'll go too. My leg can handle a short ride now. If there's a time rift, we're all invested."

Victoria frowned. "WilCarter might not be pleased. He's still anxious about a possible Braxton attack."

Paul shrugged, tapping his parchment marked with orchard locations. "It's within Kentwood territory, near the border but not outside it. We can do a quick check. No crossing domains."

Maya glanced at Ethan, who listened with unwavering attention. "All right. Let's propose a small team and keep WilCarter informed. The last orchard fiasco was too big to ignore."

WilCarter received them in the great hall, though his mind seemed occupied with war updates. At the mention of orchard scorch marks, he waved them away with little interest. "Go if you must, but be quick. The harvest is nearly done, and Braxton's men prowl the west. Take a couple of knights. I don't want more stories of 'sky-lights' unless they threaten us."

His dismissive tone revealed how tired he was of balancing orchard mysteries against looming battle. Lady Althea gave them a supportive nod, but remained silent. Maya suppressed a groan. At least they had his grudging permission.

By midday, the scouting group set out: Maya, Carter, Anna, Tomás, Jason, and two knights—Sir Alden and Sir Maurice. Ethan, unhappy, stayed behind with Nina and Victoria, who had tasks in the castle. He made them promise that if they discovered anything truly strange, he'd come along next time.

They rode south along a winding dirt road framed by autumn's golden hues. The knights chatted about minor raids, not terribly invested in orchard hunts. Maya and Carter kept their voices low, watching Anna scan the horizon as though bracing for any threat. Jason's back was straight in the saddle, determined to test his leg's resilience, while Tomás kept an eye out for scorched fields.

By mid-afternoon, they reached a cluster of small farmsteads. Smoke curled from chimneys while villagers wrapped themselves in layers against the chill. The target orchard was beyond a low ridge, rumored to be abandoned after a plague. Locals called the place cursed and stayed away. Without a guide, the group advanced alone.

Maya felt her pulse quicken with a faint, half-hopeful charge. If a phenomenon had flared, maybe they could learn more—or end up disappointed yet again. She inhaled the crisp air, every sense alert.

They ascended the ridge, spotting a narrow valley lined with leafless apple trees. Fruit had fallen to the ground and rotted. At the orchard's center, several trees looked blackened, as if scorched by unnatural fire. Sir Alden whistled under his breath. "Something burned those trees, but it doesn't look like lightning or a normal blaze."

Carter dismounted, moving carefully over the damp grass. The orchard smelled of decay mingled with something caustic. Maya followed, crouching beside the burned patch. She sifted through ash and uncovered a half-melted piece of metal—a rivet or screw, certainly not from medieval farm tools. Her heart tensed. Another artifact from a storm, perhaps.

Jason approached, favoring his injured leg. He studied the rivet in her palm, letting out a quiet sigh. "Same pattern as before. A vortex must have flared here and vanished, leaving this behind."

Sir Maurice glowered at the charred ground. "No sign of devilish lights now. Could be old."

Maya frowned. The ashes felt cold, the damage possibly days old. "We might camp and see if anything else appears tonight," she said.

Sir Alden shrugged. "Your choice. But if Braxton's men wander close, we'll have trouble."

They agreed to stay. The orchard provided modest shelter, with a small stream winding past gnarled trunks. Evening settled in, the sky bruised purple. Maya's thoughts darted back to Ethan, safe at the castle but probably yearning to be here. She hoped the night would bring no battle and no heartbreak.

They lit a small fire. Carter examined the rivet and a few other twisted metal shards discovered in the ash. "Nothing significant," he murmured. "No big seats or panels. Maybe just a tiny rift."

Maya nodded, staring into the flames. "It's more proof the storms persist, but scattered—like elusive ghosts."

Night wrapped them in a cold hush. Sir Alden and Sir Maurice rotated patrols. Tomás discussed theories on time tears and cosmic folds with Jason, though neither had solid answers. The orchard's scorched patch loomed like a dark memory. By midnight, the only sounds were the crackling fire and the wind sighing through barren branches.

Maya dozed, haunted by dreams of swirling violet storms chasing them through centuries. She woke near dawn to hushed voices. Carter stood with Anna at the orchard's edge, speaking urgently. Maya's pulse fluttered—had something happened?

She rose, stepping carefully over damp grass. The two fell silent as she approached. Anna gave a small smile. "We thought we heard something in the orchard. It was only the wind."

Maya nodded, folding her arms against the pre-dawn chill. "No sign of another rift, then?"

Carter shook his head, scanning the horizon. "Nothing."

They lingered in silence, the orchard glistening with early dew. The scorched patch, under first light, looked even starker against the pale grass. There was something beautiful and devastating in that contrast—a testament to a mystery they still couldn't unravel.

After sunrise, they swept through the orchard one last time, finding only a few more twisted bits of metal. Perhaps a bracket from a seat, or a piece of overhead storage. Not enough to solve anything. They packed their gear and rode back, the knights clearly eager to return to routine. Maya felt disappointed, a weight settling in her chest.

On the way home, they stopped at a small hamlet where a tired farmer claimed to have heard thunder a few nights prior—yet saw no storm. Another rumor. Another dead end.

They reached Kentwood at dusk. Their discovery amounted to more scraps but no gateway. WilCarter would likely dismiss it as useless. Carter gave Maya a look of mingled sorrow and frustration as they dismounted. "Just once," he whispered, "I'd like to see a stable crossing. Something we could actually use."

She offered a weary nod. "Me too."

They reported to WilCarter in the great hall. He glanced at the melted bracket and rivet, unimpressed. With a humorless snort, he waved them away. "Scraps. Nothing of value. I have more urgent matters."

Tomás bristled, but Maya urged him to keep calm. They retreated to the tower's upper chamber. Ethan rushed in, demanding details, his eyes too bright with longing. They told him everything, but their exhaustion was clear. He sighed. "No big discovery?"

Carter eased onto a stool. "Not this time. Sorry, kid."

Ethan pressed his lips together, refusing to fold. "We can't give up." The hush that fell afterward was heavy with unspoken sadness.

Over the following weeks, life returned to its precarious normal. The event in the southwestern fields dwindled into a whisper of history. Winter approached, overshadowing all else. Braxton's war efforts quieted, stifled by the season. A collective sense of waiting settled over Kentwood—as though everyone braced for either the storms' reemergence or the next conflict.

Maya found a fragile acceptance she wouldn't have imagined when they first arrived. The clinic thrived, saving peasants with new medical techniques. Guilt still gnawed at her for not relentlessly pursuing the storms, but she had responsibilities now: healing, teaching, preserving hope in quieter ways. Carter joked about them becoming "medieval civil servants," a phrase too close to reality.

One afternoon, Ethan burst into the clinic, breathless. "Maya! You have to see this!"

She stood from examining a peasant's sprained ankle. "What happened?"

"A traveling tinker showed up," Ethan said, voice shaking with excitement. "He found something by the roadside. It looks modern."

Her heart kicked. She followed him into the courtyard, where a ragged man stood beside a small donkey, showing off a battered piece of plastic. A cluster of curious onlookers murmured. Carter and Victoria were already there, staring. The plastic sheet was charred at the edges, a faint brand logo in the center: "Samsung."

Maya's breath caught. Another relic from the future—a phone or tablet's back plate, scorched. She forced her pulse to steady. "Where did you find that?" she asked quietly.

The tinker shrugged. "Out west, near a stream. I thought it was demon metal, but it's so light I figured it might be worth a coin."

Carter made a swift trade, offering a few silver pieces for the panel. The man seemed delighted, repeating that he'd found it half-buried in silt. Possibly washed downstream from an older vortex site.

Once the tinker moved on, Maya exhaled shakily. "We keep stumbling on reminders of home, but never anything we can use. Just fragments."

Ethan, at her elbow, spoke softly. "We'll lock it away so no one freaks out or tries to melt it down."

She placed a hand on his shoulder. "That's right. And we keep watching."

Time continued to roll forward, winter clutching the land in its cold embrace. Snow blanketed fields, caravans slowed, and Braxton's forces quieted. Even the storms seemed to sleep. No sightings of violet lights. No orchard burns. The war paused, leaving Kentwood to its own rhythms of survival. In the stillness, the survivors realized they had woven themselves into the castle's life. Despite longing for modern comforts, they had tasks here that gave them purpose: forging, healing, educating. Ethan thrived, bridging both worlds as though he'd never known differently.

As midwinter approached, a quiet evening found Maya, Carter, Victoria, and Tomás gathered in the tower's highest chamber. A small fire crackled while they sipped warm cider. They spoke of forging stable improvements, renegotiating trade, boosting literacy among peasants. The conversation slowed, drifting into a reflective pause.

Maya stared at the dancing flames. "Sometimes I lose track of which century I was born in. This place... it changes you."

Carter's gaze flicked to the battered Samsung panel on a nearby table. "I wonder how many travelers get pulled through these storms and never find anyone. Planes vanish all the time in our world. They might be out there, lost in some distant valley."

Tomás nodded. "Or in another realm entirely."

Victoria lowered her eyes. "We can't force open a path if one doesn't exist." She looked at Maya. "Have you made peace with the idea that we might stay forever?"

Maya's chest tightened. Images flashed—modern streets, coffee shops, urgent care clinics. She bit her lip, then nodded slowly. "I still watch the sky, but I'm not sure I can live in endless waiting. We belong here now."

They all agreed in silence, each wrestling privately with the idea that if another storm opened a doorway, they might leap through—or hesitate, unwilling to abandon these people who relied on them. Acceptance wasn't a single moment but a winding road.

Winter's long nights brought a swirl of routine and fellowship. By torchlight, they told stories of the modern world to Ethan and curious villagers—tales of planes and the internet, half-myth to medieval ears. The survivors often felt haunted by those memories, yet also found themselves warmed by the simpler life here, though war threatened at the edges.

After a light snowfall, a messenger from Harlow confirmed the uneasy quiet. No new storms. No major battles. The orchard near the watchtower lay dormant, the southwestern orchard likewise silent. Their original seat frame remained in WilCarter's storeroom, gathering dust.

One frozen dawn, Lady Althea appeared at the tower door while Maya stirred embers in a small brazier. Carter dozed nearby. Althea's urgent expression made Maya rise at once. "What is it?"

Althea spoke with a respectful bow. "Braxton's forces might move against Harlow. They'll likely cross our western fields. WilCarter wants us ready—medical help, forge support."

Maya's stomach clenched. War, the constant threat, had returned. She roused Carter, and soon the entire group learned they had to brace for an attack. Frantic preparation took over: forging weapons, organizing triage, warning peasants. A fresh wave of dread replaced the winter calm.

By dawn the next day, WilCarter's knights lined the walls. Carter worked on arrowheads, Maya stocked her infirmary, Tomás prepared peasants to evacuate if necessary. Then, a scout reported Braxton's men had struck a border outpost near Harlow's lands instead of Kentwood. They might not threaten Kentwood after all. The collective relief felt like letting out a long-held breath.

Twilight fell. In the courtyard, Ethan found Maya and clutched her hand. "It never ends, does it? The wars?"

She knelt, pulling him closer. "There's always conflict in any world. But we do everything we can to protect people."

He nodded, reflecting a maturity beyond his years. "I believe in you."

That night, the survivors gathered in the tower's top room, subdued by relief and lingering fatigue. Carter turned the scorched Samsung panel in his hands, the brand's letters fading like a memory of another life. Maya thought of all the half-chances they had chased—storms flaring and disappearing, always leaving behind scraps, never an open portal.

Tomás poured mulled wine, passing cups around. They sipped quietly, each lost in thought while the wind rattled the shutters. Finally, Victoria broke the silence. Her voice held a note of raw emotion. "We keep finding these fragments of home, but it's been over a year—maybe longer. We have real lives here now. People need us. Even with the wars, we're... part of this place. And I'm not sure I want to leave."

Maya's throat tightened. She felt Carter's warm hand on her shoulder. Everyone nodded, though no one spoke at first. Tomás said quietly, "I'm always curious about the rifts. But if none reappears, I'll stay. The people here are my family, too."

Paul released a breath, as though freeing a deep tension. "That's how I feel as well."

Maya let a few tears slip. She pictured the day of the crash, her frantic hope that the next storm might take them home. Everything had shifted since then, forging them into new versions of themselves. "I'll never stop watching the skies," she whispered. "But I can't live only for that. We have a duty here."

They fell silent, each tasting the bittersweet truth: the modern world might be gone for good, and yet these stone walls and the people within them had become home. Storms had taught them that hope could take many forms, not always the one you expect.

Below the tower, the castle settled into another winter's night. Hearth fires glowed, casting dancing shadows on ancient stone walls. The survivors—modern exiles—existed at a boundary of two eras, compelled to protect what they had found. War might darken the horizon, storms might spark again, but in the calm of that collective acceptance, they discovered a flicker of peace.

Ethan dozed by the hearth, lulled by hushed conversation and the comforting warmth of people bound by more than blood or time. Outside, the moon shone on snow-laden battlements, illuminating the hush of an untroubled evening. Tomorrow might bring fresh rumors of rifts or new threats from Braxton. Tonight, they drew close, hearts aligned in an unspoken promise to face whatever came.

If the storms returned, they would meet them with open eyes. If not, they would remain, forging a legacy of healing, teaching, and unity—an unplanned destiny in a realm centuries behind their birth. In that moment, they drifted closer to acceptance than ever before, no swirling lights overhead, only the endless tapestry of time enfolding them.

CHAPTER 11

The autumn snow had melted weeks ago, leaving the roads muddy and the chill wind sharp as a half-drawn sword. Maya stood in the castle courtyard, a swirl of damp air tugging at the edges of her cloak. Nearby, a cluster of peasants waited anxiously, their gazes shifting between her and the battered wagon loaded with provisions. She regarded them with compassion. War's threat had retreated from Kentwood's doorstep for the moment, but the peasants from outer villages had endured frequent raids and poor harvests. Now, they came seeking supplies, or a bit of healing for the wounds she alone had the skill to treat.

A hush seemed to fall whenever Maya appeared—an awed quiet woven with both fear and gratitude. That uneasy reverence weighed on her, a thousand unspoken pleas lingering in the damp breeze. With each passing month, her label of "sky-doctor" mingled with something almost mystical in these people's eyes. She drew in a slow breath and forced a reassuring smile. "We'll see to your needs," she promised gently, motioning for them to follow her toward the small side yard that served as a makeshift clinic.

From the ramparts overhead, Carter descended the stone steps, his brow etched with the strain of the day's labor. Even beneath streaks of soot, she could see his concern. "Just reinforced a wagon axle for them," he said, nodding at the peasants. "Bandits keep ambushing folks along the southern track. It's a miracle they got here at all."

Maya exhaled, feeling the chill bite at her cheeks. "At least those bandits aren't Braxton's knights," she said. "Still, we both know that if tensions heat up again, WilCarter can't patrol every road."

Carter's gaze flicked across the lines of weary peasants. "Chaos of war," he murmured. "So many displaced. You need help with triage?"

She shook her head, giving him a tired but grateful look. "I have Tomás for translation, and Nina's been gathering extra supplies. Get some rest if you can. I see the exhaustion in your eyes."

He mustered a small smile. "I'll rest once I finish the orchard saw. Fences need mending." Even in that weary expression, there was a spark of deep care for these people. By day, he forged new tools and replaced broken plow blades; by night, he fashioned arrowheads to arm those sworn to protect Kentwood. It weighed on his conscience, yet he did it for them.

They parted ways—Carter heading toward the smithy with a heavy step, and Maya ushering the peasants toward the low-roofed side yard. She rolled her shoulders, steeling herself for another round of healing in this medieval tapestry they'd come to call home.

***

By midday, Lady Althea summoned Maya to a small council chamber. Narrow windows let in a stripe of cold sunlight. Lord WilCarter sat in a high-backed chair, expression set in stern lines, while Althea stood near the table, her face tense. Opposite them were Victoria and Paul, conferring in hushed voices. The moment Maya stepped inside, her stomach twisted with the fear that news had broken—or war had stirred yet again.

"My lord?" Maya asked, dipping her head in respect.

WilCarter's sharp eyes flicked over her, then he beckoned her closer. "Braxton's domain stirs again," he said, his voice rough. "He's rallying mercenaries, possibly rogue knights, and arming them with unusual weapons. Word suggests relics from these storms—like those fragments you've encountered."

A faint chill traveled along Maya's spine. She remembered the dangerous shards of metal that had fallen from the sky, remnants from some unknown modern source. If Braxton had discovered a more powerful piece... "We've seen bits and pieces before," she replied carefully. "Someone found a battered gun once, melted scraps from seats, bits that caused injury. If Braxton has found something bigger—something still functional—this could upend everything."

Victoria gave a single nod. "Rumors say he's forging alliances and testing weaponry to launch a significant push this winter. He hopes to catch Harlow and WilCarter unprepared."

Paul's voice lowered. "If it's a near-intact modern weapon—like an explosive device or a gun in good condition—it could be catastrophic."

Althea's cheeks paled. "War with swords is savage enough. I tremble to think of advanced contraptions raining terror."

Maya pictured how small scraps had already caused tragedies, each out-of-time relic setting medieval life on a collision course with modern horrors. "So you'd like us to help confirm the rumors?"

WilCarter gave a curt nod. "My knights will ride west to glean what they can. In the meantime, if you uncover anything—any sign of more modern debris or storms that might bring these 'relics'—I want to know immediately. Is that understood?"

His gaze flicked between them, a silent command. They all nodded. The meeting concluded, leaving Maya with a sense of foreboding thrumming in her heart.

***

Walking along the castle's corridors with Victoria and Paul, Maya felt the cold stone floors echo beneath them. Torch sconces sputtered, casting shadows that flickered like uneasy spirits. Victoria's posture was rigid, frustration in her every step. "Every time we manage a lull, war stirs anew," she muttered.

Paul raked a hand through his hair. "Braxton might truly be arming himself with advanced relics. We'll be stuck in the middle—WilCarter wants our knowledge, Harlow wants our loyalty, and Braxton wants an edge. We can't keep everyone happy."

Maya's voice was subdued. "If Braxton wields a fully operational firearm, it's not just a medieval clash anymore. It's slaughter. We'll have to decide how involved we become."

Victoria's gaze hardened. "We may not be warriors, but our knowledge is enough to tilt the balance. If Braxton holds something more lethal than swords, none of us will be spared the consequences."

A taut silence followed, each turning separate corners to handle duties while questions loomed: How far would they go to prevent modern technology from fueling a medieval war?

***

That evening, the survivors gathered in the tower's uppermost room—Maya, Carter, Victoria, Paul, Tomás, Ethan, Nina, Sarah, and Jason. A single lantern glowed, throwing wavering light on the ancient stone walls. The atmosphere was tight with shared apprehension.

"So Braxton might really have found something big?" Nina asked, alarm making her voice tremble. "Something that fires like a real gun?"

Tomás stood near the narrow window, arms folded. "Rumors don't start from nothing. Even a damaged modern weapon, if rebuilt, would be enough to spread chaos."

Carter leaned against the wall, rubbing the back of his neck. "We all know how destructive guns can be in modern times. Here? It's an unthinkable advantage."

Ethan gazed at them with somber eyes. "We can't just let them do it, can we? So many innocent people could die."

Maya's throat constricted. She touched Ethan's hair in a tender gesture, mindful of how young he still was to face war's ugliness. "We'll try to help," she said softly. "But we're just a handful. This world thrives on knights and lords, fealty and betrayals. Still, we can't ignore what's happening."

Jason, tapping his cane, added, "If Braxton truly has modern weaponry, we need to figure out how functional it is—and fast. Maybe it's just scattered pieces, but we can't assume."

Victoria sighed. "And we're stuck between WilCarter and Harlow. They want our knowledge, but trust is always shaky."

Their words trailed off, replaced by the quiet crackle of the small hearth. Each person wore the same expression: a mixture of dread and resolution. In the end, reality was clear—somehow, they had to investigate and, if possible, prevent a medieval war from becoming an unimaginable slaughter.

***

Over the following days, WilCarter's knights rode west and returned with fragmentary reports: Braxton was gathering soldiers, but no one could confirm if an attack was imminent. Harlow's domain chimed in with rumors as well: travelers spoke of "fire-lances" in Braxton's camp, though details were murky. The air in the castle vibrated with unease. Maya buried her worries in medical duties, treating blacksmith burns, scythe accidents, bruises from minor disputes. She prayed that no wave of wounded from a battlefield would show up at her door.

One late afternoon, Carter entered the clinic, weaving among the cots of bandaged villagers. His expression was strangely tight. "A knight from Harlow's domain arrived," he said. "He's waiting in the courtyard. Says he has urgent news about Braxton."

Alarm rippled through Maya. She gathered her supplies and followed him outside.

***

In the courtyard, the routine bustle carried an undercurrent of tension, as if each person sensed the precarious calm. A lone knight in a green-and-white surcoat—Harlow's colors—stood near the stables. Tomás joined them, ready to interpret as needed. The knight, introducing himself as Sir Reynard, bowed with grave courtesy before speaking.

"Braxton's scouts were sighted near a remote hamlet between our lands," he explained. "Locals claim Braxton's men tested a 'metal tube' that spat fire with a thunderous roar. Livestock fled in terror. My lord Harlow requests your expertise. He believes you might recognize these devices better than we can."

Maya's lips went dry. She and Carter exchanged a glance of dread. It sounded dangerously close to a rudimentary cannon or gun—something beyond the medieval norm. "We'll come," she told Sir Reynard. "We need to see it ourselves."

He bowed, relief flickering in his eyes. "Then be swift. They say Braxton's men may move soon. The hamlet is called Willowbend, a day's ride from Harlow's fortress."

***

Word spread. Lord WilCarter's brow darkened upon learning of Harlow's summons, but he didn't stop them; he wanted any intelligence that might help him outmaneuver Braxton. Plans came together quickly. Maya, Carter, Tomás, and Paul would ride with Sir Reynard. Two of WilCarter's knights would accompany them to ensure their safety—and to guarantee WilCarter got a full report. Victoria, Ethan, Nina, and the Wus remained behind, each with roles to fill if hostilities broke out sooner than expected.

They set off at first light, bracing against a low gray sky. The wind was sharp, a constant reminder that winter had come, though snow wasn't currently falling. Maya's thoughts churned with each hoofbeat. If Braxton had indeed pieced together a weapon—perhaps from the orchard scraps or other modern debris—how many lives hung in the balance?

By midday, the terrain turned rugged, the fields giving way to leafless copse and half-frozen streams. Sir Reynard pointed to a gentle ridge beyond which Willowbend lay. "A scattering of huts," he said in a hushed tone. "No walls, no garrison—just ordinary folk."

They reined in their horses, scanning the sparse landscape. The knights drew swords with quiet determination, and Maya felt tension coil in her gut. As they reached the ridge and peered down, they saw a modest hamlet hugging a creek. Smoke drifted from a few thatched roofs, but nothing else stood out—until they noticed a wide, scorched ring of earth behind one hut. Wooden stakes jutted up haphazardly around it.

A chill traveled down Maya's arms. She swung off her horse and beckoned the group to move carefully. That blackened patch in the ground looked too deliberate to be a cooking fire.

They approached and found smoldering embers, lumps of ash, and a battered wooden barrel with multiple small holes in it. A trembling villager appeared, his face etched with apprehension. Tomás murmured gentle words, coaxing details. The villager spoke in halting phrases, describing how Braxton's men had arrived days earlier, tested a "metal tube" that roared like a beast, and then vanished, carrying away their contraption.

Paul set a hand on the barrel, eyes grim. "They're on the verge of creating a rudimentary firearm or cannon, using black powder and whatever modern scraps they salvaged."

Maya picked up a twisted shard of metal. It was partially melted but still carried the shape of something that didn't belong in this century. "They might be forging bits and pieces together, refining them."

Tomás finished translating the villager's words about Braxton's men. They'd promised to return once the tube was perfected. The villager's voice shook with fear, describing how the thunderous blast had rattled the huts.

***

Investigating further, Carter discovered a half-spilled crate of black powder in a sagging storehouse, the substance suspiciously refined. Possibly gleaned from older modern caches or improved with knowledge gleaned from the storms. Another villager pointed out a "cylinder with a handle," though he had no words to describe it beyond that. Enough clues for Maya, Carter, and Paul to realize Braxton's men were dangerously close to a workable weapon.

Sir Reynard urged haste. "We should continue to Harlow's fortress and share this," he said, anxiety woven through his voice. "If Braxton perfects this device, he could flatten knights in the field."

They left the hamlet at dusk, giving what small reassurances they could to the frightened residents. The travelers rode hard, hearts hammering with the knowledge that war might be only days away—and armed with more than medieval steel.

***

They reached Baron Harlow's keep near midnight, the fortress alive with lanterns. Guards patrolled in heightened vigilance, as though sensing an attack might come any moment. Sir Reynard ushered Maya's group into the baron's private hall without delay.

There stood Harlow, tense beside a brazier. Sir Lionel, his trusted retainer, hovered at his shoulder. The baron's expression flickered with relief and worry when he saw them. "What have you found?"

Maya, Carter, Paul, and Tomás explained their discoveries: the burned ground, the battered contraption, the crate of powder. Carter mentioned how it could be a mash-up of modern fragments and medieval forging techniques. Harlow's lips thinned with anger. "If Braxton deploys such a thing, my men's armor is nothing but a shell."

Sir Lionel's voice trembled with urgency. "Is there no way to defend against it? Could you craft some new plating that resists this 'gun'?"

Carter shook his head. "We don't have the means to make bulletproof steel. Even thick plates might fail if the device is strong enough. Our best chance is to keep it from functioning."

Maya spoke up, voice soft but firm, "If we could find and disable it... sabotage it before it's used in battle... that might prevent widespread slaughter."

Harlow studied them with narrowed eyes. "Braxton will be heavily guarded. You'd be risking capture, worse even."

Carter nodded, a grim set to his jaw. "Still better than letting him run rampant with something no one can match."

***

The next day, Harlow convened a war council in a drafty hall thick with tension. Knights in mismatched armor circled a rough-spun map that showed Braxton's stronghold in the western frontier. Tapped fingers on wooden tables, the scrape of chairs, murmured oaths—signs of men preparing for a confrontation that felt both ancient and alarmingly modern.

Maya stood alongside Carter, Tomás, and Paul. Harlow pointed to a fortress marked as Blackstone Hill. "Scouts say Braxton's men gather here," he explained. "They've carted strange metal gear into the old workshop. If that's the 'fire-lance,' we must act before they finalize it."

Maya's throat tightened. This was no simple raid—this was infiltration to sabotage a new kind of weapon. "A stealth mission might be best," she suggested. "A direct assault could lead to chaos, especially if they manage to fire that thing."

Paul nodded. "We're no military experts, but we might sabotage the mechanism. Carter's forging knowledge, my engineering background—between us, we can guess where to weaken it."

Sir Lionel squared his shoulders. "We'll form a small strike team and slip in by night. If you can disarm or sabotage the weapon, we'll destroy their powder and retreat. It's still a gamble, but open warfare is worse."

Carter's expression was hollow. "War is never clean, but we'll do what we must to save lives."

Harlow leveled a firm stare. "Then we move quickly, under cover of darkness. Every moment we delay, Braxton grows bolder."

***

Preparations flew by in a blur. Maya felt her pulse hammer as she helped Carter gather small tools—chisels, acid from a local alchemist, anything that could degrade metal or rust rivets. Meanwhile, Sir Lionel picked five knights adept at slipping behind enemy lines. They would move in lethal silence, but the survivors' knowledge of modern technology would be the key to crippling Braxton's "fire-lance."

Anna gripped Maya's hands with trembling worry. "You've done so much. Please be careful." Maya offered a determined smile that failed to hide her fear. She knew the cost of meddling in these battles, but turning away felt worse.

By dusk, their group left Harlow's fortress: eight knights, plus Maya, Carter, Paul, and Tomás. With no torches, they relied on the wan moonlight as they wound through forests and narrow passes. The night was dreadfully quiet, each step crunching old leaves, each snapping twig setting them on edge.

***

Near midnight, Blackstone Hill rose ahead, a silhouette of stone walls perched atop jagged rocks. Torches glimmered from within. The infiltration party circled to the fortress's rear, where a ravine offered partial shelter beneath a canopy of leafless trees. Maya's heart thundered against her ribs. She'd never expected to become a saboteur, sneaking into medieval strongholds to disable a warped piece of modern weaponry.

Sir Lionel nodded to a knight whose arrow whistled through the dark, silencing a sentry on the rampart before the man could shout a warning. The body slumped out of sight. Maya swallowed a wave of nausea. They pressed forward, footsteps muffled by damp soil.

Paul and Tomás stayed at the perimeter, crossbows ready, while Maya, Carter, Lionel, and three knights crept toward a lesser-used postern gate.

It was unguarded, or so it seemed, the thick wooden door slightly ajar. Anxiety squeezed Maya's chest as they slipped inside.

In the dim courtyard, only a few torches sputtered. No large gathering of men—perhaps Braxton had his main force camped elsewhere. Still, the hush felt ominous. They skulked beneath shadows, hugging the walls, scanning for any sign of the workshop. A stable sat to one side, empty but for a few anxious horses. To the right, a squat stone building reeked of sulfur and the pungent odor of burnt powder.

"That must be it," Carter whispered. The knights nodded, swords drawn.

They advanced. Voices sounded from within. Two of Braxton's men. Sir Lionel signaled; his knights moved, swift and silent. Steel shimmered, and the men collapsed with only faint gasps. Maya clenched her fists, forcing herself not to linger on the sight of fresh blood. War demanded ugly deeds.

Carter tested the door. It groaned lightly but wasn't barred. They eased inside. A smoky torch flickered on the far wall, illuminating barrels, stacks of powder sacks, and a monstrous metal cylinder mounted on a crude wooden carriage. The muzzle was banded with gleaming modern scraps. It was a horrifying marriage of eras—a "fire-lance" that could redefine combat.

Maya swallowed, the stench of chemicals thick enough to burn her throat. Carter moved closer, beckoning her to examine the cylinder. "They've hammered modern steel onto medieval iron," he murmured. "If they pack this with refined powder, it might get off a lethal shot—even if it's prone to backfire."

Sir Lionel's lip curled in disgust. "Destroy it."

Carter nodded. He and Maya quickly set about sabotaging crucial points. They found the seams and rivets, using the fine chisels to create hairline cracks. Carter smeared acid along weak lines, ensuring the metal would fail under pressure. In near silence, they slit open every powder sack they could and doused the contents with water, turning the black grains into sludge. The tension in the air was stifling, each second a risk of discovery.

Suddenly, footsteps echoed in the corridor. Shouts. A patrol was incoming. Sir Lionel hissed, "We're out of time."

Gathering their tools, they slipped through a side door into the courtyard. Shouts rose, and torchlight brightened. "Intruders!" someone yelled. Archer silhouettes appeared along the ramparts. Sir Lionel roared, "Run!" The knights bolted, Carter gripping Maya's hand as they dashed across open ground.

Arrows hissed overhead. One struck a knight, who dropped with a choked cry. Maya's stomach lurched, but she forced herself to keep going. They reached the postern gate—locked from outside now. Lionel cursed under his breath. They raced for a low stretch of wall and climbed. Another arrow whistled, finding a second knight. Blood stained the stones.

Paul and Tomás emerged from the perimeter, firing crossbows to cover the group's retreat. Maya scrambled up with Carter's help, pain lancing through her shoulder as an arrow grazed her. She choked back a cry, letting Carter haul her over. They tumbled into the ravine outside, rolling on cold mud.

Lionel, Paul, Tomás, and one remaining knight followed, faces twisted by the desperation of escape. Two knights were lost inside. No time to grieve. The fortress came alive with alarm bells, but their sabotage was done. The "fire-lance" would betray anyone who tried to use it.

They fled through the dark forest, stumbling over gnarled roots and half-buried stones. Maya's shoulder burned. Carter pressed a rag against the wound, his breath ragged. Paul looked pale, eyes wide in shock. Tomás whispered prayers in Spanish, voice trembling. Lionel drove them onward, scanning the shadows for pursuit.

Eventually, they found a shallow hollow and collapsed in exhaustion. Wind rattled the bare branches above. Maya winced as Carter bound the cut. It was a clean graze, but it hurt enough to hammer home the reality of what they'd just done. Lionel stood guard, grieving for his fallen men but resolute. They had completed their mission. Braxton's weapon was compromised; for now, the realm was a fraction safer.

***

At dawn, they reached Harlow's fortress. Lionel's swift report drew the baron himself. Harlow's face was pale with relief as he listened. "Your bravery spared countless lives," he said soberly. "Braxton's new toy is finished?"

Carter nodded. "We ensured the barrel will fail if they try firing it. We ruined as much powder as we could."

Harlow inclined his head with respect. "I'll send word to WilCarter. This may buy us time. Thank you."

Still, Maya couldn't push away the haunting memories of bloodshed. Two knights hadn't returned. The moral toll weighed heavily on them all.

She left the baron's hall feeling simultaneously triumphant and hollow: war's cost had never been so evident.

**

That afternoon, Maya and the others rode back to Kentwood, the sky streaked in pale gold as if trying to soften a harsh world. Upon entering the courtyard, Ethan sprinted forward, relief flooding his young features. Victoria, Nina, and the Wus followed with worried eyes. The returning group dismounted, stiff and sore.

Ethan latched onto Maya in a gentle embrace, mindful of her bandaged shoulder. "You're all right?" he asked, voice unsteady with relief.

She nodded, giving him a weary smile. "We are. We had to do something, and we did."

Within hours, they told their tale, describing the infiltration in hushed tones. The orchard fiasco and watchtower illusions paled next to the near-reality of a modern weapon unleashed in medieval combat. WilCarter listened, offering curt praise and a solemn vow to bolster defenses. Yet behind his gratitude flickered a calculating gleam. Knowledge was power in this world—and he wanted as much of it as he could get.

That night, the survivors gathered once more in the tower's top chamber. Carter settled beside Maya, carefully checking the fresh dressing on her shoulder. Though exhausted, they all felt a measure of grim accomplishment. War had been kept at bay for now. Braxton's monstrous contraption would likely explode on his own men if they tried to use it.

In the quiet, they found resolve: storms or not, this was their life now. They would protect Kentwood, bridging eras if necessary, forging hope amidst the shadows of war. Together, they would endure, united by a purpose beyond time.

CHAPTER 12

Winter's final breath lingered in the castle courtyard, a crackling frost upon the mud. Maya stood with Sarah Wu near the main gates, their exhaled breaths forming pale clouds in the early light. They watched as a slow trickle of travelers arrived—peasants from remote hamlets carrying meager goods for spring planting, or battered refugees escaping Braxton's distant skirmishes. Worry and determination coexisted in every drawn face. Maya felt a twinge of empathy that gnawed at her heart: the realm had endured so much already.

Sarah tucked a loose strand of hair behind her ear, wearing an expression both resolute and thoughtful. "Every day, we get more requests for help. People trust us now, see us as problem-solvers rather than strangers from the sky."

Maya nodded, recalling countless struggles since their arrival. "We've come a long way—forming alliances, preventing catastrophes—but war still roils. Braxton's leftover forces remain a threat." She cast a glance at the horizon, her mind flashing back to the sabotage mission that nearly claimed their lives. The so-called "fire-lance" was destroyed, yet Braxton's cunning lingered like a dark shadow.

The crowd pressed forward, forming a gentle swell of bodies. They parted ways with murmured goodbyes, and a tall figure emerged from the gathering—Paul, beckoning them inside. "Victoria's called a meeting," he said, voice tight with urgency. "Something about our future. She wants everyone there."

In the tower's top chamber, the survivors assembled: Maya, Carter, Victoria, Paul, Tomás, Nina, Sarah and Jason Wu, Ethan, and Anna. A small fire crackled in the stone hearth, while candlelight cast elongated shadows across the circular walls, revealing fatigue etched in every face. They bore heavy burdens—war worries, orchard catastrophes, sabotage—and the press of it weighed the air.

Victoria stood at the center, arms folded in a stance of quiet determination. "Thank you all for coming," she began, voice clear. "I've been thinking about our next step. This realm depends on our knowledge, but we're wedged precariously between WilCarter, Harlow, and Braxton's looming threat. Neutrality won't protect us forever. We may need to choose a side—or create our own domain."

Tomás lifted his gaze. "Our own domain? We're not exactly landed nobility. We can't easily abandon WilCarter's protection, especially not with Braxton prowling. Unless you're suggesting we actually relocate?"

Victoria hesitated, eyes roving over the circle of familiar faces. "Not necessarily. But we need a stable base of operations, somewhere we can live without being sucked into constant feudal battles. If we establish farmland, shelter refugees, build a school, a proper clinic—maybe we can transcend the local disputes. We'd still show loyalty to WilCarter or Harlow, but with fewer entanglements."

Maya felt an electric current of intrigue spark inside her. "A community, you mean? We have advanced knowledge—agriculture, medicine, forging. People do trust us. Question is, would WilCarter allow it?"

Carter, brow furrowed, shrugged. "He might, if we remain loyal and pay taxes. He understands our value. Harlow might sponsor us too, though we'd have to weigh that risk."

Anna looked around, her eyes reflecting a mixture of longing and optimism. "A true settlement of our own, where we can raise children beyond the constant gloom of war?"

For a moment, no one spoke. The idea was as bold as it was daunting.

Debate rumbled like distant thunder. Tomás proposed a lightly populated region near the river—fertile and ripe for development. Paul worried about jealousy from local lords if their independent settlement thrived. Nina reminded everyone that the orchard disasters could flare up in any location, so they might as well choose a place with fewer hostilities on the horizon.

Victoria resumed control of the discussion, voice resolute. "Before we approach WilCarter or Harlow, we need to be united. No half measures. We do this together or not at all." Her gaze landed on Sarah and Jason Wu. "Your thoughts?"

Sarah, eyes bright, offered a hopeful nod. "I love it. Blending our modern skills with medieval resources to create a safe haven from war. But leaving the castle walls is a gamble."

Jason flexed his newly healed leg, the lingering stiffness a reminder of past injury. "I'm good to help. But yes, we'd lose WilCarter's knights for day-to-day defense, so we'll have to negotiate carefully."

Maya's heart lifted at the idea. She cast a glance at Ethan, whose hopeful expression all but glowed. He yearned for someplace permanent. "Let's explore it," Maya said softly. "We can approach WilCarter first—offer him a share of produce or forged goods in exchange for land and relative autonomy."

***

That afternoon, excitement and apprehension collided in every step as they went to present the idea to Lord WilCarter. Doubts prickled in the back of Maya's mind: Would he suspect betrayal? Yet staying forever in the castle's orbit, chained to feudal strife, grew less appealing by the day.

They found WilCarter in his council room, stooped over a map with his knights. Lady Althea stood to one side, her posture graceful but alert. At a curt gesture from WilCarter, the knights withdrew, leaving him to regard the newcomers with guarded curiosity.

Victoria stepped forward, offering a polite bow. "My lord, we have a proposal. We'd like to establish a small settlement under your banner—an outpost that focuses on knowledge and craft. We'd stay loyal, pay taxes, but handle local governance ourselves."

His eyes narrowed. "Why?"

Maya spoke up, tone soft yet insistent. "This castle is crowded, and we can do more good if we're free to farm and build. We'd share what we produce—grain, forged goods, medical help—in exchange for a measure of independence from direct war duties."

WilCarter's calculating gaze flicked between them. "You'd operate a miniature fief under my sovereignty?"

Paul dipped his head in assent. "Yes, my lord. We remain your subjects. But we need enough autonomy to maximize our knowledge. We'd be more useful to Kentwood that way."

Lady Althea's expression showed cautious encouragement, though she said nothing.

A tense silence descended, broken only by the faint crackle of the council room's hearth. WilCarter stroked his chin in contemplation, occasionally exchanging a pensive glance with Althea. At length, he fixed them with a steel-like stare. "This might benefit Kentwood, if you supply surplus grain, advanced forging, and medical support. But betray me—ally yourselves with Harlow or Braxton—and I'll crush you."

His threat weighed the air. Carter swallowed hard. "Understood, my lord. Our loyalty stands. This is purely about building something stable."

WilCarter exhaled, a curt sign of acceptance. "I'll grant you farmland near Summerfield, by the river—a neglected parcel. You'll owe me a tenth of the harvest or an equivalent in forged goods each season. My knights won't guard you daily, so beware of bandits and Braxton's raids. Agreed?"

Maya's pulse surged with relief. She managed a respectful bow. "Agreed, my lord. Thank you."

A faint grin tugged at WilCarter's mouth. "Don't squander this. Lady Althea will finalize the documents."

They departed in a swirl of excitement, nerves, and optimism. The dream was becoming reality.

***

That evening, in the tower's welcoming glow, the survivors gathered to celebrate in hushed voices. Flickering lanterns revealed their buoyant smiles, their shared sense of triumph. Ethan's eyes sparkled like a child offered a wondrous gift. "A whole new place—our own farm, real houses!"

Maya ruffled his hair fondly, feeling a renewed sense of purpose. "Yes, but it'll take a lot of work—building structures, clearing land, preparing to defend ourselves."

Carter, arms folded, nodded. "We can bring peasants who want a fresh start. We'll teach them improved farming, forging. Paul can handle logistics, Tomás can organize schooling, Nina can help plan orchard layouts. Everyone contributes."

Victoria sipped tea and leaned into the conversation. "Finally, something positive instead of just reacting to war. Still, we can't ignore the risk. Braxton lurks, and Harlow always might meddle."

Nina's voice trembled slightly with emotion. "At least we're giving these people—and ourselves—hope. Even if the storms never return to carry us home, we'll have done something meaningful."

***

The remainder of winter blurred by in a frenzy of preparation. Sarah and Jason pored over architectural sketches, brainstorming structures that melded medieval simplicity with modern efficiency. Tomás drafted recruitment notices for peasants in search of new land. Paul inventoried every resource—building materials, seeds, forging tools—while Carter toiled at his anvil, shaping plow blades and nails. Maya gathered herbs, linens, and medicines for a bare-bones clinic.

As spring's first thaw arrived, a ragtag caravan took shape: wagons laden with lumber and sacks of grain, crates of forged tools, plus twenty or so peasants, all pinning their hopes on this new beginning. WilCarter's knights escorted them for the initial leg of the journey, scanning for bandits in the misty dawn. When the knights parted ways, the real test began. Maya's stomach fluttered at the unknown, but exhilaration hummed just beneath her nerves.

Their destination near Summerfield unfolded in gentle slopes along a tranquil bend of the river. Whispers of a thinly wooded area hinted at possible orchards or pastures, though much of the land lay fallow. An old millhouse, partially collapsed by neglect, crouched near the water's edge. Defenses were practically nonexistent, a point that left Maya uneasy. Yet the realm felt surprisingly calm in that first moment of arrival.

They came to a halt at midday. Tired but brimming with possibility, the peasants fanned out to explore the tall grasses and broken timbers. Carter dismounted, running his fingertips across the millhouse's weathered stone. "It's rough, but it's ours," he said. "We can rebuild."

Maya surveyed the expanse, inhaling the fresh scent of damp earth. "There's a tangible sense of renewal here," she murmured. Across the clearing, Tomás stretched his arms wide as if to embrace the land. "It's roomier than I expected—good soil for planting, with some effort."

Victoria stepped over to the battered mill, assessing the waterwheel's rotting spokes. "If we repair this, we might grind grain or channel water power. That alone could revolutionize production out here."

Ethan scampered along, exclaiming over every patch of wildflowers, while his mother watched with a hopeful smile. Nearby, the Wu couple consulted parchment notes, gesturing excitedly at potential building sites. Nina joined them, her eyes shining with a mix of relief and promise.

They would name this place Riverbend Haven—a sanctuary shaped by both medieval realities and modern insight.

Work began at once. Carter established a makeshift forge, hammering metal near the ruined mill, while volunteers hauled debris out of the structure. The clamor of scraping timbers and clanking nails filled the air. Maya organized a humble clinic in what remained of the millhouse's southeast corner, stacking bandages and salves. Tomás and a cluster of peasants measured plots for planting, exchanging ideas for more efficient field layouts. Victoria tallied stock in a makeshift storehouse, ensuring every tool or supply was logged.

In the early days, the excitement felt electric, like each hammer strike drove them further from the shadow of war. By sunset, though, every muscle ached, and they gathered around a crackling fire to share simple meals of bread, dried meat, and foraged roots. Exhausted yet eager, they found solace in the knowledge they were constructing a new world—small, perhaps, but brimming with promise.

***

Days blurred into weeks, and Riverbend Haven matured in spirit and shape. The millhouse roof was patched, the waterwheel partially restored. Simple shelters sprang up in orderly rows. The memories of orchard disasters and war sabotage receded for a time, replaced by daily concerns: carting lumber, forging plowshares, hauling water. Braxton remained an ever-present specter, but rumors hinted that his forces were weakened by the failed superweapon, keeping him temporarily at bay.

Despite the cautious calm, the survivors didn't let their guard down. They organized small patrols at dawn and dusk, scanning the landscape for bandits. Carter erected stout wooden stakes around the settlement's perimeter—primitive but better than nothing. Even peasants trained with spears, determined not to be helpless victims. Meanwhile, Maya took time each afternoon to gaze at the horizon, half-expecting swirling lights to appear—yet none came.

***

One mild afternoon, Ethan sprinted to Maya while she finished stitching a peasant's minor cut. Excitement radiated from him. "Mom wants you to see something—there's an orchard near the river that might be salvaged!"

Intrigued, Maya followed him past neatly organized tool racks and the humming forge until they reached a cluster of gnarled trees, their bark peeling with age. Sarah and Anna knelt by the trunks, studying them as if they held hidden treasure. The orchard showed signs of long-standing neglect, but also potential for renewed life.

Sarah brushed away some moss. "We can graft modern techniques onto these older rootstocks. Prune them carefully, encourage new growth. With a bit of luck, we'll have a harvest in a year or two."

Maya traced a withered branch, feeling an unexpected swell of hope. "We're literally planting our future here."

Anna nodded. "If the storms never return, at least we'll have something real to sustain us."

That idea settled into Maya's chest like a gentle warmth. Once, they had staked everything on finding a vortex home. Now, there was life here—expanding, blossoming.

Their progress drew attention. Word of Riverbend Haven drifted along trade routes and tavern gossip. More families arrived, haggard from displacement or drawn by the "sky-people's" rumored wonders. WilCarter dispatched an envoy to see the settlement's success and collect an early levy. He remained distant but not antagonistic, content as long as taxes flowed. A note arrived from Baron Harlow—politely congratulatory, tinged with a hint of curiosity.

Amid the day-to-day hustle—Carter hammering metal, Maya tending the sick, Tomás teaching letters—everyone realized they had formed a new community that fused knowledge from two eras. The children bounded from English lessons to waterwheel repairs without batting an eye. Ethan was the bridge between worlds, bright-eyed and brimming with easy acceptance.

***

One evening, a hush swept through the settlement when a small band of ragged refugees stumbled in. Their clothes were singed, their eyes haunted. They spoke of Braxton's men torching their village. Fear rippled through Riverbend, bringing back memories of the sabotage mission. Carter rallied the few volunteers who practiced with spears. Maya felt her stomach knot at the thought of another assault.

But no raiders came. The refugees blended into the settlement like lost souls seeking a harbor. Each new arrival shared disquieting tales: Braxton might be regrouping, or perhaps lashing out in sporadic violence. Yet, for now, Riverbend's calm endured.

Slowly, the settlement earned a reputation. Some local peasants scoffed at such "strange ideas," but others visited out of curiosity. The orchard grew green shoots, fields promised healthy yields. Even WilCarter's demands for grain or forged tools felt manageable as the settlement's capacity expanded.

***

As spring advanced, a messenger from Kentwood brought unsettling whispers: another orchard in Braxton's territory had exploded into flames under suspicious circumstances. Sabotage? Another eerie event like those orchard events? The messenger didn't know. Worry flashed in Maya's mind—were the devil-lights involved again? Or was it common warfare masquerading as supernatural sabotage?

Gathering in Riverbend's crude meeting hall—a refurbished section of the millhouse—they debated whether to investigate. Ultimately, caution won out. They had no illusions about their vulnerability. If Braxton had discovered some leftover power, it could be unleashed unpredictably. But so far, rumor outpaced reality.

Still, the news gnawed at Maya. One evening, after the sun slipped behind rolling hills, she walked beyond the settlement's wooden stakes, seeking comfort by the softly gurgling river. The lavender sky reflected off lazy currents. She couldn't help thinking about the orchard, the watchtower storms, all those tantalizing glimpses of possible gateways to another world.

Footsteps stirred behind her. She turned to find Carter, who gently rested a hand on her shoulder. "You're thinking about the storms again," he said quietly.

Maya exhaled, acknowledging the lump in her throat. "I can't help it. Part of me expects another vortex to tear open at any moment."

He gazed at the river. "If another appears, we'll deal with it. But our lives can't revolve around that threat. We've built something too important here."

She let his words settle, the last of the daylight reflecting in her eyes. "You're right. I just don't want to be caught off guard again. But yes, building Riverbend is our priority now."

He squeezed her hand gently, no more words needed.

***

Time flowed, weeks merging into months. Riverbend Haven blossomed from a rustic camp into a village that felt alive. The orchard's blossoming buds promised fruit, rows of vegetables thrived under careful tending, and the people—both native peasants and the "sky-people"—began forging a shared identity. To preserve fairness, the group formed a village council that included local families as well as the survivors. Carter's improved plows boosted harvest expectations, Maya's clinic handled everything from fevers to broken bones, and Tomás quietly introduced literacy lessons using battered modern pamphlets.

Distant war rumblings flared now and then—Braxton occasionally clashed with Harlow—but Riverbend remained a sanctuary. Vague rumors of devil-lights or scorching reached them, but never approached their borders.

Come mid-summer, Lady Althea arrived from Kentwood, her small escort gazing in wonder at the bustling settlement. Maya guided Althea along tidy rows of huts, showing her the repaired millwheel spinning lazily in the current, demonstrating how the forge created sturdy iron tools.

Althea marveled aloud, her eyes alight with admiration. "You've achieved something remarkable here," she said.

***

That night, they welcomed Althea with a modest outdoor feast. Lanterns and torches bathed the clearing in warm, wavering light. Peasants strummed a simple melody, and children—Ethan among them—chased each other, laughter echoing through the settlement. Freshly roasted vegetables and newly baked bread were passed around as neighbors and newcomers mingled.

Althea confided quietly to Maya, "Lord WilCarter remains wary, but he sees the benefit in your settlement. He might test your loyalty again, though."

Maya nodded, unsurprised. "We'll keep delivering our share, keep the peace. As long as Braxton doesn't strike us directly, we should be fine."

In the bonfire's glow, Carter and Maya exchanged a look—relief, pride, and a hint of caution. They had forged a new home, safe and thriving so far. Yet, like an undertow, the faint risk of war and storms still lingered.

***

Althea departed at dawn, promising to relay good impressions to WilCarter. Standing at the wooden gates, Maya watched the entourage diminish in the distance. She realized just how intertwined their fates were with this medieval land. They had come as accidental visitors, desperate to go home; now, they stayed by choice, building roads to a future that seamlessly blended two worlds. A wave of acceptance coursed through Maya, both comforting and bittersweet.

They had not abandoned the idea of the storms altogether, but those swirling lights no longer consumed their every decision. If the vortex reappeared, they would face it—and if it never did, they were forging something worthwhile here.

***

Late one twilight, Maya climbed a gentle hill overlooking Riverbend's orchard. The sun's departure spread a wash of purple and orange across the sky, illuminating rows of budding apple trees. Ethan, now nearly thirteen, trailed behind, settling next to her in companionable stillness. They watched the orchard's leaves sway in a soft breeze.

After a while, Ethan spoke in a pensive tone. "I hardly remember the plane ride anymore—just blurry flashes. It's all so distant."

Maya's throat tightened as her own memories stirred: the turbulence, the confusion, the unearthly lightning that had delivered them to this realm. "Time does that," she replied gently. "You've grown up here, learned the language, found real friends." She paused, voice quavering with warmth. "I'm proud of you, you know. You've been so brave."

He leaned against her. "I'm happy here. Sometimes I wonder if Dad would have liked it. I still miss him."

Maya wrapped an arm around his shoulders. "So do I. He'd be proud of the man you're becoming. We honor his memory by living on."

A hush seemed to descend on the orchard, carrying the faint rustle of leaves and the quiet hush of the summer wind. Bathed in the moon's gentle glow, the trees stood as a testament to their perseverance—fragile yet determined, mirroring the settlement itself. Maya closed her eyes, letting gratitude wash away the old ache. In that moment, she sensed they had made their choice. Whether the swirling vortex appeared again or not, Riverbend Haven was the future they had chosen to shape.

The orchard fiascos, the watchtower storms, even the scraps of modern wreckage scattered across this world felt like echoes of a life once lived. Now, the orchard whispered of hope, the wheel of time turning toward peace and possibility. If fate opened another doorway, they would be ready. If not, they had forged a quiet kind of love and purpose in this land, one strong enough to span centuries.

Ethan sighed contentedly, gazing at the orchard as if he could already envision the harvest to come. Maya looked to the horizon one last time, half-expecting a flicker of violet brilliance. Only the night greeted her. She felt no pang of disappointment—only the serene knowledge that, in forging Riverbend, they had discovered a crossing into a life that was its own miracle.

CHAPTER 13

Morning light spilled across the rolling fields of Riverbend Haven, illuminating rows of lush crops that rustled in a soft wind. Maya walked the perimeter, her boots crunching on gravel. Seven months into the settlement's founding, the farmland now thrived: green shoots and budding fruit trees stood as living proof that the survivors' fusion of modern agricultural methods and medieval tenacity could yield wonders. She breathed in the crisp air, a flicker of pride warming her chest.

A year ago, the swirling storms felt all-consuming. Now, the orchard here remained quiet—no violet glows or metal debris, only blossoming branches and the promise of a harvest that might sustain dozens of families through winter. Indeed, they'd created a haven, though the shadows of war and cosmic phenomena still loomed beyond.

Maya's gaze drifted toward the southern horizon, where Kentwood Castle lay. Occasionally, WilCarter's knights stopped by to check their progress, ensuring that taxes would be ready on time. So far, the lord seemed content to let Riverbend grow. For him, it served as a valuable outpost; for them, it was a precious sanctuary.

She spotted Ethan racing across the fields with local children. His laughter reminded her of how far they'd come—once a frightened boy on a doomed flight, now a vibrant presence bridging two eras. Smiling, she continued her patrol.

Near the old millhouse—currently the bustling heart of the settlement—a cluster of people gathered around Carter, who hammered away at a sturdy waterwheel's gear mechanism. Sparks arced through the air as he refined the metal teeth, explaining each step to the wide-eyed peasants clustered around him. They had grown used to these "innovations," forging an identity that melded blacksmith craft with futuristic ingenuity.

Maya approached just as he straightened, wiping sweat from his brow. "Any luck?"

He flashed that earnest grin she adored. "Almost. The wheel's sticking with the old wood gear. I replaced part of it, but we might need an entirely new one fashioned from stronger iron. We'll get there."

She rested a hand on his shoulder. "You're unstoppable, you know—bringing new tools to a place still reeling from war." The peasants murmured their gratitude, eyes flicking between Carter and Maya with cautious wonder. Carter gave her a gentle look.

"Just doing what I can," he said. "It still feels surreal sometimes—mixing centuries. But if it helps them live better, it's worth every blow of the hammer."

Afternoon sun found Victoria and Paul in the newly raised communal hall—a spacious barn-like structure with planked walls and a thatched roof. There, they managed the storehouse inventory and the settlement's small council, made up of local villagers who had earned their trust. Paper scrolls and modern-style ledgers crowded a makeshift table.

Victoria studied the accounts with a furrowed brow. "This year's wheat yield is surpassing our estimates. We can pay WilCarter's tax and still store enough for winter. Maybe even trade with Harlow's domain."

Paul tapped the quill he held. "Good. Diversifying trade might keep us from relying too heavily on WilCarter. But let's not appear disloyal, either. It's a tricky balance."

A villager approached, bowing respectfully. "Mistress Prescott, travelers from the south have arrived—refugees again. They seek shelter."

Victoria exchanged a glance with Paul. That single word—refugees—carried heavy implications. War in Braxton's territory never truly ended. "Show them to the guest huts," she said gently. "We'll do what we can."

When the villager hurried off, Victoria exhaled. "Every new arrival strains our resources, but we can't turn them away."

Paul's expression softened. "We built this place to offer hope. We just have to manage carefully. Riverbend's success might be a beacon—and a target."

Twilight descended in lavender and gold across the sky. Tomás, once a historian and now Riverbend's teacher, gathered children—including Ethan—near a half-finished wooden stage. Tonight marked the first "harvest festival" the settlement had dared to host, a show of confidence that they were not just surviving but thriving. Torches glimmered, music from a rustic lute drifted on the cool breeze, and the children chattered excitedly about the skit Tomás had written. It was a playful tale weaving local myths with stories of the mysterious "sky-people."

Near the stage, Nina and Sarah arranged seats and set out fresh bread and roasted vegetables. The settlement's growing vitality shimmered in the gathering dusk, torchlight revealing the eager faces of peasants, survivors, and children dancing in bright arcs.

Maya joined them, her gaze lingering on Ethan's flushed grin. "A festival. This feels almost... normal."

Sarah let out a soft laugh. "We've come a long way from orchard fiascos and medieval warfare. Though neither threat is truly gone."

As evening deepened, the festival began in earnest. Peasants and survivors shared a starlit feast, sampling mead from local honey and breaking loaves of crusty bread with spiced fruit. Children hurried onto the makeshift stage, and Tomás narrated a whimsical performance about how sky-people once fell from the clouds to guide them—braiding half-truth with legend. Applause and laughter rippled through the gathered crowd, tension lifted for a precious moment.

Maya watched with an ache of gratitude. This was what they'd yearned for: a community that bridged two centuries, all learning from one another in a peace unbroken by storm or war—if only for a night. She could still feel the faint scar on her shoulder from the infiltration at Blackstone Hill, a reminder of how fragile that peace was. Tonight, however, joy prevailed.

Partway through the skit, Ethan took the small stage with a wooden sword, playing a daring hero who shielded a village from something called "fire-lances." The crowd giggled at the gentle satire of Braxton's rumored weapon. Even Carter and Victoria clapped, though the memory of that sabotage mission remained a tender wound.

When the performance ended, music swelled, and villagers tugged one another into dancing around the bonfire. Sparks flitted upward to the star-laden sky. A collective sense of relief, almost like a lullaby, enveloped them before another uncertain dawn.

As midnight neared, families peeled away toward their huts, the festival gradually winding down. Only a few adults lingered by the embers, speaking in hushed tones. Maya, Carter, Victoria, Paul, Tomás, Nina, Sarah, and Jason shared a final mug of spiced ale together, a quiet camaraderie binding them.

They reminisced about disasters that once drove them to the brink. Now, they shaped a world less dependent on fervent hope for rescue and more rooted in building a stable future. Ethan dozed at Maya's side, his head tucked against her arm.

Eventually, the group dispersed. Riverbend lay silent, moonlight casting a soft glow over the farmland. No cosmic storms marred the sky, no violent glimmers haunted the orchard.

With summer sliding toward autumn, the settlement's work shifted to the harvest. Carter's waterwheel repairs finally succeeded—grain was milled more efficiently than ever. WilCarter's men arrived to collect taxes and rode away impressed by the settlement's bounty. Rumors spread that Baron Harlow might send merchants to barter for Riverbend's surplus. The orchard's first bushels of apples, plucked by eager hands, brought fresh excitement. The swirl of war gossip stayed subdued, and if Braxton's territory festered with conflict, it was far from Riverbend's boundaries. Any storms existed only in stories whispered around distant campfires. Perhaps the time rifts had fallen dormant, or perhaps they prowled another century altogether.

Then, on a crisp autumn morning, a rider arrived at full gallop, the watchman's horn blaring a sharp alarm. Victoria and Maya rushed to the palisade, their stomachs twisting in dread. The messenger—disheveled, breathing raggedly—identified himself as a Kentwood scout. "Braxton's troops... massing again," he rasped, voice raw. "Near the southwestern pass. Lord WilCarter requests aid from the sky-people. Strange weapon sightings..."

Maya's pulse lurched. Another new weapon? Her mind flashed to the orchards. Had Braxton's domain uncovered a fresh trove of debris?

Carter joined them, face grim. "We can't pretend this isn't happening."

Tomás hovered nearby, worry etched on his brow. "We have a settlement to protect. If Braxton's men swing around the southwestern route, Riverbend might be vulnerable."

Victoria pressed her lips together. "We need to confirm WilCarter's claim, but we can't risk ignoring him. We also can't leave Riverbend unguarded."

Their hush spoke volumes. War beckoned once more, refusing to let them slip into an easy peace.

They convened an emergency council in the millhouse. The peasants, frightened, begged the sky-people not to abandon them. The survivors reassured everyone that defenses would remain in place. Jason and Sarah offered to stay and coordinate protective measures with Nina's help. Anna chose to remain as well, keeping her son safe.

Maya, Carter, Victoria, Paul, and Tomás resolved to answer WilCarter's summons. If Braxton had discovered a new relic capable of mass destruction, they had to act. Ten volunteers from Riverbend—now a small but determined militia—insisted on joining them. Though inexperienced, these locals refused to watch their new home face danger alone.

By midday, the group departed, the Kentwood scout guiding them over farmland that rolled into Kentwood's domain. In the dusty glow of twilight, the castle's silhouette appeared on the horizon. Lord WilCarter received them in the great hall, tension carved into his face. Lady Althea stood beside him, her eyes reflecting a fierce concern.

In curt words, WilCarter explained: "Scouts say Braxton's men have an advanced relic again—small but powerful, able to fire multiple projectiles. An informant claims it's smaller than the 'fire-lance' you sabotaged but more lethal in close quarters."

Maya forced down a wave of nausea, imagining a modern submachine gun lying in medieval hands. She glanced at Carter, whose jaw tightened at the thought.

Paul spoke carefully. "Do we have any clue where Braxton found it?"

WilCarter shook his head, anger sparking in his eyes. "Possibly more wreckage from storms. Or contraband that slipped out of the orchard fiascos. All we know is they'll test it soon, possibly within a fortnight. If it works, they'll launch an attack. My lands, or Harlow's—whoever they believe they can overrun."

Victoria's voice came out low and steady. "We must neutralize it."

Althea inclined her head. "Yes. We suspect they keep it at an outpost near the southwestern pass. Our scouts couldn't infiltrate. We need your expertise—before they unleash more bloodshed."

Another infiltration. Another small band creeping behind enemy lines. The survivors exchanged somber glances, recalling the knights who died in the last mission.

Carter exhaled. "We'll do what we must. If Braxton has harnessed a working firearm, we can't let it reshape the battlefield."

Tomás frowned. "What if we ambush them before they can test it, rather than sneaking in?"

WilCarter's impatience flared. "If you can teach me how to best a relic that fires projectiles, speak up. Otherwise, infiltration stands as our best shot. I'll send my knights to draw Braxton's men away. You strike from within."

Maya's stomach churned. Images of a medieval battlefield torn by bullets were too terrible to dismiss. "All right," she agreed quietly. "But we'll need more than a handful of knights this time. And a plan if it goes wrong."

WilCarter nodded once. "My knights stand ready. Braxton will regret scavenging your sky-devils' scraps."

That night, the survivors pored over sketches of firearms, mentally piecing together how a crude submachine gun might be forged from orchard debris. This had shown them that partial relics often misfired, yet if Braxton's smiths adapted them properly, they could become stable and devastating. Their plan solidified: slip into the southwestern outpost, destroy or seize the weapon, ensure no further copies could be made.

Later, in a dim corridor, Maya turned to Carter. "This is madness. We keep getting pulled back into war. Riverbend needs us. But if we turn away, we risk a slaughter of medieval soldiers by modern bullets."

He cupped her cheek, his eyes reflecting that same resolve she had seen so many times before. "We can't hide from it, Doc. If there's a chance we can save lives, we owe it to them. Then we go home, to our haven, no matter what else happens."

She clung to him, memories flitting by of orchard fiascos, watchtower storms, infiltration at Blackstone Hill. All had seemed impossible, yet each trial only deepened their commitment to this place. Perhaps they no longer fought for a route back to the twenty-first century. This realm, for better or worse, had become their home.

Two days later, WilCarter mustered a strike force of twenty knights in addition to the survivors. At dawn's pale light, they rode west. The plan was simple: the knights would feign an assault on Braxton's border fortress, drawing defenders away. Meanwhile, Maya, Carter, Victoria, Paul, Tomás, and a smaller squad of stealth knights would infiltrate the southwestern outpost rumored to store the new relic.

Fear weighed heavily on them. Victoria rode beside Maya, voice subdued. "We push forward, always. One step of progress, then two steps dragged back by war. Let's hope this ends the pattern."

Maya gripped the reins, her heart pounding. "If Braxton fails again, maybe they'll abandon these twisted relics. Let them stick to swords and catapults."

They pressed on until the farmland gave way to rugged hills, dotted with abandoned villages that bore scars of earlier raids. By dusk, they camped beneath a canopy of trees, the knights huddling for final plans. The survivors braced themselves for another infiltration under the cover of darkness.

Night smothered the countryside like a cloak. The main knight contingent advanced along a distant road, creating a diversion. The clash of steel echoed across the fields, just enough to draw Braxton's watchers away. Meanwhile, Maya, Carter, Victoria, Paul, Tomás, and a handful of stealthy knights crept toward the targeted outpost. In the still air, Maya half-expected the crackle of a cosmic storm, a swirl of unnatural light. Instead, the hush seemed to pulse with a more terrifying tension: the threat of lead cutting through medieval armor.

They crouched behind thick shrubs, studying the outpost—a timber-walled structure with a small gate and a watchtower. Torchlight flickered, revealing guards barking orders. From the other side came muffled shouting, presumably Braxton's soldiers responding to the knights' feint. Good. This was their moment.

In a swift move, they overpowered two gate sentries, rendering them unconscious. Inside, they pressed themselves against the rough walls. The central building glowed from within. Peering through a narrow slit, Maya saw blacksmith tools, barrels of powder, and, resting on a crude workbench, a metal object about the size of a modern submachine gun.

Carter approached it cautiously, heart pounding loud enough for Maya to sense. The weapon bore medieval iron plating hammered over mechanical parts. A magazine of small bullets lay beside it, each looking jagged and incomplete. Maya's breath stilled. Were these bullets pulled from orchard wreckage?

A scrawny blacksmith with singed hair stepped out from behind a row of barrels, eyes widening at the sight of intruders. He lunged toward the weapon, but Victoria blocked him, sending it clattering to the floor. The man let out a strangled cry of fury, only to be subdued by one of WilCarter's knights.

Carter picked up the warped gun. "They're close to making this functional," he murmured. "Give them another month..."

Maya rifled through the ammo box, spotting bullets stamped with half-legible letters—"WIN..." from some brand or airline code. Her gut twisted.

Sir Bernard, the knight in charge of this infiltration, nodded to Carter. "Destroy it now. Then help our men outside."

They moved with steady urgency. Carter jammed open the weapon's mechanism, pounding at the breech with a chisel. Maya located a small powder stash and drenched it with water. The sabotage was quick but thorough, every critical piece hammered into useless fragments.

Shouts erupted from the courtyard. Braxton's men poured in. Swords clashed and steel rang in the torchlight. Maya clutched the dismantled relic, refusing to let anyone reclaim it. Paul intercepted a soldier, steel scraping as both men struggled. Tomás ducked behind crates, felling an attacker's leg with a precise slash. Victoria took down a mercenary with a sharp blow, while Carter bludgeoned another into submission using the splintered haft of a spear.

They fled as flames spread in the workroom. The infiltration team burst into the courtyard, where WilCarter's knights pressed hard against Braxton's scattered defenders. Enough confusion reigned that the survivors managed to slip out through the battered gate. Behind them, the outpost's interior glowed with hot sparks. Another short, furious battle outside, and they withdrew altogether, leaving Braxton's forces stunned and divided.

At dawn's first light, they regrouped on a wooded rise. WilCarter's men had lost a few knights; many survivors nursed bruises, cuts, or worse. Yet they had destroyed the new weapon—no small victory. Maya gazed at the ruined scraps of the gun, her mind echoing with the fear that orchard fiascos, though distant now, continued to haunt this land. Each relic they discovered brought devastation.

Satisfied enough that Braxton's immediate threat had been contained, WilCarter's men pointed their horses homeward. The survivors parted ways near Kentwood's border. WilCarter offered curt but heartfelt thanks, bound once again in an uneasy alliance to keep cosmic horrors off medieval battlefields.

Riverbend Haven greeted them at dusk, lanterns bobbing along the walls as watchmen called out in relief. Ethan sprinted to meet Maya, tears shining in his eyes. His mother hovered behind him, guiding them to the communal hall. Gasps rose among the villagers at the sight of bruises and dried blood, but Nina and Sarah hurried to fetch bandages and comfort. By lamplight, the survivors recounted the sabotage of yet another relic-based weapon. Awe and apprehension spread through the onlookers. War, it seemed, might never truly end—but for now, the "sky-people" had prevented a massacre.

In the days that followed, wounds healed, and routine settled over Riverbend. A weariness tinged with relief weighed on everyone. Twice, they had dismantled Braxton's attempts to harness modern weaponry. Twice, they had spared the region from more expansive bloodshed. If orchard storms or swirling cosmic distortions still flung debris into this time and place, they did so quietly—far from Riverbend's sight. Perhaps the rifts had shifted to some other corner of the world.

One balmy evening, Maya accompanied Carter to a rise overlooking the orchard by the gentle curve of the river. The fruit trees rustled, heavy with apples, their leaves catching the last light of day. She clasped Carter's hand, watching as twilight spread across the settlement. Memories of orchard fiascos, watchtower storms, and infiltration missions felt at once near and far. Peace teased the edges of her mind, free of swirling violet lights or strange hums from the sky.

CHAPTER 14

Early autumn cast long shadows across Riverbend Haven, each morning a tapestry of shifting gold as the sun rose over fields brimming with near-harvest crops. Maya walked the main path, greeting villagers who bustled by with baskets of apples and wheat. The entire settlement hummed with a renewed sense of purpose. New huts dotted the edges of the village, a refurbished barn sheltered livestock from upcoming chills, and the modest orchard sagged under the weight of ripe fruit. Even the palisade seemed sturdier, as if warding off the ghosts of past battles.

The troubles of orchard storms, watchtower disasters, and infiltration missions were seldom mentioned now—dim echoes of a life everyone hoped was behind them. Day by day, the settlement's harmony outshone the horrors that had once defined their existence. Ethan, taller than ever, eagerly honed his reading and writing skills, leading the local children toward literacy. Carter refined the waterwheel mechanisms, producing rudimentary yet vital inventions. Victoria and Paul managed trade, forging ties that softened WilCarter's once-harsh demands. Tomás oversaw lessons in a simple schoolhouse. Nina offered assistance in the clinic, which Maya ran with calm and steady efficiency.

Still, sometimes at dusk, when the wind whistled through the orchard's heavy branches, Maya would feel an undercurrent of unease. A prick of intuition hinted that the old orchard catastrophes weren't entirely gone. She did her best to dismiss those concerns, dedicating herself to the tangible tasks of bringing in the harvest and supporting the settlement. And yet, in moments of silence, the hush of foreboding remained.

One crisp afternoon, Lady Althea of Kentwood arrived on horseback, accompanied by a single knight. The watchman's horn echoed through the settlement, and Maya hurried to the gate with Carter and Victoria. Althea dismounted, her expression tinged with urgency.

"Forgive the sudden visit," she said, her voice fraught with concern. "I bring news: Baron Harlow requests a meeting—he's heard rumors of fresh orchard scorchings beyond Braxton's territory. Folks claim these incidents might be linked to what you once called orchard storms. Harlow wants your help investigating."

Maya's stomach lurched. More orchard scorchings? Again? "Has Braxton harnessed them somehow?"

Althea shook her head. "We're not sure. The baron only said villagers reported scorched earth and strange lights in a remote valley. No definite sign of Braxton's men, but Harlow fears they'll arrive soon enough."

Carter's jaw tightened. "We can't ignore this. Any new orchard phenomenon might spawn destructive weapons."

Victoria's eyes flickered with resigned understanding. "We're always chasing these anomalies. But if we want to keep peace in the realm, we have no choice."

Althea's gaze swept over them. "Will you answer his summons?"

They convened a council that same day in the millhouse. Maya, Carter, Victoria, Paul, Tomás, Nina, Sarah, Jason, Anna, and the other survivors gathered around a large table bearing a map. A glass weight pinned the area in question—a forested valley beyond Braxton's western border. If these new scorchings were true orchard anomalies, someone might already be scavenging scraps for war.

Nina's brow creased. "We just want to prosper here. But if another anomaly threatens to unleash modern fragments, we can't look away."

Sarah nodded. "Our settlement is strong, but not if we allow Braxton or others to seize advanced relics again. We have to stop it."

Ethan spoke up, eyes lit with determination. "I want to come, too. I'm old enough."

Maya felt a pang of worry. "It could be dangerous. This might be more than a simple orchard scorch. Let's see how it unfolds."

In the end, they decided that Maya, Carter, Victoria, Paul, and Tomás would go. Ethan, disappointed but understanding, stayed behind to assist with the schoolchildren. While Nina, Sarah, Jason, and Anna ensured Riverbend's day-to-day affairs continued in the group's absence, they would also remain vigilant for any bandits or warlike stirrings.

At first light, Maya's group set out with Lady Althea, joined by a handful of Kentwood knights. Cool autumn air braced them as they traveled east. With every mile, the feeling of déjà vu thickened—they had chased these orchard anomalies before, always ending in heartbreak. Would this be another endless loop?

As they rode, Althea explained that Harlow had been monitoring rumors of orchard storms. For months, nothing credible had arisen, but this recent account from a remote valley matched familiar signs—scorched trees, faint humming at night, glimpses of twisted metal. Carter caught Maya's eye. Neither had to speak; they understood each other's dread. The orchard storms never truly ended. They only paused.

They arrived at Kentwood Castle by evening. WilCarter awaited them in the great hall, demanding to know the plan. Althea quietly reminded him that Harlow had requested the survivors' expertise, but WilCarter refused to be sidelined.

"If more storms conjure relics," he declared, "I want them accounted for. My domain's security depends on it."

Maya schooled her features, masking the fatigue she felt. "We'll keep you informed, my lord. The location is neutral land, according to Harlow."

WilCarter leaned forward, gaze sharp. "Braxton might dispute that neutrality. You won't go alone. My knights will ride with you."

Victoria and Paul exchanged resigned looks. They couldn't deny WilCarter's right to defend his own territory, yet the prospect of juggling multiple lords' interests weighed heavily. Ultimately, they formed a precarious three-way alliance: WilCarter's knights, Harlow's domain, and the survivors who best understood these mysterious orchard phenomena.

Two days later, they set off from Kentwood with a detachment of WilCarter's knights in tow. Riding southeast along a winding road, they neared a river marking the border to Harlow's land. Clouds zipped across the sky, and a nervous tension simmered among the knights—some resented the survivors' leadership, while others feared the alleged "demonic" orchard storms. The survivors did their best to ignore the muttered suspicions.

By twilight, they reached a broad crossing. Baron Harlow awaited them with his own retinue, Sir Lionel standing at his side, face impassive. The two factions set up camp in uneasy cooperation. Over a simple supper, Harlow presented new intelligence: local peasants had reported flashes at night, blackened trees by morning, and strange metal fragments in the scorched zones. Maya's sense of dread grew. She remembered how the southwestern fields and the original orchard had nearly destroyed their lives. After a deceptively calm respite, it seemed these storms were stirring once more.

At dawn, the combined forces advanced into the forest. Fiery gold leaves closed overhead, turning the road into a tunnel of flickering light. Harlow and WilCarter's knights rode at the front, scouting for hazards. The survivors followed close behind, scanning for signs of burning or unnatural damage. Around midday, the forest thinned, revealing a narrow valley pockmarked with wild orchard trees—twisted apple, pear, and plum tangled in brambles.

A charred swath of land came into view, splitting the orchard in an ugly scar. Smoke clung to half-burned trunks, the bark ruptured as though struck by lightning. Yet the sky was clear, the midday sun shining overhead. A tense hush descended on everyone.

They dismounted, hearts pounding. Maya, Carter, Victoria, Paul, and Tomás approached the devastation while knights fanned out, keeping watch. Harlow and WilCarter lingered a few paces back, studying the scene. The burned orchard reeked of ozone, reminiscent of the storms that had once terrorized them. Kneeling, Maya brushed aside ash. Embedded in the singed earth was a twisted chunk of metal. She lifted it, dread buzzing at the base of her skull. Modern scrap again.

Carter joined her, his expression grim. "Looks like an engine casing or part of a seat brace. Not rusted. This can't have been here long."

Victoria, voice unsteady, said, "We thought the storms had stopped for good."

Tomás carefully picked up a melted piece of plastic with ghostly lettering. "The writing's almost destroyed, but it's definitely from our time."

Paul exhaled sharply. "We can't let these scraps fall into the wrong hands again. If Braxton—or anyone—builds weapons from this..."

Maya drew a shaky breath. "We won't let that happen."

They ventured farther into the blackened grove, stepping between the remains of trees. Some stood miraculously upright, while others had been blasted to stumps. In a half-ring near the center, the soil crackled with residual energy, forming a peculiar crater. WilCarter's knights muttered about unholy magic, while Harlow's men looked to Maya and the others with wary respect. She pressed her palm to the ground and felt a lingering warmth. Whatever had happened here, it was recent.

All at once, a faint violet flicker rippled near the center of the clearing. It pulsed again, bright enough to make them pause. A hush fell; adrenaline spiked. Could this be the beginning of a vortex?

Harlow commanded, "Hold positions!" as WilCarter's knights slid swords from scabbards, scanning the tree line.

Maya locked eyes with Carter. They shared the same thought: we must tread carefully. Creeping toward the shimmer, they felt static raise the hair on their arms. A few arcs of electricity danced across charred bark, forming a swirling haze that drifted in the midday light.

Victoria's gaze swept the orchard. "I feel it, too—like walking under power lines."

"We have to watch it," Maya said hoarsely. "Maybe we can disrupt it before more debris spills out."

Paul spread his hands. "But we've never found a foolproof way to seal these. We only know how to minimize their impact."

"Maybe bury it, or scatter the center," Carter offered, though his voice lacked conviction. "We can't just leave it for bandits."

Harlow and WilCarter's knights stood behind them, confusion clear on their faces. Maya steadied herself, struggling for a solution. "We try to disrupt the ground. If that fails, we guard it until it dies."

Suddenly, the whistle of arrows tore the air. One embedded itself in a scorched stump with a solid thunk. The orchard became chaos. Knights raised shields as more arrows rained down. Shouts rang out—bandits, or maybe Braxton's men. Swords clashed. The orchard's hush erupted into a furious skirmish.

Maya ducked behind a charred trunk. Carter grabbed her arm, pulling her clear of a second arrow. WilCarter's knights rushed forward, engaging silhouettes in the undergrowth. Harlow barked rapid orders to his men. Through the tumult, a few attackers sprinted toward the flashing haze, clearly trying to snatch the modern fragments for themselves.

Carter sprang to his feet. "They're after the scraps!" he shouted. Blade in hand, he raced forward. Maya followed, her pulse hammering in her ears as stray arrows hissed overhead.

Two bandits crouched amid scorched bark, stuffing pockets with twisted metal. When Carter lunged at them, one brandished a pitted sword, meeting him with a furious clash of steel. Maya slammed her shoulder into the second bandit, sending him stumbling and dropping a melted hunk of plastic. Victoria and Paul rushed in to fend off another attacker, while WilCarter's knights closed ranks, pushing the infiltrators back toward the tree line. The orchard anomaly crackled ominously, arcs of electricity dancing close to the melee. The danger was terrifying—one stray spark could ignite a devastating surge.

At last, the enemy scattered, some wounded, others fleeing into the dusk. The orchard belonged to the knights again. Panting, Maya scooped up the precious fragments the bandits had tried to steal: a bent cylinder with faint "O2" scrawled along the side. She recognized it as a piece of an oxygen tank. Modern relics, once so ordinary, now hazardous in this medieval world.

WilCarter and Harlow strode through the orchard, livid with the bold attack. Sir Lionel and Althea helped the knights fortify the perimeter. Carter ventured toward the flickering vortex, scattering loose soil over the epicenter. Sparks licked at the dirt, and the glow faded, as though starved of energy.

Maya felt relief wash through her. "Maybe it was already dying, but at least it seems to be dispersing."

With darkness looming, they gathered what scraps they could find, piling them out of reach of any potential scavengers. Harlow and WilCarter insisted on cataloging every piece. Working by the light of torches, the survivors painstakingly sifted ash, collecting lumps of metal, plastic, and half-burned tubing. Another orchard crisis, if not entirely stopped, was at least contained.

By nightfall, they had subdued the site. Bandits either lay captured or long gone. Harlow proposed torching the entire grove to ensure no energy remained, but Maya convinced him that burying the scorched zone and clearing debris was likely enough. They compromised, dumping earth over the central crater and uprooting dangerously charred trees.

Later, the knights and survivors set up camp near the half-burned orchard. Exhaustion etched every face. Maya sat in a small circle with

Carter, Victoria, Tomás, and Paul, staring at the battered cylinder in her hands, the faint letters "O2" flickering in the firelight. This battered scrap reminded her just how fragile peace could be.

Victoria sank onto a fallen log, rubbing tears from her eyes. "Will it ever end? These storms keep stirring up our past."

Tomás removed his hat and exhaled. "Each orchard anomaly reopens wounds we thought were healing. But we can't ignore them."

Paul rested a reassuring hand on Victoria's back. "We're doing what's right. If those bandits had gotten away with these fragments, who knows what they'd have built. We saved countless lives tonight."

Maya closed her eyes, recalling the devastation that brought them to this world. The orchard anomalies had shaped them—perhaps even defined them. Now, with Riverbend thriving, they had no choice but to keep standing guard, no matter how weary they felt.

"One day," she whispered, voice trembling slightly, "maybe the storms really will stop. Until then, we protect what we've built—what we call home."

CHAPTER 15

D awn mist wreathed the blackened orchard patch, curling in pale ribbons through the lingering debris of the recent storm. The ground, still scorched and studded with half-buried shards of twisted metal, exuded a cold hush that made every breath feel sharpened by an unseen tension. Maya and Carter stood at the orchard's edge, shoulders squared as if preparing for some final confrontation. Workers from Baron Harlow and Lord WilCarter toiled behind them, loading heaps of warping, melted metal onto a heavy cart. A few of WilCarter's men stood guard, awaiting orders to transport the fragments away for safekeeping.

Maya braced a hand against her heart, willing herself to be calm, though her pulse thudded in her ears. "That's the last of it," she said, voice subdued in the hush of morning. "No more of that strange buzzing, no flickers."

Carter surveyed the jagged lumps of steel loaded onto the cart, his expression cautious. "We've declared victory like this before, though." His deep voice reverberated with the exhaustion of too many false endings. "These watchtower and orchard portals or tears or... they never truly end, do they? They only fade until the next time."

She pressed her free hand gently to his arm, hoping the pressure would speak of unity, of finding solace in each other's presence. The orchard portals remained a looming uncertainty—a threat they could only keep contained. Still, for now, the swirling energies had quieted, leaving them space to breathe and regroup.

Behind them, Baron Harlow's armored knights—some battered and bruised—exchanged solemn nods with WilCarter's equally weary men. The alliance was tentative and tense, a ceasefire formed under the duress of greater danger. Whatever differences existed between their lords, both groups recognized the orchard fiascos as a threat too dire to handle alone.

***

By midmorning, that tenuous alliance dissolved back into polite neutrality. Harlow's men retreated to their domain, and WilCarter's contingent resumed their well-practiced vigilance. Parting words were stiff: Baron Harlow thanked all who had survived with a kind of grim courtesy, acknowledging that without their combined strength, the battle over the orchard might have tipped in favor of total devastation. WilCarter insisted on a detailed inventory of each item salvaged—every shard, fragment, or twisted relic documented to the last ounce.

Maya and Carter stood with their close companions—Victoria, Paul, and Tomás—observing the exchange. The orchard was a crater of ruin behind them, silent as a tomb. War had not erupted in a grand, conventional sense, but it had flickered at the edges of possibility. Now, with the orchard fiasco smothered and the scattered cosmic debris collected, everyone seemed to sense that true peace was only borrowed time.

"We should return to Riverbend Haven," Victoria said, her tone resolute. She scanned the orchard, where the last of the scraps was being locked into a metal-bound trunk. "There's nothing more for us here."

Carter gave a curt nod. "Agreed. Another one contained, but not destroyed. Best we keep ourselves prepared for whatever comes next."

Before they departed, WilCarter approached, his expression stony. "Remember your oath," he warned, voice hoarse from nights of little sleep. "If storms erupt again, we will call upon you. No surprises. The stakes are too high."

They acknowledged him with a silent nod, tension rippling beneath the surface. The orchard events had proven themselves cosmic wildcards. No one—Harlow, WilCarter, or Braxton—could ignore them or harness them without risking annihilation.

***

Under a sullen sky, the small band—Maya, Carter, Victoria, Paul, and Tomás—headed toward Riverbend Haven. Their mood was weighed down by weariness, each orchard having cut another notch into their collective resilience. They had seen lights swirl in the sky like restless spirits, had heard the staccato blasts of energies colliding with medieval farmland. This realm, pinned between old-world feuds and new-world anomalies, felt precarious at best.

Tomás, riding beside Victoria, mused about how future generations might record these events. "Will the tale be told as a grand quest? A cautionary legend? Will people think we lied about lumps of modern metal and cosmic storms?"

Victoria's quiet laugh held a note of grief. "By the time the story's retold, rumor may overshadow fact. Maybe we'll become myths ourselves—phantom warriors from another time."

Maya couldn't shake the last images. She saw it as an unstoppable swirl of color, singeing the orchard ground until it blackened, leaving lumps of debris that belonged to a different era. Closing her eyes, she pictured a stable crossing home, some cosmic corridor that might take them back. But a deeper voice in her heart whispered acceptance: they might never see home again. Perhaps they were guardians in this medieval world, forever chasing down cosmic flotsam to protect innocent lives.

Riverbend Haven appeared at dusk. The wooden walls, lamps lit at the gates, seemed to glow with reassurance. As they passed through, familiar faces—Nina, Sarah, Jason, and Anna—hurried forward, voices laced with relief. Ethan himself dashed into the courtyard, eyes shining. The communal hall erupted with subdued celebration: they had survived once again.

Later, in the millhouse's largest room, they gathered around a rough-hewn table. Torches flickered, casting warm shadows over the group as they relayed news of the orchard fiasco's final moments. Carter presented a distorted oxygen tank fragment for all to see. It looked like a relic from an alien invasion, not something from Earth.

Ethan ran a curious hand over the warped edges. "I can't believe that used to be part of your world."

Maya tousled his hair. "It may come from our past, but it's nobody's treasure now. Things like this should stay locked away, so they can't be turned into weapons."

Ethan nodded, biting his lip. "I'm glad you're here, though. It feels safer."

She smiled, comforting him as best she could. They were anchored—no, she corrected herself, they were bound—by a new life in Riverbend, one that demanded courage, resilience, and acceptance.

***

In the weeks that followed, day-to-day routine at Riverbend returned. Harvest approached. The orchard—this one healthy and free of cosmic intrusion—was heavy with fruit, branches bending under the weight of apples ripening in the crisp air. Harlow and WilCarter maintained an uneasy peace, as though each side was as exhausted by near-disaster as the other. Meanwhile, Braxton and his forces remained silent. Perhaps repeated sabotage had frayed Braxton's ambitions, or perhaps he was waiting for a more opportune moment. Whatever the cause, stillness descended on the region.

With each sunrise, the survivors blended modern techniques with medieval life. Carter improved irrigation channels, helping farmers water their fields more efficiently. Nina continued her innovative herbal experiments, guided by Maya's medical background. Tomás expanded the small school, taking local children under his wing. Victoria nurtured new trade routes, channeling Riverbend's modest surplus into neighboring villages.

***

One breezy twilight, Maya found herself back at the orchard. The day's warmth had begun to slip away, leaving a hint of chill on the breeze. She leaned against a newly built wooden fence, letting the sweet scent of ripening apples fill her lungs. Behind her, trees shimmered with the deepening gold of late afternoon sun.

Quiet footsteps approached. She turned to see Ethan, hugging his arms around his slight frame. His cheeks were pink from the cool air. He stopped beside her, gaze lingering on the orchard as though searching for something—perhaps reassurance that this place was indeed safe.

He cleared his throat. "Mom—can I call you that?" The shyness in his voice tugged at her heart. "I know I have one, but you are a second mom to me."

Maya's eyes glistened. She drew him into a gentle embrace. "I'd be honored," she whispered. The boy had clung to her for guidance since the plane crash. Now, his voice was deeper, his shoulders broader—but inside, he was still that little boy.

He exhaled with relief. "Thank you... Mom. I was just thinking how this orchard feels nothing like those... those fiascos we chased. This one's peaceful."

She stroked his hair. "We've nurtured it. No cosmic storms, no swirling lights, no chaos." Her voice caught on the last word, memories of devastation flaring for an instant. "We've created something real here, haven't we?"

He nodded. "Sometimes I wonder if a stable vortex—like a safe passage back—might still appear. If it did, would you go?" He paused, glancing at her with a hesitant hope, as though afraid of the answer.

Maya's heart squeezed. Her mind flashed to her old life, but the images felt like half-forgotten dreams. "I couldn't leave this place. I wouldn't leave you."

Ethan smiled with relief, leaning his head against her shoulder. The orchard leaves shivered in the soft breeze, as if murmuring agreement.

***

Days slid into weeks. Crisp mornings heralded the orchard harvest, which turned into a communal event. Villagers formed small teams to pick apples from dawn until dusk. Children gathered windfall fruit, laughing as they jostled each other in friendly competition. At night, the people of Riverbend celebrated with dancing, music, and hearty meals. The swirling storms, so threatening mere months ago, felt like distant nightmares.

While villagers pressed apples into cider and laid out crates for storage, the survivors turned their energies to settlement improvements. Carter, Paul, and Tomás supervised the construction of a second smithy, hoping to expand their capacity for forging tools. Nina and Maya laid plans for a dedicated infirmary, capitalizing on Maya's modern training and the local herbal wisdom Nina was amassing. Victoria, with a keen eye for trade opportunities, arranged for surplus textiles to be exchanged for regional delicacies and stronger metals. Everywhere, there was the hum of life, the sense of forging something that could outlast any cosmic storm.

***

Late in the harvest season, a messenger from WilCarter arrived, bearing a folded piece of parchment. His horse was lathered with foam, testament to an urgent ride. He handed the note to Tomás, then stood aside, wiping sweat from his brow.

Gathered in the communal hall, Tomás read the dispatch aloud to an expectant circle of survivors. "Braxton's domain is in turmoil—rebellion in the northern provinces, discontent in his own ranks. Reports suggest Braxton himself has fallen out of favor, possibly due to his failures in harnessing modern weapons."

Victoria let out a breath she hadn't realized she was holding. "So his ambition might be losing its power. That's... good news, right?"

Maya exchanged a thoughtful look with Carter. Relief pulsed through her, cautious but definite. If Braxton's grip faltered, the appetite for cosmic relics might fade. Perhaps orchard fiascos would cease to be anything more than an inexplicable phenomenon—one that no longer tempted power-hungry lords to exploit them. They might recede into the realm's folklore, becoming echoes of a time when storms raged and travelers from another world fought to contain them.

***

In Riverbend's orchard, the final leaves had turned to fiery gold, drifting to the grass like silent confetti. Children played among the downed foliage, raking them into piles, then scattering them with peals of laughter. Maya joined in, occasionally stooping to gather bundles for compost or to help the younger kids form neat mounds. Carter repaired fences further down the row, his hair glinting in the slanted afternoon light.

At midday, Nina approached with a bright smile. "The clinic is quieter than ever," she reported. "No major injuries, mostly colds and small mishaps. I almost feel useless—like I'm out of a job!"

Maya laughed. "I'd rather keep you bored than swamped with wounds."

Victoria and Paul arrived, having negotiated a small but meaningful trade agreement with a nearby settlement. Their eyes shone with pride, as if every successful conversation proved they could thrive here, despite any barriers between modern knowledge and medieval tradition.

Twilight fell gently, bringing cooler winds. Anna sought Maya in the orchard, eyes clouded with worry. "Ethan's restless," she confided. "He puts on a brave face, but I see the questions in his eyes. He wonders if the storms will reappear... if his grandparents back in the old world are still waiting for him. It stings, not knowing how to help him let go."

Maya's sympathy rose like a tide. "I think all of us wonder sometimes. We left so many people behind. But these orchard fiascos can't be controlled. If we haven't found a stable passage by now..."

Anna offered a wan smile. "He's grown so close to you and Carter. I want him to find peace here. I just hate seeing that shadow in his eyes."

Maya squeezed her hand. "We'll remind him he's loved, that this is his home. Maybe in time, those old ghosts will soften into memories." Inside, though, she understood too well that longing—both comforting and painful—had no simple cure.

***

Soon, the orchard stood bare, skeletal branches exposed to the coming winter. Riverbend's attention turned inward: storing grain, preserving produce, preparing firewood. Nights ran longer, days shorter. In the orchard's dim hush, Carter found Maya late one evening, her breath visibly puffing in the chill air. He set a hand on her shoulder, voice low.

"I keep expecting another swirl of cosmic lights," he admitted. "It's like every time I see a flicker in the sky, I brace myself."

Maya let out a trembling sigh. "I do the same. But maybe—just maybe—we've contained them. Or scared off whoever kept trying to exploit them."

He gave a heavy nod. "If only we could seal them forever. But we don't have that power. We just keep watch."

Her gaze swept the orchard. The moonlight turned the branches a ghostly silver. "Riverbend is more than survival now, Carter. We've got families and friendships, a life that feels... complete, almost." She paused, lips curving into a gentle smile. "We just have to trust that if another opening appears, we'll handle it."

His eyes met hers, understanding reflected there. "As long as we're together."

A quiet rustle interrupted them. They turned, hearts pounding for an instant, ready to face intruders. Instead, Ethan stepped into view, cheeks pink from the cold, cloak pulled tight around his shoulders. His voice was timid, as if he'd eavesdropped by accident. "Sorry to scare you. I couldn't sleep."

Maya motioned for him to join them. He hesitated, then sidled closer, hugging his arms. "I was dreaming about my grandparents," he said in a whisper. "I pictured them in our old home, waiting. But then I woke up and realized... this is my home now."

Carter's eyes softened. "You can miss them. That's natural."

Ethan nodded and cast a look at the orchard's dark silhouette. "I used to see the orchard as a curse, but now... it's where we grow food, where we laugh and play. It's peaceful."

Maya took his hand. "No fiasco tonight," she said gently. "Rest easy."

He nodded, letting out a small sigh of relief. Together, they made their way back to the village, the only sound a soft wind stirring the branches overhead.

***

Winter's arrival brought a hush. Snow fell in gentle flurries, blanketing Riverbend in white. The orchard's dark trunks stood in stark contrast to the drifts, as if guarding the settlement through the cold months. Fewer travelers arrived with rumors of war, and no messengers spoke of new cosmic tears. Even Braxton, once a looming threat, seemed embroiled in troubles of his own making.

By candlelight in the communal hall, the survivors gathered often, spinning tales of the storms for children and newcomers who had never witnessed the storms firsthand. Swords and armor rusted slightly from disuse, replaced by simpler day-to-day tasks: forging new iron pots, weaving thicker blankets, mending wooden roofs before the heavy snows came. War's echoes felt almost dreamlike now, overshadowed by the crackle of logs in the hearth.

On one particularly cold evening, Tomás pushed his chair closer to the hearth and proposed that they record everything—a true chronicle, so future generations might learn from their experiences. "We owe it to those who come after us," he said fervently. "If any new tear appears, people should know what they're facing. They should understand it's not magic, but something that can be managed—cautiously."

Paul concurred, retrieving a small stash of modern stationery he had scavenged from the wreck of the plane. Though some sheets were partially damaged, he treated them like priceless artifacts, complementing the local vellum. They would blend the two—modern and medieval—into a single testament.

Thus began a slow, introspective project. By day, they managed settlement affairs: stoking fires, distributing food, teaching lessons in the school, or helping with meager winter farming. By night, they wrote. Some nights, Carter dictated from memory, describing each orchard fiasco's chaos: swirling lights, arcs of strange energy, the desperate measures they took to bury or sabotage modern technology. Nina contributed medical notes, recounting injuries and treatments with meticulous detail. Victoria added the political angle—battles and truces with Harlow, WilCarter, and even Braxton. Tomás organized these narratives, weaving them into a coherent tale.

Maya found herself reading and rereading those sections, marveling at how fully they had consumed her thoughts not so long ago. She saw them now as chapters in a larger story—her story, Carter's, Ethan's, and everyone else's—one that did not conclude with triumphant rescue. Instead, it led here, to an unexpected sense of belonging.

Anna and a few villagers also contributed accounts: glimpses from afar, the rumors that spread, the ways they had rationalized or misinterpreted events before the survivors provided clarity. The final product, a large sheaf of parchment mixed with modern pages, represented a bridge between times.

***

Weeks passed, snow piling on rooftops and roads. When the final sentences were written, the "Chronicle of the Sky-People" stood as a testament. They sealed it in a wooden chest, lined with waxed cloth to protect against damp and decay, and stored it in the millhouse.

That same night, a soft snow dusted Riverbend's fences and orchard rows. Maya and Carter found themselves at the orchard gate, each holding a lantern. The rest of their tight-knit group joined them—Victoria, Paul, Tomás, Nina, Sarah, Jason, Anna, and Ethan himself—forming a loose half-circle beneath the whispering wind. The orchard stretched behind them, stark branches laced with frost.

For a moment, no one spoke. They simply let the hush of winter cradle them. Maya closed her eyes, letting slow breaths steady her heart. Memories flickered—of orchard fiascos roaring to life, of the frantic fear that the next swirl might devour them. Tonight, there was only peace.

Snowflakes drifted in the lantern glow, like miniature stars falling to earth. They stood that way for several minutes, letting the finality of one chapter and the promise of another settle in. This orchard had once frightened them—now it was a symbol of survival, of continuity. If the fiascos ever reawakened, they would be ready. But for now, at least, the swirl of cosmic storms had passed beyond the horizon of their daily lives.

They shared one last glance, a unified promise in their eyes: to watch over this land and its people, to protect against old dangers should they return, and to embrace the future they were forging together. They had led to something none of them had anticipated: acceptance, belonging, and the kind of strength that no cosmic storm could shatter.

In the silent hush of a snow-blanketed night, the orchard stood as a testament that sometimes, out of the greatest chaos, comes the sweetest harvest of all. And as the survivors turned away from the gate, they carried within them a resolute peace—a faith that whatever cosmic storms might rage in the future, Riverbend Haven would endure, its orchard flourishing as a beacon of hope and unity.

CHAPTER 16

Twilight bled into the sky above Riverbend Haven, painting the horizon in gold and rose. Maya stood on the orchard's gentle slope, inhaling the sweet air. A year and a half had passed since the first seeds of this settlement took hold in fertile soil. Now, orchard rows stretched in orderly lines, leaves rustling with the promise of the next harvest. She remembered when the notion of a peaceful orchard seemed impossible—when seemingly endless catastrophes and swirling storms overshadowed their every step.

A hush settled over her thoughts. Their biggest threats had simmered down: each disturbing swirl of cosmic debris intercepted, each relic of war locked away. Yet she couldn't shake the sense that some final, discordant note still hung in the air—an unfinished chord from a half-forgotten song.

Footsteps scuffed the earth behind her. She turned to see Carter, hair dusted with sawdust from the carpentry shop. He gave her a tired smile, setting a small wooden beam aside. "I see you found your favorite spot," he said, voice low as the rustle of orchard leaves.

She nodded. "After everything we've been through, this orchard is a symbol of what we've built—a haven against so much chaos. But sometimes, I sense... I don't know, a calm before another storm."

His expression softened, concern woven into his gaze. "Perhaps we've finally earned peace. The war's been quiet, Braxton's domain has collapsed, most cosmic upheavals are contained. Riverbend's thriving. Isn't that enough?"

She attempted a half-smile. "It should be. Maybe my nerves just haven't adjusted to tranquility yet."

They stood side by side, watching the orchard yield to the violet hush of dusk, each remembering the nights of infiltration, sabotage, half-glimpsed cosmic lights. Though much had changed, a faint tension hovered in the evening air, like an echo of old fears.

Within the settlement's wooden palisade, twilight signaled the official end of the workday. Villagers returned from the fields, children giggled at play around the well, and a contented hum drifted in the cooling breeze. In the old millhouse—now a repurposed office for trade—Victoria and Paul pored over tallies and ledgers. The pages documented everything from apple shipments to flour production and exchanges with allied villages. Victoria tapped her quill on the rough table, listening to the crickets chirp beyond the open door.

"Productivity's up twenty percent from last season," Paul noted, scanning the neat columns. "We could support more refugees if necessary."

Victoria nodded. "As long as WilCarter's taxes remain steady. He's grown quite used to our surplus." She sighed, recalling the precarious nature of alliances. "Sometimes I think we rely too heavily on his goodwill. We're halfway to independence, but never truly free."

Paul offered a wan smile. "It's still better than being pawns in a war. This arrangement keeps knights off our fields. That counts for something."

Victoria's gaze flickered, her tone contemplative. "Yes, it's progress. Yet I can't erase memories of cosmic debris raining down, fueling war-lust. I want a future where swirling lights and bizarre shards can never threaten us again."

He leaned back, letting out a small breath. "We're forging that future, step by step."

***

Down by the river, Tomás supervised a group of older children, all collecting driftwood for the settlement's winter stores. Every resource mattered, whether for building materials or firewood. Ethan, nearly fourteen now, stood among them, taller and more self-assured than ever. He chatted with his peers, mixing modern mathematics with the local dialect. Tomás found himself smiling at the boy's transformation—once a frightened child from Flight 207, now a teacher's assistant.

Before darkness set in fully, Tomás dismissed the group, commending them on their work. Ethan lingered at the riverbank, where the water glimmered pink in the sunset. "Do you miss the old troubles, Tomás?" the boy asked softly.

Tomás blinked. "Miss them? They were terrifying."

Ethan shrugged, shifting on his feet. "I just wonder... we used to chase every strange sign in the sky, hoping for a rescue. Now that it's all quiet, I worry we'll never see home again."

The historian-turned-teacher set a gentle hand on the boy's shoulder. "It's natural to wonder. But sometimes, peace means we can finally put down roots." He met Ethan's gaze with warmth. "You have a home here, friends, a future. Don't forget that."

Ethan nodded, though his eyes lingered on the fading horizon. "I know. It's just... I still dream about the plane sometimes. About Dad... the crash."

Tomás exhaled gently. "Dreams keep our memories alive, even the painful ones. But you've found a new family here." He guided the boy back toward the settlement, the quiet orchard behind them offering an unspoken reassurance.

Night arrived in earnest. In the communal hall, the warmth of a small feast—roasted squash, fresh-baked bread—fended off the autumn chill. Nina joined Sarah and Jason Wu at one end of a long wooden table, discussing new medical protocols with Maya. Their voices were low but eager as they covered advanced herbal treatments for fevers and infections. They exchanged knowing looks, recalling how primitive medieval healing once seemed, and how the cosmic disruptions ironically pushed them to apply modern knowledge in saving lives.

Sarah sipped her cider. "We're finally at a point where local healers trust our methods. Master Gerald from Kentwood even cites our approach in his notes." She remembered, with some amusement, how suspicious he'd once been.

Nina nodded. "We've come so far. Not long ago, we struggled to triage burns from the cosmic debris. Now we're training apprentices in sanitation and antiseptics."

***

By early morning, a crisp wind ruffled the settlement. Maya rose from her cot, rummaging through her sparse supplies—bandages, a stethoscope, antiseptics that were still precious. A soft knock at the door made her pause. Answering it, she found Anna, face etched with worry.

"Maya," she whispered urgently, "Ethan had another nightmare last night—about swirling lights. He woke up scared. Could you speak with him?"

Maya's heart grew heavy. "Of course."

She followed the woman to their hut, where Ethan sat on a simple wooden stool, shoulders taut. He looked up with haunted eyes. "I'm sorry," he murmured. "I keep seeing that vision of swirling glow and hearing Dad's voice. It's... messing with me."

Maya knelt, taking his hands gently. "Don't apologize. Trauma flares up in strange ways. We can talk, or try some calming exercises." Her modern medical training felt basic here, but it was enough to guide him through anxiety. "Remember, you're not alone."

He swallowed hard. "I know things are peaceful now, but the dream felt so real. Like a giant chasm opening again, bigger than ever. I could almost hear my dad calling."

She touched his cheek, her voice warm. "Grief has a way of twisting our dreams. If something unexpected happens, we'll face it together. You have your mother, and all of us."

Ethan blinked back tears, nodding. "Thanks, Mom," he whispered, the word binding them. He hugged her, and she embraced him with a vow that felt like solid promise.

Elsewhere in the orchard, Carter oversaw the second harvest cycle. He inspected rows of trees for signs of disease and ensured the irrigation channels still worked. The orchard stood as a testament to Riverbend's hard-won success. A handful of farmhands joined him, carefully picking fruit destined for trade.

At midday, Carter leaned against a fence post, surveying the neat rows.

A voice drew him from his reverie. Victoria strolled up, her cloak elegantly trailing behind her. "You all right?"

He forced a small grin. "Just thinking. Hard to believe we once lived in fear of cosmic storms. Now, these rows of apple trees feel almost safe."

She nodded, her arms tucked around herself. "We should be thankful. Yet I can't shake the feeling that everyone's tense, like we're bracing for something."

His gaze darkened for an instant. "War and chaos taught us caution. But maybe we owe ourselves a bit of peace too."

***

That evening, the watchmen spotted a small group of travelers approaching the western gate, carrying a white cloth of truce. Maya, Carter, Victoria, and a handful of militiamen hurried to investigate. The travelers were peasants from a distant hamlet, looking exhausted and frayed. They spoke of trouble left behind—Braxton's former brigands threatening their homes—and begged for refuge at Riverbend.

Victoria and Paul took them aside in the courtyard, quietly asking questions. The newcomers mentioned hearing vague rumors of cosmic anomalies in distant valleys, but nothing confirmed. "Probably old wives' tales," one weary man said. "We're more worried about bandits."

Maya breathed a sigh of relief. Another rumor, nothing immediate. They welcomed the peasants, offering warm meals and shelter in one of the communal huts. Though a nagging concern lingered—true or not, these cosmic relics had a way of resurfacing.

Days slipped into weeks, calm remaining unbroken. The orchard's final harvest ended with the sweet promise of abundant stores. Winter crept closer, and Riverbend's second year concluded with remarkably little drama. At times, the survivors almost allowed themselves to believe they had tamed their unpredictable fate.

But one crisp morning, a rider arrived from Kentwood, face pale with urgency. Lord WilCarter demanded immediate help—an old feud with a minor baron near Braxton's territory had flared. The baron reportedly possessed "foreign metal tubes," likely scavenged from past cosmic debris. That was all it took to stir old nightmares.

Tomás read the message aloud to the council. Weariness clouded their faces. The realm expected them, the so-called "sky-people," to solve each crisis sparked by relics from those storms. The orchard might be tranquil, but the rest of this medieval world remained restless. With heavy hearts, Maya, Carter, Victoria, Paul, and Nina prepared to ride out yet again, leaving Sarah, Jason, and the others to safeguard Riverbend.

At Kentwood, WilCarter paced like a caged lion. He ranted about the petty baron—Lord Reynall—accusing him of hoarding cosmic scraps to craft monstrous weapons. Scouts reported a device halfway between a cannon and a musket, powered by these strange materials. Tension rippled through Maya's chest as she imagined infiltration after infiltration, sabotage after sabotage. She wondered if this would ever end.

WilCarter insisted they launch a covert strike to destroy or confiscate the relics before Reynall unleashed havoc. Victoria proposed diplomatic talks, but WilCarter scoffed at the delay. "He could attack at dawn," he growled. "No time for niceties."

In the corner, Carter clenched his jaw. "All right. One last time. We'll handle this, but then we're done."

They slipped away under a moonless sky, accompanied by a handful of WilCarter's knights. Hearts pounded with the painful familiarity of another infiltration. They reached a small border village near Reynall's fortress, dismounting in shadow. If these metal tubes truly existed, they had mere hours to prevent widespread destruction.

Nina stayed back with extra knights, ready to treat any wounded. Maya, Carter, Victoria, Paul, Tomás, and a small infiltration squad crept closer to the fortress walls. Torches flickered along battlements, casting wavering pools of light. Inside, the rumored armory—brimming with cosmic scraps—waited to be sabotaged.

Maya felt her pulse hammer as she recalled previous missions. How many times had they risked their lives to keep some power-hungry lord from unleashing cosmic horrors?

A sleepy sentry dozed by the postern gate. They slipped past him, mindful not to rattle the heavy iron bars. The fortress interior was a maze of corridors lit by guttering torches. Faint voices echoed from distant chambers. Each step felt weighted with tension. Carter's knuckles went white around the hilt of his short blade, Paul gripping a small pouch of sabotage tools he'd grown too accustomed to using.

A heavily bolted door loomed at the end of a narrow hallway. WilCarter's knights got to work on the lock, prying it open with hushed determination. Inside lay a dimly lit storeroom cluttered with crates and barrels: casks of powder, containers scribbled with runes, twisted scraps of jagged metal. In the center stood a half-assembled contraption with a thick barrel fused from mismatched steel.

Their hearts sank at the sight. Another vile creation fusing modern steel with medieval forging.

A lone blacksmith guarded the device. He gaped at the intruders, then lunged for his sword. Victoria was quick to parry, steel ringing in the silent chamber. Carter knocked him to the floor while Tomás bound and gagged him. The relic stood vulnerable, a horrifying testament to how greed could warp technological fragments.

Maya and Paul raced to sabotage it. With chisels and hammers, they removed vital parts and poured water into the powder casks. Crates of spare metal pieces—once collected from cosmic debris—would go unused. Beyond the door, the clang of swords and the roar of voices signaled WilCarter's knights clashing with Reynall's men.

Panicked footsteps thundered in the corridor. Reinforcements, perhaps. Maya's throat tightened. They had to hurry.

A brief but brutal fight erupted when two of Reynall's guards burst in. Carter deflected a savage blow while Victoria and Paul dodged to either side. Maya brandished a short dagger, adrenaline surging. Tomás tackled one guard, sending the man stumbling into a crate of suspicious metal scraps. The collision created an ominous sizzle as the fragments collided.

"Careful!" Maya hissed, yanking Tomás aside before he or the guard could trigger a spark. One of the men tried to seize a battered piece of an airline seat as an improvised weapon. The team wrestled them down, leaving both guards unconscious. Hearts pounding, they returned to their desperate task, ensuring the partially built cannon was beyond repair.

With the device ruined, chaos exploded in the corridor outside. Shouts echoed through the fortress as Reynall's men discovered the infiltration. WilCarter's knights roared in retaliation. Maya and the others knew their window was closing fast. They couldn't risk leaving any cosmic scraps that might be salvaged, so they scooped up as many twisted shards as possible. The blacksmith glowered from his bindings, powerless to stop them.

"Move!" Carter urged. He led them through a side passage, the flicker of torches guiding their frantic steps.

They navigated the winding corridors, the fortress itself trembling with the thunder of pitched combat. Another infiltration. Another confrontation with a weapon forged from otherworldly materials. When would it truly end? Maya's mind raced, exhaustion weaving through her limbs as they ducked a stray crossbow bolt. Her gaze caught a mural on the wall—a medieval saint brandishing a sword—an oddly fitting image for the life they'd been forced into.

They emerged into a courtyard where WilCarter's knights grappled with Reynall's defenders. Sparks flew in torchlight. Reynall himself—a stout figure in battered armor—bellowed curses. His best threat lay in pieces, undone by the infiltration squad.

In the tumult, Carter thrust a bulging sack of metal fragments at a loyal sergeant. "Lock these up," he shouted. The last relics from this cosmic trove would be sealed away, never to fuel another lord's ambition.

***

At dawn, the fortress lay in ruin, its defenders either surrendering or fleeing into the hills. WilCarter forced the humiliated baron to kneel and forfeit every scrap of foreign metal in his possession. The threat—at least this one—had been quashed. In a huddle near the fortress wall, Maya, Carter, Victoria, Paul, and Tomás exchanged drained looks, the hollow triumph souring their relief.

WilCarter approached, his expression surprisingly subdued. "You did your part. The realm is in your debt again." A pause lingered. "I wonder how long we must chase these relics."

Maya let out a shaky breath. "We wonder the same."

He nodded. "Then return to Riverbend. I'll handle the rest. Let's hope those scraps are the last of them."

They bowed stiffly, grateful to leave. Another storm had passed, yet their spirits felt heavier with each repetition of this cycle.

They rode back to Riverbend in weary silence, the chill wind biting. Upon arrival, Ethan met them at the gate, eyes filled with concern. They mustered reassuring smiles, explaining that the threat was over—this time. The cosmic fragments were confiscated, the baron's weapon destroyed. Yet a deep fatigue pulsed through them, as if they'd been conscripted into an endless war.

That evening, the survivors gathered in the orchard—just them and Ethan, who insisted on being included. Moonlight washed over the rows of apple trees, their leaves trembling in the breeze. In this place, once the epicenter of swirling danger, all seemed calm. But the hush felt too profound, too aware of how quickly fate could shift.

A hush settled over the group. Carter's voice finally broke the silence, quiet but resonant in the night. "Is this all we are now? Guardians against every stray relic left behind by the storms?"

Victoria's eyes glistened with unspoken sorrow. "It feels like a calling we never chose. But who else will do it? We know how dangerous these fragments can be."

Paul rubbed his temples. "I daydream about normal life—just farming, teaching, crafting. No more risky missions."

Maya's eyes drifted to Ethan. In the boy's face, she saw both the fear of his past and the determination of someone who had come too far to turn back. She squeezed his shoulder. "If new trouble ever arises, we'll face it together. Until then, we keep living. That's our purpose."

In the orchard's subtle rustling, they solidified an unspoken vow: protect this land from any future threats, keep building a life worth defending, and accept that though the cosmic storms might one day return, they would stand ready.

Over the next week, no new summons came. No whispered warnings, no glimmer of swirling lights. Braxton's old domain remained in shambles; Lord Reynall, thoroughly subdued. Riverbend Haven thrived under the onset of winter, the orchard shining as a symbol of resilience. Burnt once, it now flourished with the promise that hope could rise even from scorched soil.

In those quiet days, Maya found her routine again, taking evening walks through the orchard's winding paths. Carter often joined her, and they spoke in hushed tones about the repeated missions—sabotage here, infiltration there, endless attempts to secure leftover fragments. But the orchard soothed their lingering anxieties, its rustling branches offering a gentle lullaby.

One evening, Ethan approached them, curiosity bright in his eyes. He asked if he could read the written Chronicle they'd assembled, detailing every cosmic event and mission since the crash. Maya hesitated, then agreed. "It may help you understand—and heal."

He pursed his lips, nodding gravely. "I want to see how it all connects. How we came to live like this."

***

That night, in the millhouse lit by warm lantern glow, Ethan pored over the Chronicle's pages. The survivors gathered around, prepared for his questions about the cosmic storms and past infiltration missions. The final entries made his eyes well with tears, but a quiet acceptance replaced the sadness in his expression. "We really have come so far," he murmured, voice thick with feeling.

Maya hugged him gently. "Yes, we have. From tragedy to rebuilding, from turmoil to this orchard that has become our home."

CHAPTER 17

A brittle hush enveloped Riverbend Haven that winter dawn, the orchard's leafless branches etched like black filigree against a pale sky. Maya stood on the orchard hill, breath steaming, gazing across the settlement's snug huts. Smoke curled from chimneys, and the quiet of early morning felt both comforting and unnerving. She couldn't dismiss the feeling of an unresolved chord vibrating in the icy air.

On mornings like this, the recollection of swirling cosmic lights across orchard fields lingered in her mind—portals that once ripped open and hurled modern debris into this medieval realm. For months, there'd been no major orchard disturbances, only scattered scraps found far from the settlement. WilCarter's domain thrived, and no new infiltration missions loomed. Yet, in the back of her thoughts, doubt hovered: Could the danger truly be over?

She pulled her cloak closer, a subtle tightness in her chest. After so many harrowing orchard episodes, calm itself felt disconcerting. Rubbing her arms briskly, she turned toward the settlement. The day's routine awaited her: a medical check in the new infirmary, orchard expansion plans, and the arrival of Harlow's winter trade caravan. For once, life seemed peaceful.

Carter stood in a lower clearing of the orchard, loading a crate of tools onto a handcart. Over the past few weeks, he had refined the watermill gears, ensuring Riverbend's success in milling grain—a critical element of its newfound prosperity.

Cold air stung his cheeks as he directed a few workers bundling lumber. Soon, Tomás arrived with several older children in tow. Carter mustered a friendly grin. "Morning. You're here just in time to watch me dislocate my back hauling these boards."

Tomás returned the smile, but his eyes held a trace of gravity. "The harvest is in, the orchard seems quiet, the settlement's stable. I can't shake the notion that we're in the calm before a storm. Perhaps my historian's instincts are warning me."

Carter nodded slowly. "You feel it too. I keep telling myself the orchard trouble is finished, but there's a lingering tension." He forced a casual shrug. "Maybe we should just accept this peace."

Tomás laid a hand on his shoulder. "Peace is a daily choice, I suppose."

They stood for a moment, surveying the orchard floor, dusted with frost, its branches stripped of leaves. This silence felt like a separate world from the earlier cosmic chaos—yet memory remained a fragile bridge.

In the makeshift millhouse that doubled as a community hall, Victoria and Paul were finalizing ledgers with the village council. Relief touched every face as they closed the meeting, which focused on plans for orchard expansions, fence repairs, and road improvements—remarkably mundane topics compared to the old cosmic storms.

"We're stable," Paul murmured, tapping the ledger with his quill. "No major orchard incidents for months, no infiltration missions since Reynall's fiasco. People seem... content."

Victoria's gaze flicked over the council members. "Contentment can turn to complacency. But maybe that's acceptable if it brings happiness."

The villagers nodded. They had survived cosmic storms, war, and infiltration. If serenity reigned now, they would embrace it. Yet once the meeting adjourned and Victoria stepped outside, her heart felt unaccountably heavy. The hush after so much turmoil felt aimless, as though a vital energy had fizzled out. This was what they had fought for, so why did it feel incomplete?

Near midday, Nina spotted an unfamiliar rider approaching Riverbend's gate. She alerted the watch, then fetched Maya, Carter, and the others. The orchard's otherworldly episodes had taught them to stay alert; any stranger might carry news of cosmic or martial threats.

They gathered behind the palisade. The traveler—a middle-aged man in a threadbare robe, hair streaked with gray—guided a tired horse. He dismounted and bowed politely. "I am Brother Kaylem, a monk from an abbey near Harlow's lands. Word has reached us about your knowledge of... unusual orchard storms."

Maya and Carter exchanged tense looks. "Orchard storms." Carter cleared his throat. "We have some experience. What brings you?"

Brother Kaylem exhaled, worry etched on his face. "Our abbey stands near a remote orchard that once burned under a strange storm. Now, that orchard glows at night, flickers of light dancing among the branches. We've tried prayers, we sealed the perimeter, but nothing stops the glow."

The settlement members grew quiet. Could another cosmic event be brewing? Maya's heart sank. She forced her voice to remain measured. "Where? Have you seen any wreckage?"

"Only a faint hum and eerie lights," Kaylem said. "A few novices swear they glimpsed twisted metal in the dirt, glowing by moonlight. They're convinced it's unholy."

The hush deepened. Perhaps their relief had been premature. Maya drew in a slow breath. "We'll talk in the millhouse."

Over a modest lunch, Kaylem recounted how the abbey had endured smaller disturbances in the past—burned patches and flashes in the night—but never a persistent glow like this. Wild animals avoided the orchard, and travelers veered off the roads.

"We beg your aid," Kaylem said. "We've heard of the 'sky-doctor' and her allies who quell these... storms."

Maya's fingertips grazed her temple. "We'll investigate. Carefully. If this phenomenon is active, it could be dangerous."

By late afternoon, the settlement's trusted figures convened. WilCarter's domain was at peace; Braxton's war lay dormant. Thus, no immediate threat demanded their presence here, freeing them to explore the abbey's distress. Carter crossed his arms and paced. "If it's glowing nightly, it might be a stable rift—something bigger than what we've seen before." He glanced at Maya. "Could it be a door home?"

The question pressed on every heart. Long ago, these cosmic ruptures had fueled hope of returning to their own century. But time had changed them all. Maya's throat grew tight. "I... can't dismiss that possibility. But we've built a life here. Leaving everything behind—"

Victoria pressed her lips together. "Riverbend depends on us."

Ethan, standing nearby, looked up. "If it opens a way back... do we really want to go?"

Unease rippled in the circle. They ultimately agreed to travel under the guise of helping the abbey. Half of them would remain at Riverbend—Anna, Nina, Sarah, Jason, and part of the militia—to watch over the settlement. The expedition would consist of Maya, Carter, Victoria, Paul, Tomás, and a few volunteers, guided by Brother Kaylem.

That evening, Ethan approached Maya at the orchard gate, his voice trembling. "I want to join you. I can handle whatever we find."

Protectiveness swelled in her chest. "It could be dangerous. We don't know if this is stable or explosive."

He lifted his chin. "I'm not a child anymore. I'll stay close. I swear."

After a moment, she relented. He had earned a place by their side. "All right. But do not wander off."

His grateful smile tugged at her heart.

Dawn arrived, pale gold behind thick clouds, as the group rode out: Maya, Carter, Victoria, Paul, Tomás, Ethan, and six volunteers. Brother Kaylem led them east. The orchard in question lay two days' journey from the abbey, near a winding river. Frost shimmered on the bare branches, and their breath hung in the frigid air as they traveled. Conversation remained muted. Every orchard event they had faced before had ended in tragedy, sabotage, or heartbreak, never the neat rescue they once dreamed of.

They camped that night in a small hamlet. The villagers recognized them: the "sky-people" who had contained orchard storms. Over a shared meal, locals whispered about the strange glow and the metallic howl it sometimes emitted. The hush around the fire mirrored the dread in each traveler's heart.

On the second day, they arrived at the abbey: a sturdy stone structure huddled against a hillside, with a modest tower peeking above the leafless forest. Monks in plain robes met them in uneasy silence. The abbot, an elderly man named Father Cedran, led them into a courtyard and described the orchard's nightly glow. Some watchers had reported crackling static, but not the explosive bursts that once defined earlier fiascos. It was as if a slow, unrelenting energy had settled in the orchard.

"That slow burn might be a stable gateway," Carter said, frowning. He cast a glance at Maya and Victoria. None of them knew if that possibility brought hope or fear.

Ethan hovered at the edge of the group, listening.

That evening, Father Cedran guided them along a winding path through barren woodland. In the twilight, they reached a shallow depression ringed by twisted apple trees. Already, a faint violet haze shimmered amid the leafless branches, pulsing like a hidden heartbeat.

Maya's pulse pounded. She stepped closer, Ethan at her side. The orchard felt alive with a humming energy that made the hair on her arms rise. Tomás rubbed his palms together. "You feel that charge? Stronger than anything we've encountered before."

Paul set down a metal rod. The tip sparked. "This place is saturated with static."

Victoria surveyed the perimeter. "We'll need people on guard if opportunists or hostile lords hear about this."

They established a small camp nearby. Abbot Cedran and several monks joined them in uneasy vigil, flinching at even the faintest crackle. Ethan stayed awake, transfixed by the orchard's glow. Maya, Carter, Victoria, Paul, and Tomás set up instruments—compasses, rods, remnants from previous sabotage kits. As midnight drew near, the orchard's violet haze intensified. Sparks hissed across skeletal branches, crackling like tiny lightning bolts. A deep hum grew, reminiscent of a distant jet engine. The watchers trembled, some monks fled to safer ground, crossing themselves.

The haze ballooned into a swirling ring, stirring dead leaves into a sparkling cyclone. The sight clutched Maya's heart. Could this be the vortex they once prayed for? Then, with a sharp snap, the ring collapsed, shrinking to a calmer glow. The orchard remained unscorched, the watchers trembling with relief.

Come morning, they collapsed onto makeshift beds. Over a sparse breakfast, they debated. Carter hypothesized the phenomenon might be partial—assembling energy each night, flirting with a full opening but never completing the tear. Maya dreaded the thought of a stable rift that might pull in or spew out large fragments of the modern world. She saw Ethan's conflicted expression, hope and fear battling behind his eyes.

The abbot prayed for deliverance. The watchers prepared for another night's vigil. Meanwhile, monks scoured the orchard floor for stray debris. They retrieved a small hunk of warped plastic bearing half a familiar brand name—a sign that the orchard might indeed be forging a pathway to the time they'd left behind.

On the second night, the glow brightened even sooner. Violet arcs danced from trunk to trunk. Ethan stood close to Maya, promising he would follow her instructions. When midnight came, the orchard erupted with greater force. A crackling swirl rose high, forming a ring in midair. Leaves spiraled upward, jolting with static. Carter shouted for everyone to stand clear. The abbot clutched his rosary, whispering prayers as the ring seemed to flicker with half-glimpsed shapes—a suggestion of twisted metal or an otherworldly view. Then the swirl shrank on itself, vanished with a thunderous boom, and left only a few new scraps of scorched metal behind.

Carter and Victoria cautiously retrieved the fragments, hearts heavy. Maya found Ethan trembling, tears pooling in his eyes. She wrapped an arm around him, murmuring, "It's all right. This was never easy."

Night after night, the pattern repeated. At dusk, the faint shimmer began. By midnight, it swelled into a near-gateway, threatening to open wide, only to collapse again. Debris sometimes rained out: seat cushions, twisted brackets, shards of plastic. Tension mounted. The monks debated exorcisms. Others suggested burning the orchard itself. Maya vetoed that plan. "That might only strengthen whatever energy is forming. We can't risk innocent lives." Abbot Cedran, though wary, abided by her judgment.

At last, on the seventh night, the orchard's glow outdid every previous display. Sparks jumped between trees, scorching bark and filling the air with the pungent scent of ozone. The watchers arranged themselves in a wide ring—Maya, Carter, Victoria, Paul, Tomás, Ethan, and a few volunteers. The abbot and monks kept a safer distance. The orchard floor trembled beneath them as the clock neared midnight, and the swirl rushed upward in a towering column of light.

Ethan gripped Maya's sleeve, torn between terror and a lingering wish that a miracle might appear. The ring expanded more quickly than before—two meters, three, four—roaring with the force of a jet engine. Dust and broken twigs surged into its glowing center.

Carter's shout cut through the chaos: "If it holds, is this our way home?"

Maya's heart thundered. Over the years, they had built a life here: a village that depended on them, a sense of belonging that grew out of adversity. Could they abandon it? She caught Ethan's stricken gaze. He still wondered if this rift might lead them to lost family, to a world of modern convenience.

At that instant, the ring stabilized—an eerie, shimmering portal. Through the violet haze, they glimpsed what might have been bright fluorescents, the corner of a corridor that looked almost... modern. Or was it some trick? Wind tore at their clothes, arcs of energy lashing the orchard floor. Carter clutched Maya's hand. "We have to decide now."

Time seemed to stand still. Ethan whispered, "Mom..." but he couldn't finish. Grief and longing blended in his voice.

Maya clenched her jaw. Memory after memory flashed through her mind—countless battles, the war-torn orchard, the settlement's struggles, the unsteady alliances forged through blood and sweat. She thought of the villagers looking to them for guidance. She pictured the orchard that had once felt so alien and realized it was now their home.

She shook her head. "I can't. We can't leave Riverbend behind after all we've built." She turned to Ethan, her voice trembling. "This is our life now. I won't gamble it on a storm that might be an illusion."

Victoria, tears glistening, stared at the glowing portal. "I would've jumped at the chance years ago. But we've grown beyond that. Our duty is here."

Paul nodded, though regret shadowed his eyes. "Everything we've done... has made this world ours."

Tomás murmured a prayer. "We don't belong in that other place anymore."

Carter's grip tightened on Maya's arm. "We stay together."

Then the swirling portal flashed brilliant white, a thunderclap shaking the ground. In one searing blink, the ring folded into itself, leaving darkness and the singed orchard behind. Not a single shred of new wreckage rained from the sky. At first, no one moved. The orchard suddenly seemed darker than any night before it.

Maya sank to her knees, tears slipping down her cheeks. There would be no grand rescue, no swift return to the 21st century. Ethan dropped beside her, burying his face against her shoulder, and Carter draped an arm around them both. The abbot and monks carefully ventured forward, crossing themselves in mute awe.

Come dawn, the watchers gathered a handful of final scraps—worthless debris from a vanishing dream. They secured them in a chest, resolved to hide them away. Bone-weary, they refused Father Cedran's offer to stay longer. With heavy hearts and quiet goodbyes, they rode west. Ethan stayed close to Maya, eyes lowered, still wrestling with what he had witnessed.

When they returned to Riverbend, the orchard greeted them in a hush of winter stillness—so different from the violent vortex they had left. The townsfolk rushed to meet them, relieved to see them safe. That evening, they huddled near the communal hearth and recounted the final swirl of cosmic energy, the fleeting vision of a modern corridor, and their decision to remain.

A solemn acceptance soon settled over them. No more illusions of an easy rescue. No more infiltration missions or sabotage against cosmic phenomena. They were rooted in this realm, bound to the life they had painstakingly forged. Now, they belonged here fully, no swirling light or shattered relic to stand between them and the life they had built.

CHAPTER 18

A brittle wind swept across the silent orchard at Riverbend Haven, stirring the last fallen leaves into swirling patterns of gold and umber. Maya stood near the orchard's center, a place that had once throbbed with fearsome possibility—where she, Carter, and the others had so often feared the cosmic swirl. Now, the orchard lay in gentle repose, the bare trunks silvered by a pale winter sun.

She closed her eyes, inhaling the faint scent of soil and dried bark. It spoke of both dormancy and promise, recalling the countless seasons since Flight 207 disappeared from the modern world. Those years had brought infiltration missions, desperate battles against cosmic storms, and heartbreak over swirling portals that cast out scraps of the future—or threatened to. Yet here they stood, still breathing, still forging their lives. If the orchard storms had one last trick to show them, the realm gave no sign.

Footsteps crunched behind her. Carter approached, cloak pulled tight against the freezing breeze, his boots pressing into frost-laced grass. She turned, warmed by the gentle smile that had long sustained her in this unfamiliar land. Setting down a burlap sack, he revealed a handful of misshapen metal fragments.

"I found more debris," he said, voice low, glancing toward a recently turned patch of earth near the fence. "Only small chunks—a seat-buckle piece or two—probably washed to the surface by the last rains."

Maya sighed. "All this time, and still more remnants."

He nodded, kneeling to sift through the scraps. "The storms must've scattered things in ways we'll never chart. At least no warlord's found these pieces lately."

She crouched beside him, picking up a twisted bit of plastic, likely part of a panel from the plane. Once, these shards had made her ache with desperation, craving rescue or closure. Now, she felt only quiet acceptance. This land was home, no matter what relics turned up.

By midday, the hush of winter settled over Riverbend Haven, its daily routine moving to the steady rhythm of purposeful work. In the community hall, Victoria and Paul pored over ledgers and trade lists, their faces reflecting a calm contentment. The courtyard bustled with villagers hauling flour from the mill, weaving between huts. Even in the mild chaos, no one exhibited the old, wary tension that once overshadowed every task.

A handful of refugees from Braxton's fractured domain appeared that afternoon, drawn by tales of Riverbend's security. Victoria greeted them with composed kindness, explaining that the orchard storms had quieted. She offered work on orchard expansions set to begin in spring. The newcomers looked equal parts relieved and astonished to find a settlement unburdened by either cosmic threat or feudal rage.

Once the orientation ended, Paul turned to Victoria, a faint smile tugging at his lips. "We've somehow turned our old orchard fears into orchard prosperity."

She studied the courtyard, where villagers moved with shared purpose. "It's surreal, but I'll take it. No cosmic swirl on our doorstep. Even WilCarter's taxes haven't crushed us. We're... thriving." A distant look crossed her face. "I still have dreams about orchard nights, though. Hard to shake the memory of that electricity in the air."

He nodded. The orchard had left everyone with scars—some internal, some visible—but the settlement's spirit outshone those nightmares now.

Meanwhile, in the new infirmary, Nina and Sarah were tending to a peasant child's swollen ankle. The space smelled of herbs and clean straw. Rudimentary diagrams hung on the walls, an amalgam of modern knowledge and local sketches. Sarah probed the injured ankle with careful fingers.

"Just a sprain," she said, fastening a snug wrap. "Rest a few days, stay off ladders."

Nina watched with approval. "Your skill's improving every day, Sarah."

A hint of pride lit Sarah's eyes. "Crazy to think that plane trouble and orchard storms led me here. But I feel like I'm doing exactly what I was meant to do."

Nina's lips curved softly. "The storms forced us down a path we never imagined, yet somehow we found purpose. We've all grown."

The child hopped off the cot with a thankful grin, limping away to find a sibling. Their small giggles faded in the corridor as Nina and Sarah exchanged a satisfied glance. The storms were once a source of perpetual dread, but now life revolved around healing and learning, not cosmic anomalies.

That evening, a delicate layer of snow settled over the rooftops, transforming the orchard into a ghostly sketch beneath moonlight. Tomás finished instructing older children in a simple annex on the orchard's edge. Lanternlight flickered across their hopeful faces as he guided them through half-salvaged modern pamphlets and local parchments.

When the students departed, Tomás tidied the makeshift desks, nostalgia washing over him. He remembered the days when orchard storms monopolized his thoughts: were they a harbinger of doom? A doorway to history? Now, his energies poured into shaping young minds. Stepping outside, he breathed in the sharp winter air and encountered Ethan.

The boy—more a young man now—leaned against a wooden post, studying the orchard's dark silhouettes. Tomás touched his shoulder in greeting. "Pondering those storms again?"

Ethan nodded. "I still dream about them, but the fear's gone. Sometimes I wonder if something might flare up again, or if we've truly seen the last of it."

Tomás gazed at the silent rows. "Tough to know. But we've handled so much that, if it comes, we'll be ready. Fear doesn't live here anymore."

Ethan offered a quiet smile. "Yeah. I think so."

In the days that followed, the cold of winter became an everyday companion. One clear morning, Maya felt an irresistible pull to the orchard hill. She discovered Anna already there, scattering compost at the tree bases. The woman's gaze shone with serenity, as if the orchard's hush had replaced all her old anxieties.

Maya joined in, working row by row until Anna paused. "I was just realizing... you became Ethan's mother in so many ways. I used to worry these storms might tear him from me forever."

Maya felt a twinge in her chest. "We've all been shaped by those events. I'm just grateful the storms spared us."

A reflective look crossed the other woman's face. "He's thriving here, maybe more than he would have in modern times. Hard to believe I'm saying it, but the orchard changed us for the better."

Maya let out a gentle laugh. "It changed everything."

That afternoon, two knights arrived from Kentwood Castle with an announcement from Lord WilCarter. Workers paused their labors to greet them in the courtyard. The knights exchanged weary glances as though burdened by their message.

"My lord wishes you to know of rumors in distant lands," one knight proclaimed. "North of the mountains, an orchard-like disturbance was observed—akin to what you once called a fiasco. He does not insist you investigate but felt it best you be informed."

A weight settled over the listeners. Maya's heart fluttered briefly, but the old panic did not return. "Thank you for bringing word," she said. "We'll keep watch, though we have no desire to chase illusions."

The knights bowed and departed. In the orchard, Carter found Maya tending an ancient trunk. "So there's another swirling rumor up north?"

She brushed back a strand of hair. "Yes. But we agreed we wouldn't run off chasing every tale. We've done more than enough."

He rested a reassuring hand on her shoulder. "We belong here now. Let that be our answer."

Anna joined them, relief in her eyes, as though glad the storms' mania no longer dictated their lives.

As weeks passed, the bitter cold yielded to the faint promise of spring. Frost ebbed from the ground, and tight buds peeked from branches. Not a single cosmic ripple troubled the orchard's calm. Each morning, villagers pruned branches, prepared seeds, and planned expansions deeper into the forest. The orchard fiascos that once terrified them seemed increasingly like a cautionary legend.

One mild morning, the principal figures of Riverbend met in the millhouse with various villagers. They discussed orchard expansions without a hint of dread. Maya, Carter, Victoria, Paul, Tomás, Ethan, Nina, Sarah, Jason, and Anna listened to townsfolk excitedly propose new irrigation channels and orchard rows.

"We no longer fear the orchard storms," an older villager declared. "We can plant and prosper."

Victoria nodded. "Yes, we can. We built our refuge on knowledge that once kept the storms in check. Let's press forward."

While finalizing those orchard plans, Ethan spoke up, his voice subdued. "So... we're never going back, right? No swirl's going to whisk us home?"

Maya reached for him, her expression tender. "We made that choice already. When we stood at that vortex near Harlow's abbey, we decided. This is our home."

Villagers quietly affirmed it. Tales of swirling gateways might float around, but the "sky-people" had chosen to remain. They weren't going to fling themselves into any cosmic unknown.

Tomás cleared his throat. "Let's gather tonight for a vigil in the orchard—like a symbolic gesture that we're fully here, not waiting on any phenomenon."

An excited ripple ran through the settlement. At dusk, they assembled beneath the trees, torches illuminating the developing buds. The orchard glowed under the moon, and a gentle wind stirred the branches.

Carter began, his voice carrying in the hush. "We once believed these storms would be our undoing. Over and over, they threatened us. Yet we stand here now, stronger for having faced them."

Victoria continued. "Some wonder if we ache for another cosmic swirl, a chance to reclaim our old world. But we decided to stay. We choose to cultivate this land."

Maya blinked away tears. She remembered the infiltration missions and sabotage efforts that nearly consumed them. In the torchlight, she saw Ethan's proud face, Carter's loyal gaze. "We vow to protect this orchard, this realm, and each other—whatever storms come or don't."

Around them, villagers pressed palms to trunks or knelt to touch the soil. A collective breath passed through the orchard like a hush of thanksgiving. For a moment, Maya sensed a subtle tingle of energy, reminiscent of those storms, but softer, almost benevolent. She exhaled, tears slipping down her cheeks as old fear melted away. The orchard itself seemed to accept their vow. Or maybe it was just the wind.

When spring arrived in earnest, blossoms frothed in pink and white across the orchard rows. Visitors wandered in from allied lands, marveling at the orchard's lush renewal. Lady Althea, who had once glimpsed the terrifying cosmic whirl, walked with Maya among the flowering trees, gently parting clusters of delicate petals.

"It's beautiful," Althea whispered, inhaling their fragrance. "No more storms, no more wreckage—only this."

Maya's smile shone with gratitude. "Yes. After everything, it seems almost unreal."

Althea smiled back. "WilCarter might request increased orchard shipments, but I believe he respects all of you more than ever. This orchard stands as proof that what once threatened can be turned into a gift."

In the weeks that followed, the settlement rejoiced in orchard festivities. Children played tag under the blossoms, and villagers harvested early fruit to create orchard wine and mead. Tomás organized a cultural fair, highlighting orchard produce alongside local crafts. The nightmares had transformed into orchard-inspired pride. The mood of celebration overshadowed memories of infiltration and sabotage.

One day, Carter found Maya demonstrating a modern pollination technique to a circle of farmers near the river. After they dispersed, he stepped in close, his grin soft. "You never fail to amaze me. You went from a field medic in dire storms to orchard horticulturist. Is there anything you can't do?"

She shook her head with a laugh. "We've all adapted. That's how we beat back the storms: we refused to live in fear."

He pressed her hand gently. "By the way, another traveler mentioned more rumors of swirling lights up north. We're staying put, right?"

She squeezed his fingers. "Definitely. Let others chase ghosts if they like. Our path leads here."

When summer came, the orchard boughs drooped under the weight of thriving fruit. Not once did anyone see a flicker of cosmic swirl. Prosperity blossomed across Riverbend. They forged new tools for neighboring hamlets, hosted weekly markets, and trained visiting healers. Even hostilities ebbed, as Braxton's realm lay in tatters. Life unfurled in ways no one had imagined.

One golden afternoon, Maya and Carter strolled the orchard, inspecting new saplings. Where orchard storms had once raged, sunlight now pierced through lush leaves. Carter stopped before a cluster of bright apples, wonder in his gaze.

"We truly did it," he murmured. "We've changed orchard fear into orchard fortune. Even if those storms never leave the world entirely, they no longer define us."

Maya felt tears prick her eyes. "Yes, we belong here. Chaos or not, this is our future."

He slipped an arm around her, orchard sunlight dancing over them. Their memories of infiltration missions and cosmic illusions seemed dreamlike—distant, almost unreal.

By the time autumn rolled in, the second major harvest exceeded all expectations. Harvesters bustled through the orchard, singing while they plucked apples and carted them off to be pressed into cider or traded abroad. Victoria skillfully managed trade routes, shipping goods far beyond WilCarter's lands. Riverbend's orchard was renowned for growth and renewal, not for swirling cosmic storms.

An orchard festival took shape, complete with Tomás's newly written plays and children's musical performances. Folks from allied areas poured in, eager to witness the orchard once haunted by storms. They found it brimming with apples, laughter, and stories of how the survivors—"sky-people"—had tamed the swirling chaos.

On the final night of celebration, lanterns brightened the orchard paths, turning each tree into a softly lit jewel. Gentle music drifted through the crowd, blending with the laughter of dancers. Toward midnight, a hush spread among the gathered revelers, and the orchard pickers formed a space for the survivors to address the crowd.

Victoria spoke first, her voice carrying strong and clear. "Years ago, we lived in fear. We endured infiltration, sabotage, heartbreak. But we overcame every threat."

The assembled villagers cheered, and Paul stepped up next, praising the unity that had brought them through. Finally, Maya took the stage. Her gaze roamed over dear faces, old friends and new, her heart filled with gratitude. "This orchard endured so much," she said, voice trembling with emotion. "Cosmic storms tried to pull us into another realm—or bury us in debris. But we chose each other. We chose this life. No storm can change that."

A wave of applause swept over them. Lanterns flickered, casting the orchard in a golden glow. Ethan watched with tears, letting the applause wash away any lingering sorrow from the past.

Dancing continued well past midnight. As the orchard aisles emptied, only a few figures remained in the hush. Maya and Carter found a quiet corner beneath a venerable apple tree, the stars gleaming overhead. She rested against him, shoulders finally free of old burdens. He stroked her hair, speaking softly:

"After all we've seen, everything from infiltration missions to swirling illusions, we discovered something better than a portal home. We made a home of our own."

She closed her eyes, filled with wordless relief. "If another storm ever rears its head, we'll meet it together."

He brushed a gentle kiss to her forehead, the leaves whispering in a lullaby-like hush. Peace settled between them—an abiding calm no cosmic threat could hope to destroy.

The weeks after the festival brought a new normal to Riverbend. People no longer flinched at the idea of orchard storms. They spent their days cultivating, trading, and hosting travelers who visited out of curiosity or admiration. Braxton's defeated territory posed little risk, and WilCarter's demands stayed measured. Soon, visitors regarded the orchard as a sanctuary of renewal rather than a relic of chaos.

One day, Maya, Carter, Victoria, Paul, Tomás, and Ethan gathered at the orchard's heart. They carried the Chronicle of the Sky-People, an account of their extraordinary journey—every infiltration, every flash of lightning in the orchard's midst. Together, they read the final chapter describing their choice not to jump through the last cosmic rift. Tears welled as they recalled those they had lost, the family they'd hoped to see again, and the illusions that once seemed so tempting.

When the reading ended, they placed the Chronicle in a carved chest beneath a modest shrine. If future generations heard rumors of cosmic storms, they would find the truth of how the "sky-people" refused to surrender to swirling chaos.

That night, moonlight bathed the orchard in silver. Ethan stayed among the trees, remembering how orchard storms had haunted his dreams when he was a child. Now, he felt only thankfulness that life had moved forward. He glanced at the stars, murmuring a silent farewell to his old longings. This orchard, this settlement, had become all he needed.

Nearby, Maya and Carter watched him, arms looped around each other's waists. A rush of quiet joy swelled in them. In earlier times, the orchard storms might have ripped them apart, but they had endured. Though they might still glance to the horizon sometimes, they no longer feared a cosmic swirl snatching away their lives. They lived in the orchard's glow, not its shadow.

When dawn came, the orchard shimmered in a gentle mist. Riverbend Haven stirred to birdsong and the rustle of villagers beginning another day. Stepping from their lodgings, the orchard watchers greeted each other with bright smiles. No infiltration mission loomed on the horizon, no war threatened the peace, and no cosmic swirl beckoned them away. Only the orchard, its blossoms, and the steadfast pulse of a realm they had chosen to protect.

Ethan ran among the rows, his laughter echoing. Maya watched him with a grateful heart. They had fought so hard to preserve this place—and in doing so, discovered themselves. She turned to Carter, eyes shining with relief and wonder. "We made it," she whispered.

He nodded, the breeze ruffling his hair. "Yes, we did."

With that final hush of orchard calm, their journey of cosmic storms reached its quiet conclusion, forever woven into the land they now called home.

Epilogue

Winter's last breeze whispered over Riverbend Haven, carrying the faint scent of distant pine and damp earth. In the orchard's heart—where once the world seemed poised on the cusp of another cosmic tear—rows of apple trees now stood calm and flourishing. The long months of cold had passed with soft snows and quiet labor, and spring had arrived as gently as a shy dawn, greening every branch and coaxing new blossoms from the earth.

On a mild afternoon, Maya paused beneath a venerable apple tree, the bark rough against her palm. She closed her eyes, recalling the orchard's darker days: swirling violet storms, shards of modern wreckage, and the dread that had shadowed every breath. Yet as a fresh breeze laced with blossoms stole across her face, those once-consuming fears felt more distant than ever—like a half-remembered dream.

"Are you talking to the trees again?" Carter teased from a few steps away, his laughter echoing kindly. He rested one hand on the cart of seedlings that would soon fill a new section of orchard. In the year since the last major cosmic flicker, they had expanded Riverbend's farmland, welcoming new families who sought safety—and found more than they'd ever hoped for.

Maya touched a budding branch, smiling as Carter drew closer. "They deserve gratitude," she said. "After everything they've witnessed and endured." Indeed, the orchard's gnarled trunks had withstood swirling storms and final chances at escape. They were survivors, just like her.

She turned at a shout from Ethan, who now towered over many of the villagers. In the orchard's newer rows, he was helping Tomás measure plots for irrigation channels. Once a trembling boy clinging to memories of a downed plane, Ethan now brimmed with a calm confidence. At sixteen, he had become Tomás's trusted assistant—a scholar and teacher to the youngest children who gathered for lessons at the old millhouse.

Seeing Maya watching, Ethan waved. His smile, bright and open, carried none of the old shadows that once haunted his eyes. Across the orchard, Anna tended to a cluster of saplings, chatting easily with Nina and Sarah. A group of children scurried in circles around them, giggling whenever the women teased them about one day inheriting the orchard's bounty.

Victoria and Paul stood near the watermill, conferring over trade ledgers. They looked up occasionally to watch the orchard at work, their expressions laced with satisfaction. Where once they had braced for infiltration missions and sabotage, they now negotiated trade routes with far-flung villages—an unspoken promise that Riverbend's orchard produce would keep bellies full and hearts hopeful throughout the realm. As they sealed another agreement with a traveling merchant, the hum of everyday life felt like the sweetest music.

By late afternoon, a clatter at the gate drew a small crowd: a messenger from Lord WilCarter, flanked by two riders from Baron Harlow's domain. After exchanging bows with Riverbend's watchmen, they dismounted near the orchard. Maya and Carter approached, curious if some new storm rumor had broken the peaceful spell.

But instead, the messenger produced two letters sealed with wax—one bearing WilCarter's sigil, the other Harlow's. "My lords bid me deliver these, with thanks," the man announced. "They wish only to confirm your orchard stands safe. Should any new disturbance arise, they trust you know best how to handle it—but they will not ask for your aid unless you offer it freely."

Murmurs spread through the onlookers. Maya broke the seals, scanning the lines. Both WilCarter and Harlow wrote of renewed stability: *the orchard fiasco knowledge rests*, and *no swirling storms disturb their realms*. Their letters were warm, almost regretful for past demands. Both lords concluded that Riverbend deserved its independence—no more storm duty unless there was a dire emergency indeed.

The crowd exhaled in shared relief, and Carter's grin flared bright. "I'll admit, it feels good not to be on anyone's emergency call list."

"That it does," Maya agreed softly. For so long, they had borne the weight of defending medieval lords against cosmic anomalies. Now, both WilCarter and Harlow had let them go. Their alliance arcs ended in a note of trust and freedom, echoing the orchard's own transformation from threat to promise.

That evening, the settlement convened in the communal hall, where lanterns glowed over tables laden with fresh bread and early spring fruits. Children begged Ethan to retell how the orchard once swirled with violet storms, and he obliged them with good-natured embellishments—describing seatbelts and "in-flight meals" with a grin—while the younger ones squealed in awe. For them, it was all myth and marvel, a legend that had shaped their elders' courage.

Later still, under a sky brimming with stars, Maya and Carter slipped away to the orchard's old clearing. Moonlight draped the trunks in silver, and the faint chatter of distant voices melded with the rustle of leaves. Carter drew her close, the warmth of him chasing away the night's chill.

"Think we've truly seen the last storm?" he asked, voice hushed. Maya leaned into him, listening to the orchard's soft, reassuring hush. "If another comes, we'll face it," she said simply. "But I think this land has given us its answer. We belong here."

She pictured that swirling portal they'd seen near Harlow's abbey—the final, fleeting chance to return to modern life—and the letters in her pocket, proving WilCarter and Harlow no longer expected them to swoop in whenever cosmic rumors arose. Their orchard was their own now, entirely free. In the orchard's gentle sway, she and Carter had discovered a life tethered not by fear but by purpose.

A shooting star flared overhead, fleeting and bright. For a moment, they both watched its arc vanish into the horizon. Once, such a spark might have sparked frantic hope or dread. Now, it merely reminded them of how vast the world could be—and how precious the home they had chosen.

"I think," Carter said, brushing a light kiss to her temple, "that star's giving us a blessing." Maya closed her eyes, heart steady. "We don't need any more miracles," she murmured. "We've already found ours."

In the orchard's embrace, Riverbend Haven lived free of swirling storms and cosmic dread. The story of *Flight 207* and the orchard fiascos remained in the *Chronicle of the Sky-People*, a testament to storms that once shattered time itself. Yet its final pages proclaimed a simple, eternal truth: peace could bloom after chaos. And as long as these trees bore fruit, they would stand watch over a future the survivors had built with courage and unwavering hope—untethered, and beautifully at home.

Be sure to find your next thriller by:
Scott P. Hicks

at

Please leave a review and share with others.

Thank you for reading my book.

Scott P. Hicks

Made in United States
Troutdale, OR
04/29/2025

31000699R00148